EXCESS BAGGAGE

A LOVE STORY...

Brooklyn Prairie Publishing

ISBN-13: 979-8-9908336-0-9 - ePub
ISBN-13: 979-8-9908336-1-6 -Kindle
ISBN-13:979-8-9908336-2-3 -PDF
ISBN-13: 979-8-9908336-3-0 - Paperback

Book I: *Excess Baggage* - A Love Story

Book II: *Cutting Losses* - A Redemption Story

Book III: *Mixed Messages* - A Love Story

Book IV: *Second Chances* - A Later in Life Love Story

EXCESS BAGGAGE

A LOVE STORY...

JODI CULLINEY

For Pete, without whom none of this would be possible.

PROLOGUE

It was finally going to be the day she'd been waiting for—her wedding day. She had dreamed of pledging her life and love to him since she met him almost twenty years ago. He had loved her when she was afraid to wish someone would love her like that. He'd never taken anything from her—only given. So how was it now that she stood too immobilized to make one more step? Her thoughts turned to her wedding dress, which was the stuff of fairytales—champagne colored, with plenty of beading and lace, form-fitting and also flowing. So why was she hiding?

Over and over in her head, her regrets raced and doubts circled. She had never thought herself completely worthy of him, and had proven herself right. Why had she taken so long? Why hadn't they gotten married years ago, before any of this had a chance to happen? Maybe he had been the one with cold feet all along.

All she had to do was put one foot in front of the other, and it would be closer to being over. She could move past all of this loathing she felt for herself. Without a doubt, she knew he could give her the life she had wished for all these many years. What was that saying? "It's not you, it's me"—it wasn't completely her, but since she was the only one standing here, for now it was true.

"Deep breath, deep breath, deep breath—you can do this" she whispered to herself as she rounded the corner to the doors. They had been very traditional so hadn't seen each other or each other's attendants before this moment, the night of the rehearsal. She knew who his attendants were—two of his cousins, his teenage best friend (also hers at different moments), his friend from med school, and his college fraternity brother, who she had detested on first sight; the feeling had been mutual.

"You good, sis?" Asked Ruth, not just her maid of honor (despite being married and a new mother, she refused to be referred to as "matron of honor') but her best friend and devoted older sister. "Need a drink before we go in?"

"No—just gathering myself. Everybody all set?"

"Yep, just waiting on us, and Dad. Have you seen him?"

"He was here and then vanished," and then here came her dad, rounding the corner, and holding out shots of Squirt, her favorite childhood drink.

"Got the good stuff, in honor of your sister", and they clinked cups and immediately downed the Squirt. "Now, ready, Kid?"

"Let's roll", and her sister turned the corner and started down the aisle, the notes of the cello wafting to greet them. "Dad, I may have messed up," but her dad was staring straight ahead at their mom, who he had loved and then lost and then loved again, and before she knew it, they were halfway down the aisle. It was at that moment she looked beyond her groom, and over to his groomsmen, and she stumbled.

What the hell? It couldn't be. The odds were stacked so high against this happening right now. And then his eyes locked with hers, recognition flaring, cheeks flushing, and realization dawning. How could she not have known?

CHAPTER
One

Tess

Six Months Earlier

"Where are you?" Asked Tess, on speakerphone with her sister, Ruth, while also taking out the braid she had coaxed her red curls into early this morning—whenever Tess traveled, she needed her hair firmly restrained; now that she was comfortably ensconced in her room, she could let it all hang out.

"I'm making my way to the boarding area," Ruth yelled into her phone.

"Okay, settle—why are you screaming at me? May I remind you that this is supposed to be MY adventure!" Tess laughed. "Don't be stressed. I've got snacks, drinks, and mystery novels! We are so set for this trip."

"Don't threaten me with a good time! I'm hauling my ass up the stairs now. See you in five," and with that, the line went dead.

Tess had to pinch herself back to reality so many times over the past few months. In six months, she'd be marrying her childhood sweetheart, who also happened to be the only man she has ever loved.

Currently she was riding AMTRAK, and had begun her trip in New York City. She was waiting for Ruth to board in Philadelphia, and then they'd be on to San Francisco. They were taking the train across country and from there would head up to wine country also via train to meet the rest of her friends for her bachelorette weekend. Taking the train had been her sister's idea. Ruth had been married for five years and was expecting her first child in several months; Ruth was also into her second trimester and unfortunately still experiencing morning sickness. When they had planned the trip two months ago, they hadn't necessarily considered that the morning sickness would last, but the thought of traveling on a flight for five hours was unappealing to each of them in general; both Ruth and Tess knew that once the baby was here, and Tess was finally married, that their "sister moments" would be few and far between. The sisters had been eagerly anticipating this trip and looking forward to making memories over the week. To compensate for the time they would be spending traveling to California, they were, sadly, flying home.

She and Ruth were doing it up in style, having gotten a First-Class private room. Tess had ridden a train from Germany to Prague with Josh, her fiancé a few years ago, and they had a room with two bunk beds and their own bathroom. The sisters' room was very swanky compared to that room, though: no bunk beds this time, but two twin beds on each side of the room, with double pillows lying atop them, a nightstand for each bed, and a large window framing a fantastic view of the world they were leaving behind. After checking out the small but complete bathroom, where Tess had seen two of the fluffiest robes in existence, she was thinking she could *definitely* get used to this.

Suddenly the room door flew open and Ruth breezed in, diva shades still on and strawberry blonde curls flying all around her head.

"Tell me again why we didn't just drive there?" Ruth queried. "We could've thrown all our shit in the trunk, and just headed out on I-Eighty".

Tess burst out laughing "You're nuts! Number one: we'd spend four days getting there—"

Ruth interjects "Oh, I see. AND???"

They both erupted into gales of laughter, because four days was the exact length of their train excursion. Tess replied, "Neither of us will have to exert ourselves to get to Cali, and this way we can spoil ourselves rotten until we de-train!"

Ruth slumped down onto the chair closest to her bed after depositing her belongings on the floor and sighed heartily. "So, how is everything going as far as the wedding? Any jitters yet? Questions about the wedding night?" Ruth smirked.

"Right, Ruthie, hard to have questions about someone I've been with for like seventeen years. I honestly just can't believe that it is finally on our horizon. You know, it seems it took ages for us to get engaged, and now it feels like we've been planning the wedding for a decade. I am definitely looking forward to this weekend, for sure. I haven't seen a few of my ladies for years. How many ended up saying they were coming?"

"All in all, there will be eight of us—Sarah is just coming night of, but the rest will be there the entire weekend."

As Tess's maid of honor, Ruth had planned the bachelorette weekend, using her natural skills in deducing what her sister would be into: lots of food, some wine, and no sleazy 'entertainment'. Ruth was also looking forward to spending these few days alone with her little sister. The two of them, only two years apart, had been close growing up, but now lived two hours from each other; on the East Coast, two hours could feel like twelve when traveling to see each other, whether by train or car.

"So," Ruth queried hopefully, "did you bring me anything good?"

"Since you asked, and ever so nicely I might add, I did! I've got some snickerdoodles, monster cookies, and Chex mix. Made everything yesterday, and drove myself crazy not eating any of it!" Tess was a baker and did her baking out of a commercial kitchen in Brooklyn. She supplied many of her neighborhood delis and cafes with her baked goods, and specialized in cookies and pies. Tess also shared a space at the Green Market near her apartment. "I can't believe I got all of my clients stocked up with desserts for the next week. Only stuff that can be frozen, but I won't lose any business while I'm away!"

"Are you any closer to finding a store front to rent out?" Ruth asked, "I know you've been dreaming about that since we were kids—having your own bakery. I can lend you any down payment, you know."

"I know, but I'm just full steam ahead with this wedding; Josh and I will be in a better place a year from now and then I can focus on actual life. Josh thinks I should wait to make sure I have a strong customer base, but you know I would kill for my own space. Being able to welcome customers in and talk to them about sugar—what more could I ever want?" Tess laughed.

Growing up on a farm had been lonely, as both parents worked all day, and the girls were left to their own devices during the summer. Their mom had been a nurse practitioner and their dad a vet, so the sisters had grown up learning to nurture, and now expressed themselves this way through their respective careers. Tess a baker, who loved nothing more than treating people to delicious desserts, and Ruth a speech pathologist who worked in a school district outside of Philadelphia.

"Mmm, excuse me while I bliss out right now. Seriously, you would have lines for days if you had your own place," muttered Ruth, around a mouthful of monster cookie.

"Thanks, Sis. I still need to be realistic, though. When I have a real location, that will make it hard to take a train cross-country. Should I have any desire to do so in the future, that is," Tess responded laughingly.

"Well, these are some fancy digs for the next few days; I feel so classy. Should we FaceTime Mom and thank her for it?"

"Aww, yeah, let's do it," Tess said gleefully, and rang their mom on FaceTime.

Their Mom answered immediately, "Hello, darling girl!"

"Make that two darling girls," Ruth nudged into the iPhone frame.

"Hi, Tessie, hi, Ruthie," yelled their dad into the phone.

"Take it easy, Pops, we can see and hear you just fine. So you two are spending the afternoon together, huh?" Ruth asked suggestively. Tess's and Ruth's parents, Ellen and John Lefferts, had been married for twenty-one years when Ellen had decided that, since their daughters were both in college, she didn't know who she was without being a wife and mother, so, had asked for a separation from John. The separation turned into a divorce three years later. Five years ago, however, at Ruth's wedding, their one dance turned into two, which turned into John and Ellen "sorting things out" since, but both daughters felt it was only a matter of time before wedding bells rang again for them.

"As a matter of fact, your father and I have some news of our own—we are moving in together!"

"Umm, okay, but didn't Dad already move his stuff back into the house? Not to be a smart ass or anything'" Ruth said sarcastically.

"Yes, I did, but the real news is that we are selling the house and getting an apartment in town!" John exclaimed.

"Holy hell—you're going to be city folk, huh?" Replied Tess. Never mind that the "city" was eight miles away from their childhood home, and population of ten thousand, give or take one thousand.

"We figured it was time, especially since you girls are soon to be having your own families and are living half a country away. We reckoned we could do with a fresh start ourselves, especially if we are going to be newlyweds," and with that, John pulled Ellen's hand toward the camera, and Tess and Ruth saw a sparkling emerald on their mom's ring finger.

"Absolutely gorgeous," Tess squealed.

"Oh, Mom and Dad, we are so happy for you! And excuse me, I think THIS is the 'real news'!" Ruth said excitedly.

After a minute of happy tears and congratulations, Ellen queried, "How is your trip going?"

"Well, we have only really seen our room, but look how amazing it is," and Tess panned the phone around the room, "it's so luxurious. It actually is too much, and I thank you both so much for doing this for us."

"Listen, we thought we'd be paying for an extravagant wedding for you, but since you and Josh wanted to do it yourselves, your mom and I thought upgrading your train experience would be an excellent gift. We're both so proud of both of you and nothing makes us happier than seeing the two of you at such wonderful places in your lives. Plus we have to make sure our first grand baby can travel in style, even if in utero."

"Okay, thanks Dad, thanks Mom, we are going to head out and survey the rest of the train, or at least the dining car," Tess said. "Love you guys, and we will be in touch."

"Love you, Mom, love you, Dad" replied Ruth, with tears in her eyes.

Then John and Ellen were gone, and Ruth and Tess began hugging each other. "I can't believe this! I mean, I knew they'd get back together, but to know that they will be an actual couple at the wedding? This is the best news; come on, let's go walk around and find a way to celebrate," and with that, Tess flung their door open and strode outside.

"But what about our snacks?" Ruth called.

CHAPTER

Two

Sam

What he really needed was to stretch his legs, but Sam Charles had promised himself that he would write at the *bare minimum* two chapters a day while taking the train to Reno. It was essentially the entire reason for traveling by train (other than his complete, overwhelming, and utter fear of flying—not to mention his rather bad habit while flying of cursing out fellow passengers for minor infractions, such as breathing too loudly or having the gall to merely exist in the same space as him). So for the benefit of all, he has found himself to be more human (and humane) when NOT FLYING. The benefit of being, what he called "self-employed", was the ability to take as much time as he wanted or needed in getting from point A to point B; however, he had a looming deadline for his novel to be submitted to his publisher, and that required this trip to be a working one. So, Sam was taking the train from Boston to Reno and then driving to Lake Tahoe to meet up for a bachelor party for his college fraternity brother and selected friends.

Sam compromised by standing up in his cabin, walking over to his backpack and pulling out his soda. Swigging it down, he felt some of the tension begin to ease. He'd been struggling with the third book in his series since he started. The first two had been insanely successful, which had taken him completely by surprise. He had written and sold several short stories and even published a book of poetry, but the writing of novels was where his true passion was; unfortunately, he had had book after book rejected for five years in a row, and then the magic happened when he wrote his science fiction novel, and the idea for a series was presented by his agent. It didn't help that the success of the first two books had also signaled the end of his very brief marriage. He guessed that's what happened when you married for all the wrong reasons—there was no chance for them to grow together, only apart. He had tried explaining this to Josh, his frat brother and soon to be the groom-of-honor at the bachelor party.

"Just give her a chance" or "You don't even know her" were Josh's responses when questioned about the famous Tessa. Valid questions, without a doubt, as he didn't know her and in fact had only met her once, years ago in college, when she came to visit Josh for a weekend. Sam had a long-lasting and regretful exchange with her and had come away with the impression that she was judgmental and more than willing to hold a grudge.

Enough stalling, Sam thought to himself, and sat back down at the small table in his room. As he stared at the iPad screen, fingers hovering over the portable keyboard, his thoughts took him back to Penn Station in New York City. He had been sitting in the dining car having some breakfast when he spotted her on the platform. He had never been so entranced watching a woman board a train, or at least attempting to board the train, but was struggling with her luggage. After watching her nearly decapitate a woman walking with a cane, and then almost mow down a family pushing a stroller, he couldn't stop himself from bounding out of his chair and down the stairs to help her. "Before you kill someone, can I carry this case up for you?" He asked. Then she looked up at him, huge green eyes, and he was absolutely breathless. He looked down and then noticed her lips were moving but he somehow had been struck deaf. Shaking his head helped him right his senses, and he tuned in to hear her saying "that would be amazing. I thought I left all my bricks at home, but it seems I actually packed them in my suitcase," she laughed, and the sound sent chills down his spine. "Lead the way," he muttered, and as he followed her up the stairs, he saw gold glinting through her crimson braid.

Dragging her suitcase across two cars, he realized they were now in the first-class car. "Nice way to travel, if you can," Sam observed.

She chuckled, "You'd think it would have come with a side order of valet, right? I was having such a time getting my things organized to board. I honestly thought I was traveling 'light'. Wait until my sister gets on—now that will be a complete shit show!" They both laughed and then came to a stop at Room 132. Tess checked her ticket and remarked, "Well, this is my room according to my ticket."

She turned around and he was hit again with those green eyes. "I, uh," she seemed to falter. She cleared her throat and then said, "Thanks so much for helping; you're the best."

"Yeah, no problem. Well, I better get back to my breakfast. I'm sure I'll see you some time again on the train," and with that, he turned and reluctantly strode back to the dining car, resisting the urge to turn around for a last look.

That was a couple of hours ago at this point, and they had just now pulled out of Philadelphia. Bringing himself back to the present, he was suddenly struck with inspiration, and sat back down at his table, fingers flying over the keys. Suddenly his phone lit up. A text had arrived from Liam, the organizer of the bachelor party, and also the best man at the corresponding wedding. "Dude," the text read, "have you checked the bachelor party invite on Facebook?"

Rolling his eyes, Sam texted back, "No, I don't do Facebook," resisting the urge to respond with DUDE.

"Just wanted to check that you're still coming. Josh said you weren't sure," Liam wrote.

"I'll be there Friday as planned."

"Sweet," and that was the end of communicating with Liam. Sam liked Liam, and had hung out with him many times over the years. He was Josh's cousin, but Josh had often remarked that they had grown up like brothers, and were only a few months apart in age. He had gone to college not far from where Sam and Josh had gone, so he had been a frequent visitor to the frat house both Sam and Josh lived in. Sam wouldn't say that he and Josh had been particularly close when they had first started living in the house, and hadn't expected at that time they'd remain friends for so long, but during their sophomore year something shifted and they matured. They went from drinking buddies and then dove deeper with their conversations: discussing their childhoods and often talking about what their futures might hold. Josh had always had a long-term plan as far as Tessa (who had been his high school girlfriend, then college girlfriend, and now his fiancée) was concerned. Sam often encouraged Josh to spread his wings and test the waters with other girls, but Josh stayed true to Tessa during his college years; Sam was never sure if that had been due to his true love for her or because it was the easiest solution for his plans. What really drove Josh was his career—becoming a surgeon. Sam hoped this had eased and he had a better work/life balance, because he knew first-hand what choosing your career over your wife could do. And he knew for a fact that Tessa and Josh didn't have the kind of flame needed to burn through that.

CHAPTER
Three

Tess

"Isn't it almost lunchtime?" Asked Ruth. "Please tell me our first stop on the train tour is the dining car."

"Haha, Sis, you read my mind," laughed Tess. "If there's one thing a Lefferts knows how to do, without a doubt it is finding the dining car!" They walked through the connecting car and then into the dining car, swaying with the movement of the train.

"Girl, the train looks good on you. Too bad I'm the one behind you and not Josh—he would have one hell of a show right now! Meanwhile I already feel like I'm beginning the pregnant walk," Ruth moaned.

The sisters sat down at an empty table in the nearly full dining car and looked at their menus. A smiling waiter whose name tag read "Todd" approached, and filled their water glasses.

Tess ordered a Caesar salad and an iced tea, and Ruth requested the artisan grilled cheese and a ginger ale, and the waiter was off, with a wink and a grin.

"I love it when waitstaff has a bit of cheek," Tess exclaimed. "What's with the ginger ale? Are you feeling okay?"

Ruth sighed. "It's these hormones—I always feel I am on the verge of possibly being sick, yet still hungry. I thought queasiness subsided after the first trimester, but I have been sadly misinformed. I just want to have an amazing time on this trip so hoping to calm down whatever is percolating. Hey, remember when we were growing up, and Mom insisted that mixing 7-Up and Pepsi together was the same as ginger ale? I'm not knocking it, because it is delicious, but not the same, Mom, not the same."

"Oh my god, I know. She tried to convince us a lot of imposters were just as good as the real thing. What about Cool Whip? Like, that has its place, but in NO WAY is it whipped cream, and I shall fight anyone to death who thinks so!"

Ruth snorted with laughter, "Speaking of whips, what about Miracle Whip? Like, hello, Miracle Whip, I welcome you to my macaroni salad, but stay the hell out of my potato salad!"

"I feel the same," came a voice from both above her and behind her. Tess looked up into the face she had been trying to put out of her mind since this morning.

"Oh, hi. Fancy seeing you again," she replied uncomfortably. "Here for some lunch?" Tess felt the intensity of those brown eyes deep down inside of her soul, and did this man have the longest eyelashes she'd ever seen or was it her imagination?

"No, just passing through on my way to my room. Manage to get everything stowed in your room okay?" At her nod, he looked over to Ruth and said, "this must be your sister?" Tess nodded again.

"Well, have a nice lunch, ladies, and I look forward to running into you again," and he headed toward the doorway.

"I hate to see him leave, but I love watching him walk away," then Ruth paused and waited a beat. "Okay, Sis, you have some 'splaining to do," Ruth stated. "What were you up to before I got on this train? Or did you bring a mysterious stowaway as your travel companion? How does he know about your room? Has he been to your room? Why do you look like you will need some of my ginger ale?"

"Stop, for god's sake—I can never get a word in when you fire off the questions. You know, you really should've been a lawyer; you totally missed your calling. Although, I guess you are a speech pathologist, so talking is your thing -"

"And as usual, little sister, you are the queen of evasion. Oh, nice, here's our order. Food AND drink," Ruth smiled at the waiter, "thanks so much."

Tess twisted her engagement ring around and around, getting her thoughts in order so she could explain to her sister how she happened to meet this mystery man. Well, meet isn't exactly right. Saved? No, too dramatic, she mentally dismissed. "So I was having a moment with my baggage this morning when boarding. My rolling case was tipping over, my overnight bag had somehow broken the strap, and I was also running late and trying to keep my shit together, and here comes the 'mysterious stowaway', as you called him, to my rescue. He just sort of jumped off the train, and swooped everything up before I had a moment to even catch my breath. So then he carried my bags for me to our room, and off he went. We didn't make any introductions or anything."

Ruth sipped her soda, and looked at her sister over the rim. "You always have had a way of charming complete strangers, Tessie. It's those eyes—no one can resist eyes that green. You also have a way of looking like you want a hug," she said sincerely.

Tess laughed. "Being fluffy definitely ups the huggable quotient." Tess had come to loving terms with her size when she was in college, knowing she would never be thin. Instead she focused on her health overall, and moderation; not always easy when you baked for a living. Pushing her huggability to the side, Tess proceeded to tuck into her Caesar salad with gusto.

"Well, mystery man is clearly a gentleman, and they are few and far between these days. Speaking of gentlemen, what is happening with the bachelor party weekend? Sean is totally bummed that he couldn't make it. He was so stressed about leaving his mom alone for the weekend, but Josh said he understood." Sean, Ruth's husband, had just lost his father the month before and he was helping his mother transition to an apartment, and getting his childhood home ready to sell.

"No, no, Josh was cool with it. Since he lost his mom years ago, he was sympathetic, but he was relying on Sean to keep all the guys under control," Tess laughed. "The last I heard about ten guys were going. I think his cousin, Liam, was going early to get the lake house ready. In a way, I wish we were going there. A weekend at Lake Tahoe? Josh and I went there a few years ago, and it was so much fun! His dad had thought about selling it after Josh's mom passed away, but it has been in his family for forty years. I'm hoping that after we're married and all settled, we can go out there once a year."

"And do you think that they will have a stripper-free party?" Ruth's voice had dropped an octave to a conspiratorial level. "I know that's not Josh's scene, but it usually it has more to do with the other men. Didn't you mention his college roommate was going? You had some altercation with him back in the day?"

"Ah, yes, 'Fitz'," groaned Tess. "God, just saying his name annoys me. Ugh. And the way Josh always talks about him—like he is the next Hemingway or something. And that nickname?! 'Fitz' is so aggravating—why not Fitzgerald? Why not F. Scott? It's alarming that someone I only ever met once left such a bad taste in my mouth."

"Okay, settle down—odds are he has matured somewhat in the decade that has passed. Is he also coming to the wedding?"

"Sis, he's IN the wedding," Tess replied, with her eyebrows raised for full effect.

"What? You didn't tell me that when we were talking about the wedding party last week."

"Well, Josh had asked one of his other cousins, but he wasn't sure if he could make it; some kind of drama going on. That side of the family isn't known for their reliability anyway. So, we were throwing around ideas about potential groomsmen: I suggested Sean, actually, but he thought of Fitz; he and 'Fitz' do meet up about once a year, you know. I give Josh credit, he was reluctant to ask him, knowing my feelings, but I won't have to have that much to do with him, and you know I'm not the controlling type."

And with that, Ruth choked on her sandwich. "No, you just have an itinerary for every single moment of your life, and god forbid someone changes a plan! Sends you into a tailspin, but no, I wouldn't say you were controlling," she laughed.

"Hey, I just like an organized plan. I guess if I did have to admit to any faults of mine, I can be a little rigid…" Tess paused for a moment, and then said, "remember in his senior year of college when Josh and I broke up?"

"Yeah, you said he needed a break to just focus on getting into med school. And then you guys got back together a few years later."

Tess took a bite of her salad, followed by a sip of iced tea, and then said, "Actually, that was only partially true; he did need to focus on getting into med school, but he had become so indecisive about us being together after he graduated. I had planned to go to New York for his graduation, but he was content for me to stay in California. I was so afraid of him finding someone else that I pushed. I could feel everything looming ahead after he graduated, and then I was nervous about what came after that, like me graduating. I would be done with school and then what? I hated the idea of me being untethered. In hindsight, I can see now why he broke up with me, but you know how humiliated I felt? And then to learn when we got back together that it hadn't really been Josh's decision?"

Ruth looked up from her empty plate, "Sis, in every story of your breakup, how is it that it is never Josh's fault? You always blame it on yourself or Fitz, but Josh *IS* the one who pulled that trigger."

Tess waved her hand, almost as if she was shooing any blame from Josh. "Josh has always been my 'safe space' as the kids say today. He's the only man who's ever loved me—really the only man to ever look twice in my direction. It doesn't matter, I guess, why we broke up—what matters is that we got back together and stayed together. What if I had never found that again?' Her eyes began to get misty.

"Oh, Sis, I had no idea you felt that way about anything. You are so amazing, and always have been. Screw all those men! They clearly have very poor taste! I hope you truly know how worthy you are of love? Real love? And that is what you have with Josh, right?"

Tess hesitated, watching the waiter come to their table.

"How was everything, ladies? Can I bring anything else to your table?"

"No, thank you. Lunch was wonderful," Ruth assured him, and thanked him once more. When he left with their empty dishes, she reached across the table and squeezed her sister's hand.

Tess looked into Ruth's eyes, so much like her own, yet where Tess's eyes were a bright green, Ruth's were a deeper shade, and so much like their dad's eyes. "I'm sorry, this is supposed to be a happy time. I am supposed to be a blushing bride, not a crying one! Your hormones are spreading to me, I guess. And yes, Josh has always been my one true love. I still remember the first time I met him at the library in high school. Hard to believe I was such a nerd, right?"

"Okay, Nerd, let's go back to our room for a spell. Little mama here needs a nap, and no offense, but you could use a little freshening up."

CHAPTER
Four

Sam

Sam strode back to his cabin, not believing his luck, or fate, or whatever he felt like calling it. He had hoped he hadn't seen the last of her when he left her at her cabin this morning, but he had no idea where her destination was and how long she would be on the train. For that matter, he also was clueless as to what her name was. Something about her was niggling the back of his mind—like she should be familiar somehow, but how is that possible, he wondered? There was no way in hell he would have forgotten her, or even someone *like* her. Hearing her laugh tinkling through the dining car had drawn him over to her; he hadn't known for sure it was her, but having heard the laugh earlier made him suspect it was, and Sam was rewarded in finding himself right.

"Ugh," he muttered to himself, he had one goal on this train—to finish his novel. Well, he supposed he actually had two goals: finish the novel and make it to Lake Tahoe. With that, he sat back down at his small table and pulled out his iPad and keyboard. He was actually working on a romantic subplot: his first two books had taken longer than expected in finding an audience at first, but to his surprise, after an appearance at a writer's conference, he had been hash tagged (whatever the hell that meant) and thus had gained more female readers. Book sales had been climbing since, and each had finally made it to best seller lists. After reading so many comments in online book reviews about the chemistry between his male and female protagonists, he was doing something he'd never done before, which was listening to his audience.

At that moment, his phone rang, and seeing it was his mom, he answered. "Hey, Ma, what's up?" His mom, Jane, had recently retired from teaching high school English and now had free time on her hands. A lot of free time, if the number of calls to him were any indication.

"Oh, I was just doing some laundry and thought I would call to hear the voice of my eldest son, since I haven't heard from you in a while." Subtle, Mom, thought Sam.

"Okay, I just talked to you yesterday, and I'm guessing everyone else is either busy or you have already talked to them," Sam responded, knowing that as the oldest, he was last on her worry list. He had four younger brothers and the amount of mother-henning Jane did generally increased the younger her sons were.

"Well, Jamie is busy with his new baby, Bobby had a call out at the station, Chris had a meeting with a client, and Eric didn't answer, so I guess he must be busy," and with that, Jane sounded none-too-pleased with her youngest son, who had followed his talents to Broadway and was usually out on an audition. "So, how is the book coming?"

The only one more interested in his words-per-day quota than his agent was his mother. "It's going. Just trying to work out a bug in my head about my characters. Remember when you would have me do those writing lessons in high school?"

"Oh, you mean when I would give you a topic and have you write five hundred words? Sammy, you were always so talented; really, so much better than any other student I ever had." Sam barked out a laugh.

"Jeez, Ma, not that you were biased or anything, though. Anyway, I'm back to doing that recently. I just can't seem to break through with this subplot about my characters getting it on."

"Good lord, Sam, must you be so crass?" It was always feast or famine with his mom—she was either praising you or scolding you. "That is probably the problem—you see a love story as 'getting it on' when it should be about them developing a relationship. Frankly, that's always been your problem, if you don't mind my saying so…"

"Is this about Amanda again?" Sam enquired, knowing it more than likely was, and also knowing that his mom had never actually approved of the relationship.

"It's more about all of your exes. You have never had anyone that made you feel weak in the knees, anyone who challenged you, or anyone who has fully understood your worth. All of them just took one look at that beautiful face and probably now your sizable bank account, and that was it. You are my first born, and I want the world for you, and that includes love." Jane was nothing if not biased toward all her sons.

"I was the first one to admit that marrying Amanda was a huge mistake; unfortunately, it was a choice I regretted almost from the moment I proposed, but it was like I was on a speeding train not able to get off. Ironic considering I am now on a speeding train," Sam laughed.

"Well, you were swept away, but by what I don't know. I'll admit that Amanda was perfectly nice—honestly she was just a bit too perfect all-around. You want someone with flaws, and you will love them for those flaws. It was not her personally, but this has been the way with all of your choices. Look at Dad and I, for instance"

"I hope you're not suggesting I need to find someone like my mommy, because I can't go there with you without my therapist present."

In response, his mom started laughing, and then choking. "Good lord, please no sassy quips while I'm drinking my coffee. Save those for truly dull moments in our conversation, as I've been telling you since you were about five. No, I am absolutely NOT saying you need a woman like your precious mother, but someone who makes you shine, like I do with your father. You know how serious he is—but I make him laugh and lighten him, and he grounds me. He always has—I would have floated away on some faraway dream if not for him. He showed me that he WAS my dream." Jane paused and Sam could tell by her sighing that she was immersed in thoughts of his dad. He coughed, and his mom said, "Enough daydreaming—tell me how your train ride is going. Where are you now?"

"Actually, I'm not entirely sure. I've only been out of my room twice since I boarded, and both times were to the dining car. Well, I guess technically I went outside," Sam began to say, and then swore to himself. Damn, he thought, I never should have said anything.

"What do you mean, you went outside? While the train was moving?" Having five sons made it easy for her to imagine them doing all sorts of reckless activities.

"No, we were stopped at Penn Station in New York. I was eating breakfast and happened to look out the window and saw someone struggling with her bags on the platform."

"Oh, really? Her? Just remember, Sam, a damsel in distress makes for good material in your books, but maybe not in real life. You don't want to be involved with someone who can't take care of herself. How can you be sure she isn't some kind of con artist? This is exactly what I am always afraid of—one of my sons getting taken advantage of. I mean, you are JUST out of a bad marriage. You do not need to jump into something suddenly —"

Thankfully his mom finally stopped to take a breath, so he could cut her off, "Oh, sorry, Mom, my agent is calling. I have to take this. Love you and will call tomorrow." And with that, he hung up. No matter how many times he told her that his marriage hadn't been "bad" simply because it ended in divorce after a couple of years, she refused to believe it. True, it was pretty much doomed from the beginning, but he didn't necessarily regret it, and he counted Amanda as a friend still. He guessed that since his parents had such a rock-solid union, and often could not keep their hands to themselves when they were together, it was difficult for her to imagine divorce. It was also why he felt more shame than anything when he considered his failure in his marriage. Maybe if he had tried harder? But Amanda was rising in her career at the same time that his books were taking off, and she wouldn't, or couldn't, take time off to travel with him on his book tours. You can't be a newlywed and spend weeks apart.

Suddenly Sam was struck with inspiration. Pulling on his glasses, he grabbed his keyboard, opened up his writing app, and began furiously typing. He may finally have a grasp on the romantic element, despite his mother's shade earlier, as visions of perhaps a red-headed stranger entering the lives of his characters and spicing things up came to him. Take your inspiration where you find it, Sam, he encouraged himself. Isn't that what his mom always insisted, after all, during those writing lessons?

CHAPTER
Five

Tess

Tess looked over at her snoring sister. When they had gotten back to their room, Tess had first freshened up with a steaming hot shower; then she and Ruth had watched two episodes of a true crime documentary—well, Tess had, anyway. Ruth had conked out about fifteen minutes in, just as they were past the introduction of the murder mystery. Napping certainly wasn't on Tess's agenda for her cross-country escapade, but then again, she wasn't four months pregnant. Tess still had a hard time believing that her older sister was going to be a mother, or that she herself was going to be an aunt! When they had been growing up, dolls had been a huge part of pretend play, with each sister being a "mommy" to about four dolls each. Certain she would have started a family by now was one of her frustrations with her life, and had been for several years, but one she had never confessed to anyone. Aware that it may seem desperate to others, all Tess secretly wanted was to invest her love in someone who returned it ten-fold. During her childhood (which had been pretty fantastic by most standards) she would experience intense moments of loneliness. It was difficult to live so far out of her hometown on their farm, away from her friends and classmates during school breaks and summer vacation. While their parents worked long hours, the girls had only each other and would entertain themselves. After outgrowing dolls, Tess's companions were Ruth (always), her books, and then her baking.

What she needed was some air, so Tess grabbed her latest Karin Slaughter hardcover, her phone, and the bag of monster cookies; she headed to the lounge car for a cup of tea. Monster cookies were one of the first things she had learned how to bake, and would spend an entire Saturday afternoon at her grandma Eloise's side, along with her sister and her mom, all around the kitchen table. The monster cookie recipe was huge and required the force of a strong arm to stir everything together by hand at the end. Then they would each take a smaller bowl filled with dough and scoop them out onto every cookie sheet they could find in the house. Of course, only two sheets could go in the oven at a time, so eventually Tess and Ruth would begin sampling the monster cookie dough while the cookies baked. Once baked (everyone had to ensure the cookies were NEVER over baked, but just slightly under), the cookies were transferred to newspapers to cool on the countertops and table in their tiny farmhouse kitchen. Both of her grandmas were her inspiration for her starting her own bakery, and Tess got sentimental every time she looked at the recipe cards handwritten by either one of them, Grandma Eloise or Grandma Lydia. The monster cookies are one of her top requested items by the eateries who bought her baked goods, along with Grandma Lydia's homemade bread.

Tess could feel herself getting emotional and was growing close to tears. Her grandparents had played such a huge part in her life, and all of them were gone now, except her dad's mom, Grandma Lydia, who lived in a nursing home. Tess made a small wish when she got engaged that she would be able to have her one surviving grandparent at her wedding, but last month it became clear she would not be able to make the trip to the wedding. Remembering all of her grandparents now, Tess thought about how she got her sense of humor from her grandpa Jack, who had a sarcastic comment for every event; and from her grandpa Clarence, her love of books—he would give her two dollars for books whenever he saw her.

She was thankful for all of them playing such a huge role in her formative years, but every year they were gone seemed to be more poignant.

Wiping her eyes, Tess had finally reached the lounge car, and located a small table by a window toward the center of the car. After she sat down, she looked up into the face of the waiter from lunchtime. "Oh, hi, I didn't expect to see a familiar face already," she laughingly told him.

"Well, they like to move us around, and it makes the day go faster when I get to see new people. Just you this afternoon?" Todd inquired.

"Yes, thank you. Do you have English breakfast tea?"

"We certainly do. Would you like milk and sugar or lemon?" Todd offered.

"Fantastic. Milk, please," Tess requested.

"Anything else this afternoon? Snacks or sweets?"

Showing Todd her bag of cookies, Tess smiled and said, "I think I'm covered in that area."

"Ooh, the lady is prepared. What kind of cookies are you packing?"

"Monster cookies—have you ever had one?" Tess had always known the power of her cookies and was reeling Todd in.

"No, I've never even heard from them! Don't even tell me you made them yourself! They have that homemade look, not the factory look some of our stuff has," he said with some disdain.

"Haha, you've been missing out, Todd!" Tess reached into the bag and brought out a cookie for presentation. "These bad boys have oatmeal, peanut butter, chocolate chips AND M&Ms."

"Sounds delish—how about I bring you a plate so you can class up teatime?"

"Only if I can share a cookie—want to try one?" Tess raised the bag up to Todd so he could reach in and choose his own cookie.

"Definitely." Todd plucked out the largest one and bit into the chewy cookie, and rolled his eyes, "Girl, you were not kidding—these are fantastic! Now this is what we should be serving here."

"Thank you, and wait until you try my snickerdoodles. I'll bring one by tomorrow for you."

With that, Todd disappeared to get her tea. Glancing around the car, Tess was surprised at the number of solo travelers at every table. Although most would more than likely think she was also a solo traveler, due to the absence of her sleepy sister. Suddenly Tess's phone began jingling. Seeing the caller ID read "Josh", she answered.

"Hey, Babe, how are you?" She asked Josh.

"Tessa, finally! I was expecting to hear from you this morning after you got on the train," Josh admonished her.

"Oh no, I'm sorry—I was a complete mess getting on the train, and then Ruthie got on; after that, we hung out in our room, we went to the dining car to have lunch, and then watched a couple of episodes of that new series- "

Josh cut her off, "Okay, but it's four o'clock now—you've been on the train for hours. You didn't have a spare moment to call?"

"Babe, I'm sorry. After lunch and we got back to our room, I took a shower and then when we watched that series on my iPad, Ruthie fell asleep. I just now left our room and came down to the lounge car." Tess started to twist her engagement finger, only to find her finger was now empty. Oh hell! Where was her ring? Josh would freak out if he knew she wasn't wearing it.

"You know I just worry about you, especially when I haven't heard from you—no call or text since you left this morning. It does sound like you've been busy, though. Did you give Ruth her goodie bags?" Josh asked, and then continued, "I can't believe you almost forgot them this morning, especially after you made such a fuss over making everything."

"Yes, I did give Ruth her goodies; thanks for reminding me about them. She was super excited. I actually brought a bag to have a couple of cookies with my tea."

No response from Josh after that. Radio silence was never a good look on Josh. "Hello," Tess said, "is this thing on?"

"Tessa, honey, I thought we agreed to watch the sweets intake for a few months? Didn't you have an issue at your dress fitting?"

At moments like this, Tess regretted mentioning any insecurities to Josh; he was way too matter-of-fact for her, way too "Oh, you have a problem? Well, I have a solution." When Tess had first gone bridal gown shopping, none of the gowns she loved had come in plus sizes. After being reassured that her top choice could, in fact, be ordered to be made to her size, she was extremely disappointed when the dress arrived and it was most DEFINITELY NOT in her size. Fortunately, she had ordered it far enough in advance, and alterations had started immediately. That was last week, and when she had gotten back home and told Josh about the mishap, he went on and on about them starting the Mediterranean Diet (or was it Keto, this time?) and that he could also stand to lose a few pounds before the wedding. More upsetting than the wedding dress was Josh's attitude lately, almost like he was trying to reform her or remold her into a smaller, and quieter, version of herself. Shouldn't this behavior have started years ago, Tess often thought, and not just now be rearing its ugly head six months before their wedding?

"You did have an issue with your dress, didn't you?" Josh repeated. "Honey, I'm only trying to help you here."

"What you're not understanding, Josh, is that I don't think I need help," she whispered into the phone. "You know how many years it took me to be happy with my body? Which you say you love, by the way."

"Whoa, hold on—I never said I didn't love your body. It's just that you were so upset that day. I just want to fix it, or help you fix it."

"Right, I was upset my dress didn't fit, and the problem IS being fixed. By a seamstress, not a diet. Look, my tea is here and I don't want it getting cold. I'll call you later, okay?

Josh sighed, "Sure, Tessa. I love you."

"Love you, too," and as she signed off from her fiancé, Todd placed her tea in front of her.

"Everything okay, sugar? You just seem a little down."

Tess smiled up at him, "Yep, it's all good. Thanks, Todd." As she lifted her cup of tea, a motion from across the car caught her eye.

CHAPTER
Six

Tess and Sam

Looking up from his corner table, Sam blinked to clear his vision,
wanting to make sure he was seeing things correctly. Yes, affirma-
tive, his recent source of inspiration was sitting in the dining room,
and seemingly distressed. Sam noted to himself that she had changed
clothes since earlier, and was now wearing a sunshine bright top, with her
red hair now flowing over her shoulders. Unable to stop himself (and not
particularly caring to, either) he grabbed his bag of chips and soda from
the table as she hung up the phone, and walked the distance of half the car
over to where she was sitting.

"Have you ever seen the movie 'Strangers on a Train'?" Sam asked,
and she looked up from what appeared to be a cup of tea, those green eyes
shooting sparks right into him.

"Excuse me?" Tess asked, somewhat confused.

"You know, that old Hitchcock movie…" Sam began to explain, "where two strangers meet on a train and agree to murder someone for the other person?"

Tess interrupted, "Of course, I know that movie! I love Hitchcock, but I hope you're not asking me to murder someone for you, are you?" She joked, eyes lit up with delight.

Sam laughed, "No. I was sitting across the car and noticed you seemed upset, so I wanted to try to lighten things up. Movie references always seem to snap people out of a funk. And then I also realized I never had a chance to introduce myself to you, and my mother would skin me alive for being so rude," he paused, stuck out his hand and greeted her, "Hi, I'm Sam."

"Oh, hi, Sam, I'm Theresa," and she put her hand in his. He felt his hand engulfing hers, and felt a surge of protectiveness as he ran a thumb over her knuckles., touching the softest skin imaginable.

What in the world possessed her to introduce herself to this man-Sam-with her full name? Absolutely no one, with the exception of her mom when she was chewing her out, called her Theresa. But now, on a train with a stranger (albeit a very mesmerizing stranger with the darkest brown eyes she's ever seen, and don't even get her started on those dimples) she suddenly decides to be known as Theresa? Ruth was going to die when she heard this. Upon reflection, maybe a sort of anonymity was completely within reason when riding a train cross-country?

Reluctantly letting go of her hand, he asked, "Mind if I join you? I'm harmless, I swear," he added when she seemed to hesitate.

"Sorry, um, sure. You don't seem like a murderer, but I don't know if I would categorize you as harmless," she remarked, as her eyes tracked his movements while he sat down. Glancing down, he saw her rubbing her hands together.

Sam grinned what one of his exes called his "wolf grin", aware that it had been used to disarm a woman on more than one occasion. What he wanted was to see her relax and look like she wasn't all tense. "So, Theresa, what brings you on the train?"

After a slight pause, she answered, "My sister and I are traveling to San Francisco. Kind of a last hurrah, sister bonding moment."

"Now this sounds like an interesting premise for a movie! Sisters creating all kinds of chaos on a cross-country train, maybe involving themselves in the lives of fellow passengers. Perhaps solving mysteries or creating a 'meet cute' between two unsuspecting solo travelers."

Tess belted out a laugh, and the sound of it floored him. The eyes, the laugh, that mesmerizing red hair. He was beginning to feel like spotting her out the window was his best stroke of luck in a long time. "Wow, Ruth would love this movie. Nothing she loves more than injecting herself into other people's lives. You, Sam, have a fantastic imagination."

God, the sound of his name on her lips was intense to his ears. "I should, I spend my life making things up. I'm a writer."

"Oh, really—anything I might have read?"

Sam glanced down at the table, not wanting to discuss his previous works or his current one, but noted the Karin Slaughter novel on the table. "I doubt it. That book, on the other hand, is an excellent choice. I read it in a weekend. Her imagination terrifies me, but in a good way. Have you read all of the series?"

"Of course," she responded emphatically. "I haven't had a chance to read this one yet, but *finally* got some chapters in today. I've been swarmed with my work."

"I know that feeling. What do you do?" He imagined what Theresa might do for a living—librarian? Nurse? Wow, Sam, your guesses are from a century ago, he thought.

"I'm a baker," she said proudly.

"Oh really—anything I might have eaten? I love to eat," and with that he crumpled his now empty chip packet and placed it on the table.

Tess smiled, saying, "Well, that depends—spend any time in Brooklyn? That's where I bake. I rent out space in a commercial kitchen down the block from my apartment, and I supply some neighborhood delis and coffee shops with their carbohydrate needs. Or is it carbohydratic needs?"

Laughing, Sam confessed that despite his close relationship with words, 'carbohydratic' was not one he was familiar with. "But your work definitely sounds delicious. Do you work by yourself or with anyone else?"

"My dream is to have my own bakery one day, but right now I work by myself, and I love it. I generally work every other day, but the hours are stupid. I'm up and baking at like four a.m. so I can get breakfast items delivered by the time commuters want them, and then I go back to the kitchen and bake desserts."

Sam rubbed his belly, when despite the intake of chips, it began growling. "Forgive my poor manners. I hadn't eaten anything since my breakfast was interrupted by a red-haired tornado," he looked pointedly at Theresa, who blushed. "I should have had something more than chips. What's that on your plate? Looks tasty."

"Too bad for you it's not on the menu," Theresa taunted.

Too bad it's not on the menu? Even in her own mind she sounded like a sultry throwback to the 1940s. What was she doing? Looking up, Tess saw Sam still watching her. "What I mean is that I brought these with me. My sister is pregnant and threatened me with sisterly violence if I didn't bring her some cookies for our journey. She can be very persuasive. Plus, I have this obsession to show my love through food. Obviously."

Sam looked confused, "Don't know about obviously, but you seem like the type of woman to have no problem expressing yourself. That can be a very rare quality these days. It's hard to find sincerity in the age of social media."

Tess nodded in agreement, then stated "I agree to an extent, but I must confess that I am absolutely addicted to knowing everyone else's business. I have some college friends I keep in touch with through social media; honestly, we probably would have lost touch if not for the internet. I don't know how my mom did it, but she has remained in touch with, like, every friend she has had through every stage of her life, no social media needed."

"Yeah, my mom, too, but I think people tended to make stronger connections a generation ago, and well before that. Interactions meant more then," Sam said.

"I never thought about it like that, but really it makes sense. Like how they always knew everyone's phone numbers by heart. Huh. Too deep for me to consider," Tess laughed, and then took a breath. "So, Sam, what brings you on the train?"

"I'm an absolute asshole who hates flying, I guess you could say," and with that Tess burst out laughing.

"I think I've been on planes with you. Always grumbling about layovers, connections, having to pay for premium snacks?" She guessed.

"Exactly," Sam responded, "plus I have to work, and I have the luxury of being able to take as long as I want getting somewhere. I'd take the train everywhere, if I could. I'm meeting some buddies for the weekend. Some I haven't seen in several years, so it should be a good time."

"Oh, nice. And where is your destination?" And then they were interrupted by Todd, the waiter.

"It's nice to see both of you enjoying the afternoon together. Can I get anyone more refreshments?" Tess ordered another cup of tea, and Sam declined.

"No thanks, I still have some soda left. Actually, could I get a burger? And also I guess another one of these," Sam requested , holding up his soda can. "I'm suddenly starving."

"Absolutely, I will get that in and be back with your tea, gorgeous," Todd stated.

Tess blushed and laughed, "He is going to be a fun part of the trip." Sam nodded in agreement. Tess looked at Sam as she sipped the remnants of her tea. "Before you ordered your burger, I was asking you where you are headed?"

"Oh, sorry, umm Reno. I had to be up at the crack of dawn to catch the train in Boston this morning, but I try not to travel with any excess baggage, so it was pretty seamless."

"Hey, is that a dig at me having 'excess baggage'? Seems a little personal, when we've only now just officially met, and you have no idea all of the deep, dark secrets I could be hauling around," Tess informed him.

"A woman of mystery, eh? Must be the reason I abandoned my breakfast this morning. I have always been drawn to a mystery, I do have to admit," Sam confessed, as he stared straight into Tess.

Tess chuckled unsurely, unable to tell if he was making fun of her or not. Josh had made a comment when they got back together all those years ago that one of the reasons he loved her was her ability to be an open book; he had at least once even inferred that she wasn't as deep as some of the other women he had dated during their hiatus. It had always stung her that he had been with other women during that time. Josh had always been the only man for her, even when they were teenagers. Ruth had warned her when they stayed together after going to colleges on separate coasts that she was making a mistake and had even suggested Tess break up with Josh so that she was free to explore other relationships, or at least not feel guilty for attempting to explore them. Tess, however, had no interest in being rejected by uninterested men—she had felt scathing looks from them while being IN a relationship, god forbid she were single.

"That's me, a real Agatha Christie." Suddenly her phone pinged with a text from Ruth, inquiring as to where her sister had gone off to, and then a second text appeared immediately telling Tess that she was feeling deathly ill and to please bring another soda if she could.

"Sorry, Sam, sister emergency. Mind if I take this?" And with that, Tess grabbed the new can of soda that Todd had just brought to their table. "I'll pay you back later," and flashed him a grin that melted his core.

And with that, Sam longingly watched her saunter across the lounge car, and then disappear. Although he hated to see her leave, he couldn't help but appreciate the view. In a completely non-sexist way, of course, just in case his mom was reading his thoughts.

Todd approached his table, sat his burger down in front of him, and said "Enjoy."

Sam grinned at Todd and said, "I intend to, believe me."

CHAPTER
Seven

Tess

Struggling with her room lock, Tess at last managed to get the damn door open, and promptly stumbled over her sister's purse and cardigan. "Ruthie, where are you? I'm here," Tess called, and then muttered, "obviously"

The door to their bathroom then swung open, and Tess looked over and saw her sister clutching the doorframe. "Oh no, Sis, you look like hell," Tess proclaimed to Ruth.

"Well, at least I feel as good as I look. Did you manage to bring me a soda? I need something to fizz my sick out," Ruth responded with a line their mom always said when they were ill as children. Ellen Lefferts believed carbonation was a general cure-all, using it on everything from laundry to sickness to even a braising a Sunday roast.

Handing her sister the can she had procured from Sam, she told her, "I got you this."

Ruth stared at the soda incredulously, asking, "Dr. Pepper? This is an interesting choice. When was the last time you saw me drink a Dr. Pepper? Who drinks Dr. Pepper when they're sick?"

"Interesting time to be picky about your fizz, Sis. Remember Mom used to say that any fizz would do. And anyway, you're welcome, and beggars can't be choosers, yada yada."

Chugging the soda led Ruth to burp against the bubbles. "See, it's working out the sick already," Tess said, nodding with encouragement.

"Sorry I'm being such a bitch. Until I got pregnant, you know I hadn't thrown up in seven years. Then suddenly I'm vomiting morning, noon, and night; this business of 'morning sickness' is such bullshit. What they don't tell you is that it happens all day long. Ugh!" With that, Ruth slumped down into a chair.

"Oh, Ruthie, how terrible! You were napping so peacefully when I left. I went down to the lounge car for some tea and cookies—" Tess stopped suddenly. "Crap!"

"What? What's the matter?" Ruth asked Tess.

"I forgot the cookies at my table," Tess moaned.

"Okay, no big deal. You brought a bunch, right?"

"Well, the thing is I took the whole bag of monster cookies— "

"What? I hadn't even had one yet! I only had some snickerdoodles! Why did you take the whole bag? You know how much I love monster cookies," Ruth admonished her sister.

"I know, and I'm sorry. I'm sure I can get them from Sam later, if he picks them up," Tess said to herself.

"Sam? Who's Sam? How long was I sleeping that you come back to our room suddenly knowing 'Sam'? I feel like Rip Van Winkle here."

"Oh, remember that guy from lunch? The one who helped me this morning with my bags?"

"Of course I remember the mysterious stowaway! Those eyes—you know, I've always had a thing for brown eyes. I know Sean has blue eyes, and they're gorgeous, but I could totally get down with some dark brown eyes. Total dreamboat," Ruth sighed, and then laughed at her sister's expression. "Don't worry, it's just my raging hormones. If I'm not puking I'm fantasizing."

"Well kindly keep your fantasies to yourself, or save them for your own husband," Tess advised. "Anyway, I was having my tea in the lounge car, and he came over and introduced himself; said he thought I seemed upset, which was interesting. So we chatted for a bit until you texted me about being sick."

"Were you?"

"Was I what?"

"Were you upset? What happened?"

"Did I mention that Sam was wearing glasses this time?" Knowing her sister loved a man wearing glasses, Tess was hoping to distract Ruth from having to tell her about Josh's phone call. She had been there when Tess originally tried on wedding dresses, and had then gone to Tess's first fitting after the dress arrived. That first fitting had been a complete and utter nightmare, for both of them. Ruth had to witness Tess's humiliation as the dress that had been ordered in her size had actually been too small to zip up in the back. Weight and men were sore subjects with both sisters.

Ruth snapped her fingers. "We will circle back to the glasses, but please—you were obviously upset if you're trying this hard to get me off-topic. Sis, what happened?" Ruth implored.

"Oh, Josh called, and he was none-too-pleased that he hadn't heard from me all day."

"So what? It's not even a day yet! Doesn't he have his own trip he needs to be packing for? Any medical cases he should be studying so he can get published? Anything to keep from interrupting our sister trip? I mean, I love me some Josh, but he can be so clueless."

"Exactly! He means well, but sometimes he says the most irritating things."

"Like what? What else did he say other than reading you the riot act for ghosting him?"

"Oh, I mentioned I was having some cookies with my tea, and he chose to remind me about my dress not fitting. So tone deaf. He knows how it makes me feel to talk about my weight."

Ruth responded, "First of all, so flipping what if your dress didn't fit? NOBODY'S DRESS FITS! Not unless you're one of those extremely lucky women with high metabolism, or an extremely unlucky woman with an eating disorder. Second, is this something he does often? Discusses your weight?"

"No, no, he doesn't do it 'often' but now that he's a doctor he kind of sees it as his due diligence to help me be the healthiest I can be. In his defense, he always sees some part of me I could make just a bit better, you know?"

"And by making yourself 'better'" Ruth said, using air quotes, "would you be making yourself better for him or you? Tess, I know the weight thing is a sensitive subject with you, and it is for me, too. We come from a long line of chunky women, but I thought each of us had made peace with our bodies years ago? Just like Mom taught us to do." And it was true, their mom was also "fluffy" as Ellen liked to call it, and had passed the phrase down to her daughters. She had instilled in them by example and by words that their worth was in the beauty of their persons, not their bodies.

"Ruth, no offense, but you've only ever been a *little* chunky, and that makes a difference to the world. I just want to be right with the world and myself, you know? I found my man early on, and he loved me for ME. If he wants to help me make me a better person in a variety of ways, I don't think that's a bad thing. And quite honestly, if that's what it will take for us to live happily ever after, then fine. I said what I said, and I mean it. It's not as if I've never heard Sean make suggestions to you."

"True, but not personal shit like my body size. He's not 'Eat This, Not That'. And anything we try to better ourselves on, we do as a team. What is Josh improving on? A few months ago, you mentioned that he makes plans with you and then breaks them at the last minute. Is he getting better about that?" Tess watched Ruth get worked up about Josh, and had to admit that it felt good to have her sister have her back, as always.

"Wait—that is about his work. If he gets called in or has to stay late, well, that's what being a doctor-a surgeon-is all about. Not like he WANTS to cancel our plans," out of breath, and realizing she sounded just a bit defensive, Tess took a beat and then let the tears fall, as they'd been threatening to do all afternoon, it seemed.

Ruth got up out of her chair and padded over to her sister, "Tessie, I'm sorry. Let's not dwell on this. I had no right to question Josh or your relationship. I know how much he does love you, and you love him. This week is supposed to be about you, and I come in here with my big mouth, even bigger attitude, and out of control hormones. I'm so sorry. How did your call end with Josh, then?" Ruth asked while rubbing her sister's back.

"We ended it amicably. Part of Josh's deal is that he is a fixer, and if he thinks he can fix something, he will try: it's why he became a surgeon. He fails to realize that if I want him to fix something, I will ask. He's not the greatest communicator, and he can be a bit of a know-it-all," Tess admitted while blowing her nose.

"I will agree with that, having known him since he and I were both seventeen. He could be so annoying, and I guess I kind of like that he hasn't changed much in the last eighteen years. Josh does have some really great qualities, Sis, and if you're happy, then I'm happy." Ruth kissed the top of Tess's head, and then followed up, "First question, though: if you're so ecstatic, why were you having tea with Mr. Gorgeous Glasses? Second question: Where is your engagement ring?"

CHAPTER

Eight

Sam

Although Sam was thoroughly enjoying his burger, he couldn't help but wish he still had Theresa here as his dining partner. He wondered when the last time was he had clicked with someone so instantly, and realized he had no idea. Perhaps that was the cause of his creative dry spell, and that he had been able to write so freely earlier was no coincidence after seeing her that morning. Even now he had so many ideas swirling in his head and was anticipating getting back to his room to write—he felt his fingers itching for his keyboard. Too bad he wasn't one of those writers who wrote in longhand on a notepad: he craved the clicking of the keyboard, though. What so many people didn't understand about being a writer was that it was so often a lonely profession (he didn't necessarily mind the solitude, but he did miss making regular connections) and that it was WORK creating characters and plots. When people found out he was a writer, and especially that his last two books had been best-sellers, it often made it awkward: some people claimed they had read them (when clearly they hadn't) or worse, they were dismissive and had no interest in them; this was why he had brushed Theresa off when she had asked about his books; also, Sam hated talking about himself.

Just then his phone rang, and upon seeing it was one of his brothers, he answered, "Hey, Jamie, how's my beautiful niece?" Doing a double take after picking up his phone, Sam noticed that Theresa had left her novel behind. Was fate helping him out here? Being the perfect gentleman, he of course had no choice but to make a stop at her room to return her novel, he told himself.

"Emily is perfection, unlike her old man—and I do stress the OLD bit. Awake during the night, constantly eating, and crying at a volume sharp enough to pierce eardrums. Oh wait, that's Tamzin and me, not our baby," his brother joked.

"Good to know you haven't lost your sense of humor. Or is this the beginning of what are known as 'dad jokes'?"

"A sense of humor is sometimes the only thing getting me through a day loaded with dirty diapers. How did Mom have five of us? After seeing what comes out of just one baby at any moment, I'm convinced to stop at just one," then Sam heard Tamzin in the background, before Jamie came back on, "so, we heard you made a new friend…"

Sam groaned, "Wow—Mom has to be setting some kind of world record with her phone calls. It feels like I just talked to her not five minutes ago."

"You know Mom: 'Sammy met someone'," Jamie mimicked their mother's higher-pitched voice. "I was like 'Ma, isn't he on a train crossing the country?' She says 'Jamie, where's your sense of romance?' And my answer was no romance for the next six weeks, to which she said she didn't know how Tamzin puts up with me, and she hopes Emily grows up with more class."

"Oh, so a successful call with Mom, then? Well, you did your duty by answering and then annoying her, and now she can keep moving down the line of sons."

"Believe it or not, now that I have my own kid, I get why Mom is all up in our shit all of the time. Poor Emily doesn't stand a chance with me and Tam as parents. So, tell me about the dame? I'm assuming Mom was right—there is a dame?"

Sam sighed, "Jamie, she's incredible. A baker from Brooklyn, who also happens to be a Hitchcock fan? I'm dedicating my next book to her." Sam laughed, and then said, "Bro, not kidding here—I'm floored by her every time I see her. She has these green eyes that like sear right into me; no, not even—they sear right THROUGH me. First time I looked into them I felt like I was seeing an answer for something I didn't have a question to yet. Red hair, like fire, and the most lush—" Sam stopped suddenly.

His brother waited expectantly, and finally prompted, "The most lush…"

"I'm not sure I should be talking like this. You know, with the current environment? It just feels wrong now. Maybe I shouldn't even be THINKING about it? Would she think I'm degrading her or judging her by her looks? Trust me, she is well-covered in that area, but she's more than that—she's an entire soul."

Jamie whistled, "Okay, you are definitely in deep, and you met this woman, what? A couple of hours ago? But I'm here, at home with a newborn, on paternity leave. I promise to not reveal to her our conversation. Brother code, and all, so you can tell me all the deep dark secrets. What's her name?"

"Theresa. She just seems unlike any woman I've ever met. Or at least any I have ever dated."

"Dated and married, I presume? Because if she's anything like Amanda, you're fucked."

"God, no. Amanda and I were never going to work, but for so many reasons that were my fault as much as hers, I do have to point out. Anyway, I don't want to hype this up too much. I just met her today, although we did spend some time together this afternoon. Turns out she's traveling with her sister to San Francisco, so I will have the next few days to get to know her. Or hope to, anyway."

"Well, if my opinion means anything, you deserve good things, Sam. Tamzin was just saying last night how she wishes you would find love again; you know my wife is one of your biggest fans. No more poetry, though, because I'm pretty sure that she would leave me for your iambic pentameter." And with that Sam's niece began wailing in the background. "Gotta get the kid to her mama for feeding time. Talk later," and then Jamie was gone.

He and Jamie were only eleven months apart—Irish twins was their familial term for it. His parents had their five boys in fairly quick succession, just about two years separated each of his brothers, so they were all extremely close growing up and even more so now into adulthood.

Sam was pretty solemn as a kid, taking his responsibilities as the oldest child very seriously. An overachiever in school, he excelled in his studies but was often classed as 'nerd' by other students. Now he wore the mantle with pride, but as a teenager, as a male, being studious and (even worse) a book worm, often came with deep ridicule. To overcome the teasing, Sam would settle down with a pen and paper and just write, and his world opened up then. He knew he could dream on paper, putting all his insecurities aside, and create a world in which he was the hero. Not that he would ever say he was an outcast—he was often the life of the party, but that was a facade he had created, and was egged on by his brothers—with them he was their hero; the big brother who carried the world on his shoulders and could do no wrong. Money was tight for his family when he was growing up, and when he went to college majoring in English his mom was concerned about his career opportunities, especially when he focused on creative writing. Scholarships, work study, and all sorts of odd jobs made sure not much time was left for partying, so living in the frat house made it easy to socialize and not hole himself away.

Now, thinking of his past life, he casts his memory back firmly to college. Pledging a fraternity was one of his best decisions he made, and he still kept in touch with many of his 'brothers', Josh being one of them, and probably his closest connection to that time. It was Josh who had come up with Sam's nickname "Fitz" shortly after they met. Sam always carried a copy of "Tender Is the Night" with him, which was his particular favorite F. Scott Fitzgerald novel. Being in a fraternity made getting a nickname unavoidable, but "Fitz" was one he could live with back then. He wasn't proud of everything from that time, though, with one weekend in particular sticking out. He was a senior and working on his first volume of poetry, and also trying to write his very first (and terrible) novel, and it was homecoming weekend. The frat house was alive with visiting girlfriends, hormones, booze, and anxiety. Unfortunately, he had also broken up with his long-term girlfriend, so he wasn't in the mood for any monkey business in the house. Josh had selected this weekend to introduce him to "Tessa", finally, after hearing about her for the last two years. He intended to put his best foot forward with her, because he respected Josh so much, his fellow house geek. He remembered being struck by Josh's stories of her, emotionally. He speculated Josh to be exaggerating when he bragged about Tessa so much, that even the best words could not possibly do her any justice. When they were finally introduced, so very briefly, she was utterly dismissive of him, cutting and scathing in both words and tone, that it had been impossible to juxtapose Tessa in person and Tessa through Josh. Unfortunately, Sam had responded terribly to her, and had made a few hateful comments about Josh and how he could do better; it was not his shining moment: he was drunk, stressed, and embarrassed, and he had regretted it immediately the next morning, after Josh told him that Tessa refused to come to the frat house again.

"Are you all set here?" Sam looked up and saw Todd, his waiter grinning down at him.

"Oh, sorry, I was lost in thought. Yes, thanks, I'm done."

"I see she left you some cookies?" Todd said, nodding to a bag of cookies partially hidden by the Karin Slaughter novel. "She gave me one and it was beyond."

"Oh, she had to rush off to see to her sister, I think. Thanks for the cookie tip, though. Maybe I'll steal one before I return these to her."

CHAPTER
Nine

Tess

"Let's retrace your steps—we came back to our room after lunch and then what?" Ruth had been trying desperately to get Tess to retrace her steps to locate her ring.

"I took a shower, and yes, before you ask, I just tore the bathroom apart—twice! Obviously, I put on fresh clothes, then we sat down on my bed and watched that show on my iPad. Or I did, anyway—you fell asleep at some point," Tess said to her sister, with a hint of salt in her tone. She continued, "so I turned off our marathon, and I read some of my book; then I was feeling peckish, so I grabbed my book and cookies and went to the lounge car. Now I'm here." Tess was more annoyed than panicked at this point, because she knew she just had to remember what she had done with her engagement ring. Her memory was middling at the best of times, and of course now that she was wracking her brain, she was drawing an absolute blank. She always removed her ring when she showered, and would put it back on after putting on lotion and moisturizer. At home, her routine is to put her ring in a small bowl she keeps on the bathroom sink for safekeeping.

"*And* it just occurred to me that along with your cookies, I also left my book at the table! Ugh, where is my head?" Wailed Tess.

"Wow, you actually seem to be more worried about forgetting your book than misplacing your ring."

"I mean, it IS the new Karin Slaughter." The sisters looked at each other and then burst out laughing. "No, seriously, I know my ring is here. I've been in an altered state since getting on the train and just need to re-group." Tess brought her hands up to put her hair up in a ponytail. "Oh hell, and now Josh is calling," she announced after phone began ringing. "Probably feeling the heat from our earlier call. Should I answer?" Tess asked her sister.

"That depends on how guilty you're going to sound. And right now you're getting flushed. You know you can't lie worth a shit. So unless you're going to tell him about your ring—" and then Tess's phone quit ringing. "Well, there goes that. Problem solved."

Tess fell back onto her bed, tossing her arm over her head. "I just wish we hadn't had that sucky conversation before. This isn't how I wanted to start the beginning of my wedding journey."

"Technically, I think your wedding journey began with him asking you to marry him. This is like somewhere in the middle," Ruth reassured her sister. "Listen, everyone at the bachelorette weekend knows you're engaged, so don't stress."

"I sincerely hope you are not suggesting that I am leaving this train without my ring." Why would Ruth even try to suggest that? And why was Tess herself feeling so defensive? With that, Tess stood up and went over to her bags, beginning the process of taking out each item and carefully combing through her belongings.

Ruth also stood up, and hugged her sister, then apologized, "Sis, I'm sorry I made a joke about not finding your ring—obviously, we will find it. For now, though, considering the area space of this room," Ruth started, after looking at Tess's clothing being strewn about, "multiplied by my preg-nant body, things are getting close in here. I am going to just have a waddle down to the lounge car myself. I'll go look for your book, and MY cookies.

I need to get some steps anyway." She headed to the door, blew her sister a kiss, and then went out the door.

Folding up the clothes from her suitcase, Tess placed them back in. Once she checked all outside pockets of the suitcase, she zipped everything back up and stowed it back on the valet table. That left her overnight bag and her purse, but she was suddenly feeling overwhelmed; she grabbed a bottle of water and went to sit by the window to watch the countryside dance by. She knew she should call Josh back and let him apologize for being an ass earlier (she hoped he would, anyway). He had good intentions, and that was part of the problem: he always meant well, and would hate knowing he was causing her any anguish. He had had his own weight struggles he had dealt with as a teenager, but during his first year of college, he grew three inches taller and somehow his weight had resettled in the right places. Tess had never felt like he loved her any less, or saw her in a different light, but it wasn't the same —they no longer had the same view of the world, or how they were seen by that world anymore.

Tess took a drink of her water, and thought back to the day she met Josh in high school. She and her family had lived in her hometown forever—both Tess and Ruth were born in the same hospital as their parents had been. When Tess was a freshman, she was looking to find her place in high school. After having wandered into the library, she had seen the sign up sheet for Oral Interpretation, and took a chance. So many comments of "but you'd be so pretty if you lost weight" or "I'm sorry, this uniform doesn't fit you" had worn her down, so she had counted out marching band and pretty much all sports as her extra-curricular activities. Oral Interp was an activity not relying on looks or size, only her imagination and creativity, two things she had in droves. Two afternoons later, she was back at the library for the first meeting. Glancing over, she had seen a boy who looked as out of place as she did. She was the only freshman there, and he was the "new kid". She hadn't met him yet, because he was older than her. No doubt he was cute, but heavy, like she was; Tess took another chance and walked over to his table, where he was sitting alone. "Mind if I sit down?" She asked him. He shook his head, and motioned for her to take a seat. Tess smiled at him and said "I'm Tess. I think you're new here?" And the rest was history. It turned out he was two years older, and in Ruth's grade, and the three of them became the three musketeers, until Ruth got a boyfriend the following summer, which left Tess and Josh alone more frequently. It only seemed natural when the two of them turned to each other, and by the time the school year came around, Tess and Josh were a power couple (at least in their own young minds) and both had branched out into all sorts of acting bits in school. Tess had gained a self-confidence she had been lacking, and was head over heels in love with her first (and only) boyfriend.

At that moment, there was knocking on her door. Tess got up and crossed the room, laughing, "I guess you forgot your key, huh, Ruthie," as she swung the door open. Her breath caught in her throat. "What are you doing here?" She asked.

CHAPTER
Ten

Tess and Sam

A quick glance into Theresa's room told Sam that she very likely was alone, and he congratulated himself on his impeccable timing. "I thought you might be missing something," Sam said.

"What? How did you know? Did you find it?" Tess inquired, slightly taken aback that this handsome stranger could be returning her ring to her. She also became uncomfortably aware that she was wearing a loose-fitting tank top that she would normally never let anyone but her nearest and dearest see her in.

"Yes," he answered, smiling, "you left these at the table," and he held up her book and her little bag of cookies.

"Oh, those. Okay, I thought you meant—" she faltered. "What I mean is, thanks so much for bringing them over. My sister actually headed over to the lounge car a bit ago to check if I left these there. Thank you for bringing them to me: that was so sweet," Tess paused, touched by his thoughtfulness. "Do you want to come in?" Why was she asking him in, this almost-perfect stranger (emphasis on the perfect part)? Asking a man into her room, a man with those eyes that were like pools of melted chocolate. And the glasses, oh my. Tess had avoided studying him in full until now, but he was, she had to admit, extremely attractive. Like the kind of good looking that always passed her over. Her friends were constantly telling her that she has a barrier she puts up with men, one that instantly reads as: Back off asshole. She denied it over and over, but perhaps there was some truth to that. Unfortunately, she had been rejected during times she wasn't even TRYING to get noticed, and that's what truly hurt. Some men (too many in her experience) feel that a woman's worth relies solely on their attraction to said woman, and if he isn't attracted to her, then she isn't worth his time.

"Sure, I would love to." Sam remarked as she stepped back to let him pass by her, and he caught a light scent of vanilla and something floral as he did so. He had already had the idea that if Theresa didn't invite him into her room, he would try to finagle a way in, like suggesting it would be good background for his book. Yeah, he was sneaky like that. "Wow, this room is incredible. Much nicer than my room. I mean, I have a bed and table, but it's about half this size."

Tess gestured to a chair, "Would you like to sit down?"

"Thanks. So you rushed off earlier because of your sister—is everything okay? I guess it must be, if she went down to the cafe car. I hope the Dr. Pepper helped?"

Tess laughed, "It did, after she read me the riot act for bringing Dr. Pepper in the first place. She wanted a ginger ale, but I explained to her that beggars can't be choosers. She's absolutely fine—she's pregnant, not ill or anything, but she does have bouts of morning sickness all day. She's barely showing, yet is *definitely* making the most out of her condition. That's part of the reason we are taking the train to San Francisco: Ruth didn't want to have to rush around; she's a big fan of nesting, so if you look at that bed there, you can see how she has brought her own pillow and her own blanket. Is that TMI?" Tess asked, as she once again laughed at herself.

Sam smiled in response, loving the sound of her laughter. "Well, my brother and his wife just had a baby a couple of months ago, and if you believed him, he is the one who had all the cravings and aches and pains.

Typical second child syndrome, or at least that's what our other brothers say," Sam said, shaking his head.

"How many brothers do you have?" Tess queried curiously.

"Four brothers, so there are five of us, all together. Our mom used to say she knew how zookeepers felt. Hell, she still says that!"

"Five boys—wow! My mom thought she had it rough with Ruth and I! I always wanted more siblings, though, and I know my parents wanted more kids, but they got stuck with just us." Tess pulled at her ponytail, and wondered if she looked ridiculous.

"Oh, I wanted to confess that I had one of those monster cookies, and it took all my willpower to not eat the whole bag. Seriously delicious. I could see coming down to Brooklyn to get me some of those in the future," and Sam just stared at her, letting the inferences float on the air. It seemed time was standing still in that moment, in this small room, with only the two of them, breathing the same air as each other, feeling the swaying of the train, almost like a heartbeat. Just then Tess's phone pinged.

Gasping, Tess reached over and picked up her phone from the table between them, "Oh it's Ruth. She can't find my stuff. I'll just text her—" and with that, her phone flew out of her hands, landing at Sam's feet. She bent forward from her chair the same moment that he reached down, and their hands met, with each one trying to grab the phone. Sam looked at her, his gaze sending fire into her body. She felt as if she was burning, the feeling was that intense.

Sam had gotten to the phone first, and when he placed it in her hand, he couldn't resist holding on to her fingers an extra second or two. Hell, it could've been hours and he wouldn't know any better. Theresa had him completely mesmerized—her hair was coming loose from her ponytail, her cheeks were flushed, and god help him, he had tried not to look since the minute he entered the room, but then she bent over to get her phone…

Her phone pinged again, a reminder that Ruth's text had gone un-answered. Tess cleared her throat, "I'd better answer her." She typed and then said, "Okay, I called off the dogs. Oh, now Ruth says she is going to go to the dining car and get us a table for dinner. I mean Ruth and I… Ruth and I are getting a table for dinner." Why was this so awkward? Tess was used to being genial, to being friends with everyone. And was it hot in here?

"Okay, well I should get back to my room," Sam said, even though he had made no move to rise from the chair. "I should actually thank you, you know."

Tess looked at him with confusion, "What are you talking about?"

"Well, I know I told you earlier that I'm a writer, but I didn't mention that another reason I am taking the train was so I can work before I play this weekend. I am supposed to send my editor my first four chapters; I've already postponed it twice this month."

"So what does that have to do with me?" Tess asked, moving her hand up to her throat.

"Meeting you, Theresa, has inspired a new angle in my book. I had such writer's block until you crashed onto the platform in New York. Suddenly, I have all kinds of ideas," and Sam made circling motions over and around his head, almost as if he couldn't contain his inspiration.

Tess laughed nervously, "A new angle? Like a hot mess trying unsuccessfully to get her bags onto a train? Or a head case crossing the country with her sister in tow?" Now I sound like Ruth, Tess thought to herself—firing off ridiculous questions before even one can be answered.

Sam cocked his head, and studied the woman he knew as Theresa. He could not put his finger on it, but there was something slightly familiar about her, almost like she reminded him of someone he had met before. Not that he had ever met Theresa, though, Sam mused. He would never have forgotten her, not as intrigued as he was by her.

"Can I walk you down to the dining car? I promise I won't interrupt your sister dinner; it's just that I thought I'd pick up another soda before I start writing."

Tess licked her lips, "Umm, sure, but I was going to change into something more dinner appropriate.

"Okay, I'll just step outside your room," Sam half-heartedly offered— he hated the idea of leaving her.

"That's okay—the bathroom is big enough to change. Be right out," and with that, Tess grabbed a shirt out of the suitcase on her bed, and ducked into the bathroom.

Sam stood up and, noticing another bag of cookies on the opposite bed, he walked over, opened the bag and took one out. "Are these snickerdoodles?"

Tess called out, "Yes, help yourself. Just don't tell Ruth; they're her favorite."

Mine, too, Sam thought, and bit off half the cookie, and its cinnamon and sugar melted on his tongue. "Oh my god, you're amazing, Theresa," he moaned. And then he couldn't breathe. She had redressed in a purple silky looking blouse, that draped in all the right places. The color brought out the depth of green in her eyes, and somehow made her red hair even more vibrant, which was now falling loose over her shoulders. No, he thought, still not breathing. I need to get out of this room.

"I'm sorry, yes, I'm ready," Tess said worriedly. "Are you okay? You said you need to get out of this room. Freaked me out a little bit."

"Did I say that out loud? I guess your snickerdoodle threw me for a loop. My grandma used to make these for my brothers and I when we were little, and I haven't had them in years. You are very talented, Theresa."

She blushed, thanked him and nodded toward the door, "Shall we?"

Chapter
Eleven

Sam

Although he would have loved to have dinner with both Theresa and her sister, Sam had known that the wisest decision for him would be to just head back to his own room and start writing, especially after he had become almost verklempt in such close quarters with her. One of the perks of having a private room was the option for room service, which he could take advantage of whenever he wanted. So, he had regretfully bidden Theresa farewell at the doors to the dining car and set off back to his room.

Now that he had the feeling of Theresa reminding him of someone, he wanted to ponder it. There was every possibility their paths had crossed before, especially since she had told him she lives in Brooklyn. He travels from Boston down to New York City a couple of times a year to meet with his publishing team, take in some Broadway shows, and meet up with his frat brother Josh and some of their other friends from college. Sam was good at making male friendships, since he was so close to his brothers. He wasn't a fan of shallowness, and preferred meaningful connections.

Picking up his phone, he was suddenly struck with the idea to call Josh. He was looking forward to the upcoming weekend with him and the other attendees for the bachelor party. Knowing Josh, the party was going to be fairly low-key, but filled with outdoor actives they could enjoy at Lake Tahoe; he'd been there once before during a college break, and Josh's family house was a perfect place to gather. He pulled up Josh's entry in his phone book and hit the call button.

Josh answered almost immediately, "Hey, Fitz, what's up?"

Sam chuckled—he could count on Josh to answer his phone in exactly this way every single time. "It's always good to know some things never change, Doc. Are you getting ready for your big weekend?"

"Absolutely, Fitz. I heard from Liam this afternoon, and he said he had verified your presence for the weekend. I just got a moment of down time, so I'm glad you reached out. I really appreciate you coming for my party—I know the location is a bit out there, but everyone that's coming has been there at least once in the past. I'm stoked we will all be together at one time. Not going to be a huge gathering, though; I'm sure Liam told you."

"Actually, I've only texted with Liam, so I don't know the complete details, but I'm open to whatever. It'll be good to see some of the brothers from our frat house again. How many will be there?"

"Five brothers have confirmed, a few cousins other than Liam, a couple of guys I went to med school with who could get away, and a doctor I did my residency with in Brooklyn. Tessa's brother-in-law was supposed to come, but he had a family thing and couldn't make it. Oh, man, get this—you know my cousin Daniel?"

"The chef from Chicago, right?" Confirmed Sam.

"Exactly! He said he'd do all the cooking we want at the lake house—steaks on the grill and any fish we catch, bacon and eggs in the morning; he has a whole menu he wants to make there."

"God, sounds amazing! I'm hungry already," Sam laughed. "So last time we spoke you mentioned something about starting at a new hospital? How's that going?"

"Good, good—long hours and not a lot of time off, but it's all as expected. Tessa's been fantastic, though. I know that you two don't really know each other; I guess now that I'm really thinking about it, you guys only met that time back in college. How is it that we haven't had a proper meet up with the three of us, especially since you and I see each other a couple times a year?" Sam was a bit caught off guard with this, because he had been asking Josh for all of them to get together for years, but Josh always had a reason that Tessa could not be with him. Sam had wanted to mend fences with her since college.

"Well, I've been in the midst of a divorce, and we really just see each other when I'm down in New York, or you have a conference in Boston. Plus, there's the fact that she despises me. I really need to make that first meeting up. It's one of my biggest regrets from our frat house—I know I acted like an ass," Sam bemoaned.

Thinking back on that day always made Sam feel regretful. He and Josh had just recently formed a tight bond, despite having lived together in the frat house the previous year. All Josh could talk about was either his drive to become a surgeon or Tessa. If Sam had been honest with himself, he would have recognized his feelings as jealousy. Sam had never felt that strongly about any of his previous girlfriends, or even the one he'd been dating for the past year; to have Josh talk of being so in love with Tessa, and to witness him being completely unwavering in that devotion (despite other college girls who so clearly wanted to date him), was astonishing for him. Especially for a romance that seemed doom to fail: it had begun in high school, and then Josh and Tessa had gone to schools on opposite coasts, not to mention their two year age difference, which could seem more like a decade in college. Tessa had been coming for the college's homecoming celebration, and Sam knew it was the first time she would be visiting Josh at school. Their frat house was almost like a scene out of "Animal House", and when Sam opened the door to Tessa, he failed to instantly recognize her from the photo Josh kept in his room. He could sense her insecurity, and then it seemed disdain seemed to take over; he remembered wanting to pull her into a hug, but was met with resistance, and Tessa firmly stated that she was only there to pick up Josh. It was clear she had no interest in meeting any of his brothers, or getting to know them as his friends. Josh cancelled the plan for them to double date to the homecoming ball, and they stayed on the other side of the ballroom completely by themselves, at an event that should have been social. Sam had felt so shitty for Josh, knowing he had been so excited for everyone to meet Tessa, and to show her around their house.

With the passing of time and maturity, Sam could see now that she had been a fish out of water then, and he could sympathize that it must have been completely overwhelming to an eighteen-year-old girl to be by herself in that awkward atmosphere. Unfortunately, Sam was not as mindful back then, and although he hated to recall his exact words and he knows he was out of line—in fact, he knew it back then. Twenty-one-year-old men are still boys, though, and he was an absolute prick, no doubt about it. Sam looked forward to the opportunity to make it up to Tessa, hopefully sometime before the wedding, which is exactly what he says to Josh right now.

"I know, Fitz, I know. There's also the little fact that she blames you for me breaking up with her my senior year; I mean, I have denied it every time she brings it up, but I guess it's easier for her to blame you and not me for the whole deal. I mistakenly thought that she should enjoy the rest of her college life unencumbered, especially with me then going to med school. Breaking up with her is one of MY biggest regrets."

"Yeah, I never understood why she would hold me responsible for you guys splitting up, but I guess if it causes less friction with the two of you, I can bear the burden." Sam had enough breakups of his own, he didn't necessarily want to be held responsible for anyone else's, but sometimes you had to take one for the team, right? "You made your way back to each other, though, which is the important part. Everything is cool with you guys, right? She is good with your surgeon hours and all that? I know long hours apart can be hell on a relationship. Not that I'm speaking from experience or anything."

Josh cleared his throat, and seemed to take a moment. "I talked to her this afternoon and things were a little tense, but nothing we can't work out. Listen, Fitz, I'm so psyched to see you and hang this weekend. I've got to go. See you soon."

"Peace out, Doc," Sam replied. He hung up continuing to think about Tessa now and his regret for whatever problems he had caused for his friend and fiancée, and whether it still had a ripple effect, even it was years ago.

CHAPTER
Twelve

Tess

After Sam escorted her just outside the dining car and had started back to his room, Tess had reached into her pocket and touched her ring. When she had been reaching for her phone on the ground, she had put a hand out to steady herself as she bent forward. Much to her surprise, when she splayed out her fingers, they brushed something small and metallic. After silently thanking her lucky stars she had found her ring, she had curled her hand around it and tucked it into her pocket as soon as she sat up. Since she had put some lotion on her hands after changing her shirt, she didn't want to put it back on yet—best for the prongs on the ring to not get lotion under them, right? Or at least that's what she told herself as she entered the car, and smiled at Ruth from the door. Tess walked over to her sister and sat down.

"Oh, Tessie, I love that top you're wearing. Purple is your color—you are absolutely glowing!" Ruth proclaimed.

"Am I? Must be from the walk here. Just thought I would dress up a bit; you know, dinner with my sister," Tess said in her sing-song voice. "Are you feeling any better?"

"Much better," Ruth replied. "I've had a ginger ale and some of this delicious bread—the butter is to die for. Took you long enough to get your happy ass here, though. I feel like I texted you an hour ago, but the wait was worth it." Ruth said laughingly. "In the future, don't keep a pregnant woman waiting, especially when she's been sick and is FINALLY ready to eat!"

"Yeah, sorry about that," Tess paused and took a seat across from her sister. She debated what to tell Ruth, and then went with, "You won't believe who came to our room…"

"Let's see—is he about six feet tall, sexy as hell, and has bottomless brown eyes?"

Tess looked at her sister with surprise, "Wow—news travels fast! How'd you know?"

"Oh a little birdie may have mentioned that a certain handsome, single writer was heading to your room," said Todd, who suddenly showed up at their table. "Evening ladies; you two are looking fabulous, if I may be so bold?"

The sisters laughed, and after ordering a round of drinks—another ginger ale for Ruth, and a martini for Tess—they looked at their menus. "So you must have already known why I was late. Did you know Sam was in our room when you texted me?"

"I only assumed so, considering I saw Todd almost the minute I came into the car to check for your stuff. I will admit I wasn't sure if you would 'fess up about him being with him." Ruth looked up from her menu, and said casually, "plus the flush on your cheeks tells me something is going on with you." Looking back at her menu, Ruth announced, "I think I'm in the mood for some pasta, especially with that delicious sounding Bolognese sauce."

"Ooh, yummy. I'm thinking the salmon for me—you know how I love lemon and capers," answered Tess. She was a sucker for anything tart and sour, be it sweet or savory. Growing up on the farm, they had mostly eaten very basic, stick-to-your-ribs kinds of meals, but their parents did expose them to as much of a variety as they could, especially when they traveled anywhere. As a family, they would take a big trip every summer and go somewhere more urban, where the girls could be exposed to different cultures, foods, and most importantly to the arts scene in every city. Ballet, theatre, museums, John and Ellen had given their daughters a rich childhood that taught them to appreciate both urban and rural life. Now that both Tess and Ruth lived in large metropolitan cities, their parents came to them for cultural experiences. The fact that they could stay with their daughters was even better: John and Ellen loved to save money if given a chance.

"That's it? You're having the salmon and not going to tell me any details?" Ruth looked appalled.

"Okay, I think I'm also going to save room for dessert," Tess announced to her sister. It was a time for celebration, and what said "celebrate" better than sugar? And on another note, how did Todd even know Sam was single? Thankfully, she was spared any more explaining, as Todd had reappeared at their table.

After giving him their orders, and receiving their drinks, Ruth pressed Tess more firmly, "So, were you with Sam this whole time? I mean, if Todd saw him leave before I even got here, that means he would've had to arrive at our room practically as soon as I had left? And I'm presuming that's what took you so long to get down here after I texted? You were with Sam?"

Tess felt her sister's eyes studying her, and was desperately trying not to feel guilty. She had nothing to feel guilty about, right? She hadn't done anything wrong. Sam was just a nice, fellow traveler who was thoughtfully returning something to her. Something that she had managed to leave at a table they had been sharing didn't feel like a pertinent detail to confess to her sister. Or was it? Was she over thinking this, which she had a tendency to do? Maybe she was UNDERthinking it. Was it out of line for a single (or so Todd says) man and an engaged woman to be in a room alone together? This wasn't the Victorian age, she told herself. But, she quietly asked herself, if it was perfectly innocent, why was she not sharing these details with Ruth? Also, why was she keeping her ring in her pocket instead of sliding it back on her finger?

Ruth was snapping her fingers, "Hello? Earth to Tess! Oh good, you're back with me now. Well? Were you with Sam that whole time?"

"No," Tess denied, "not the whole time. I looked for my ring and put my stuff back into my suitcase. Then there was a knock on the door, and I thought it was you, like that you had forgotten your key. But Sam was there instead. And then it seemed rude to not invite him in, especially after he had been so sweet to deliver my stuff to our room. So, he sat down and had a bottle of water and a snickerdoodle—"

Ruth interrupted, "You gave another of my cookies away? Good lord, Tessie, I might need those down the road when I am too sick from your niece or nephew to possibly be interested in any other food, and here you are giving away my backup source of sustenance! And why are you babbling? You only ever babble when you have a guilty conscience."

"Don't be ridiculous—I have nothing to be guilty about. Or maybe I do. I don't know. Maybe I just feel bad about getting into it with Josh earlier and then ignoring his call when I was looking for my ring. What kind of fiancée misplaces her engagement ring, anyway?" And yet, that wasn't true, was it? She now had her ring back, so why hadn't she told Ruth?

"Oh, pish posh. There was that story on the national news just a couple of weeks ago about some tv journalist losing her engagement ring at some awards show. On the red carpet, no less! Happens to everyone." One of Ruth's best qualities was being able to downplay even the most hair-raising of situations, which was often a blessing; however, it could also be frustrating as hell, though, if you NEEDED her to make a big deal out of something. Which was most definitely what Tess did NOT want her doing now. "Besides, you know Josh: he never takes anything too personally. You can call him back after dinner tonight back in our room. He'll be done with work and missing you and all will be right between you guys."

"Ugh, you're right. I'm not going to dwell on the ring right now. I have complete and utter faith that it will show up. Now, let's make a toast." They raised the drinks that Todd had deposited at their table.

Ruth toasted, "To the Lefferts sisters!"

Tess couldn't agree more, "To the Lefferts sisters!"

CHAPTER
Thirteen

Tess and Sam

"I'm so sorry, ladies," interrupted Todd, "as you can see, we are a packed train car tonight, and I would never want to impose on your sister time, but I have a lonely gentleman who seems to be without a place to sit. He's not bad to look at, either, so I'm hoping he could maybe join you two for dinner?" Tess looked over Todd's shoulder as he gestured to the podium by the far set of doors, and her eyes located Sam immediately, looking freshly showered, and wearing a button-down shirt in her favorite color: blue. She could be in trouble. Good thing she had only had the one martini.

"Umm, I think we're almost done here," Tess began saying, just as Ruth cut her off with "Of course—we'd love the company!"

"Fabulous," sang Todd, and he went over to retrieve Sam.

"Ruth, what are you thinking? I feel weird eating with Sam at the table," hissed Tess to her sister.

"Oh, don't be ridiculous—look how happy he looks now. I can't stand a sad-looking man, especially when he's hungry!" Ruth then looked up at Sam, and said, "Have a seat, handsome. I don't believe we have formally met—I'm Ruth, Te—"

Tess spoke over her sister, saying, "Yes, sorry, this is my sister, Ruth," woof, that was close. Should she have confessed to her sister that Sam knows her as 'Theresa'? Well, too late to do that now, without also telling Sam that she had misled him about her preferred name. How awkward was this going to be? She cleared her throat and said, "Good evening, Sam. I wasn't expecting to see you tonight. I thought you were staying in your room?" Out of the corner of her eye, she noticed her sister raising her eyebrows at her.

"Yeah, I was expecting to just order room service and eat in, but then I thought of having a cocktail, and decided that since I wrote another chapter, I had earned a night out. Sorry, that was a long explanation," Sam laughed, shaking his head.

"Ooh, you're an author, Sam? How fascinating. We both love to read. What kind of writing do you do?"

"Spoiler alert, Sam, Ruth loves asking questions. She will have your life story in about five minutes."

"Too true," Ruth agreed, "I'm a nosy little bitch sometimes, but I also won't be offended if you tell me to mind my own business."

Sam was loving Ruth—what a fireball! Theresa's hadn't been exaggerating about her. "No, I don't mind answering questions, especially about my work. I've written kind of a variety of things, but the first thing I had published was a book of poetry."

"Ooh—poetry. How romantic." Ruth's swooning was interrupted by Todd, who was carrying a tray seemingly loaded with drinks for all three of them.

"Okay, beautiful people, I have another ginger ale for mama here, another martini for cookie lady, and a bourbon for the gentleman."

Tess tried telling Todd that she and Ruth hadn't ordered more drinks, but then he delightedly pointed out that Sam had ordered a round for the table. "Your steak will be out soon, sir," and Todd was off again.

Ruth was nodding at Sam with a grin on her face, "Very generous, Sam, thank you. So tell me about the poetry you've written. I do some poetry work with some of my students."

Sam asked, "Oh, are you a teacher? My mom was a teacher."

"No, speech pathologist; I've found that rhyming poetry helps with kids learning speech rhythms, so I'm always looking for more inspiration."

"Very cool. I can send you my two volumes I've had published. Although my style is more Walt Whitman than Emily Dickinson. That's how I got started writing poems, though. I had an amazing English teacher in high school, who also happened to be my mom, and fell head over heels with Dickinson. I just began writing, and for me, non-rhyming poetry was much easier," Sam laughed.

"What a great origins story. Okay, so we have the poetry. Do you write in other genres? You seem like a well-rounded fellow."

"Haha, I don't know about that, but I have gotten around, at least where genres are concerned. So I have two volumes of poetry, a book of short stories, and two novels," Sam stated.

"And you tried to downplay your writing earlier when we were together," Tess admonished. "That's incredible. I can't imagine creating something out of thin air."

Sam told her, "You created those amazing cookies out of thin air. Now that is talent. And delectable. I will acknowledge that my books aren't for everyone, and in fact I had been having some writer's block."

"So what do you do when that happens?" Tess asked.

"I just hope to encounter inspiration; lucky for me I did this morning," and Sam gave Tess a look that shook her to her core. She felt Ruth watching the two of them, so she hurriedly said, "That happens when someone storms into your life, right? Hot mess with too many bags," Tess hoped that humor could defuse this situation.

"Oh, here comes your food, Sam," Ruth announced. Suddenly, Ruth began rubbing her belly furiously, and said, "Oh, I need to get back to our room."

"What? Why?" Asked Tess. "I'll go with you, Sis."

"No, no, I just realized that Sean is calling in like five minutes. You stay,"

"But we were going to share dessert…" Tess implored.

"Oh, I'm sure Sam will share something with you. Stay, finish your drink. Bye, Sam, I'm glad we got to meet, formally." Ruth leaned over and hugged her sister. "Have fun, sweetie," she whispered, and then she was gone.

Sam was enjoying his steak with gusto, "God, I love red meat," he exclaimed. "How was your dinner, Theresa? Looks like maybe you had the salmon? I studied the menu earlier, and was tempted by that also."

"Delicious. I love something tart for dinner," she laughed, trying to get over her uncomfortable feeling of being alone with Sam, once again. "I guess I should move to Ruth's chair."

"Why? Scared to sit this close to me?"

Tess looked into Sam's eyes and felt like she was drowning in those dark pools. The second martini was definitely a mistake. "No, but I'm sure you want to keep your options open."

Sam lifted his eyebrow in question, "What options?"

"Oh, you know, for any ladies who may have seen you on the train," and she made a gesturing motion to the car with her hand.

"Don't look now, but it seems I'm sitting with the only single lady in the place, judging by all of the couples surrounding us. Besides, it's kind of loud in here, and I want to make sure I can hear you."

Tess sputtered, "You don't seem to have had a problem with the volume yet."

"No, not yet, but it's definitely getting louder in here. Plus, how are we going to share dessert in you're on the other side of the table from me?" Sam countered.

"I really shouldn't have any dessert, especially since I've had two drinks," Tess demurred.

"Why? I don't see anything wrong with having drinks and desserts; you like sugar, right? I mean, since you're a baker and all."

"I love sugar—maybe just a little too much. I made my fia—"she stopped, and cleared her throat, not ready to admit she had a fiancé, "I made a friend a promise that I would try to make good decisions about food choices."

"You're not going to make me beg, are you? I hate eating dessert alone," and Sam smiled at her, his eyes crinkling at the corners. "But I will warn you that I am extremely good at begging," and Sam gave Theresa what he hoped was an undeniably loaded look.

Tess flushed cherry red and said, "Okay, but I'm getting my own dessert!" She hoped to tone the heat level down she felt permeating the air between them. "I never planned on sharing with Ruth anyway."

Sam reached for the dessert menu, and as he placed it in Tess's hands, his fingertips stroked the top of her hand, and she couldn't control the shiver that ran through her body.

"I hate sharing, too," Sam said suggestively.

CHAPTER
Fourteen

Tess

By the time Sam escorted Tess back to her room, Ruth was asleep in her bed. Tess had actually enjoyed having dessert with Sam, and the two had discussed his poetry in further detail, and he had made some suggestions for Tess to give to Ruth. She had told him how much she enjoyed having her sister live so close to her in Philadelphia, and she had talked about learning how to bake from her grandmothers. Sam and Tess had traded stories about growing up, and then discussed books each of them, it turned out, had both read. Their time together wasn't as salacious as Tess had feared it might be, although she did feel somewhat awkward for spending a rather intimate moment with a man who wasn't her fiancé, or related to her. She had plenty of male friends, but nothing about her encounters with Sam were similar to anything she had ever experienced, and she certainly couldn't remember the last time she had eaten dessert in front of a man who was as attractive as Sam. As a larger sized woman, mockery just wasn't something that she would ever subject herself to, and

Tess knew full well how so many people, especially the opposite sex, looked at people like her who had the audacity to act like they were enjoying their food. When she was in elementary school, she had been teased for her weight so often, and as she grew up, every year she would hope desperately that those classmates had matured. Some did, but others were too easily influenced by the kids (primarily boys) who seemingly only wanted to cause emotional pain. Sam had given off none of these vibes, though, and he truly seemed so sincere and genuine overall.

Tess sighed as she changed into her pajamas, then washed her face, brushed her teeth, and took out her contacts. It had been a long day, she thought to herself as she slipped on her glasses and sat down on her bed. She really needed to call Josh—in fact she was feeling quite disconnected from him since their call this afternoon. Lately their communication just seemed to be off; he was working such long hours, and with Tess having to be up so early in the mornings to bake, she was often asleep when he got home at night. She had known his schedule was going to be grueling once he became a surgical resident, but had not anticipated just how much, apparently, and this was the basis of so many of their disagreements. Well, that, and his latest obsession with trying to get her to be healthier; while she knew she should drop a few pounds (seconded by her doctor) she did get a clean bill of health at her last physical checkup. Josh, however, said that annual checkups don't always tell the truth about overall health, and who was she to argue with a doctor? Especially one she also happened to be marrying in six months.

Knowing her sister slept like the dead, Tess called Josh, and he answered after two rings. "Hi, Babe," she said to him.

"Tessa, you must have ESP—I was just going to call you. I miss you. How was the rest of your day?"

They chatted for several minutes about life on the train, and then Tess said to Josh, "Listen, I want to apologize for kind of freaking out earlier. I know you always have my best interests at heart."

"What are you talking about? When did you freak out?"

"You know, when you called earlier. I was eating a cookie and you reminded me about my dress. It kind of comes across to me like you're hounding me, but I know you mean well." How could he not recall this? Maybe he was trying to deflect any guilt he had?

Josh sighed, and in Tess's estimation it lasted for at least a minute. "Tessa, I ONLY ever have your best interests in mind. I knew you were upset with me before, but I figured you would work it out."

"Work what out, exactly, Josh? Work out that you were right, you mean? This isn't what I wanted to rehash when I called. I did want to apologize and get back on track, especially since we're apart for the next week, but I'm not getting into a sugar count with you or how you know best for me. I admit you WANT the best for me, but only I know what is best for my body."

"Tessa, I love you so much, and I have for so long. I never want to hurt you, but I feel like this conversation is going off the rails, once again. Listen, I have to get back to the hospital. I have a surgical consult in the morning, so I need to study up on it. I love you, and I'll call after the meeting. Maybe we can FaceTime tomorrow?"

"Sure, I'd like to see your handsome face. Love you and miss you," and Tess hung up, feeling worse than she had before. She started rubbing her ring finger, and realized she'd never taken her ring out of her pocket. Crap! She jumped up, and reached for the jeans she'd been wearing earlier, putting her hand in the pocket she'd put her ring in earlier. Pulling it out, she now saw that it wasn't her ring after all! It seemed to be an empty, key ring. What the hell?? She can see now how she mistook it for her engagement ring—it was quite heavy and relatively the same size in diameter as her ring. No stone, obviously, but she hadn't been feeling for it when she picked it up from the carpet earlier; she'd only grabbed it and slid it into her pocket. She couldn't help it, she just started laughing. Her emotions were out of whack.

"Sis, what's wrong? Are you laughing or crying?" Damn, and now she'd woken her pregnant sister.

"Hell, I don't know—both?" And then she did start laughing in full, and her sister rose and came over to her, putting her arm around her shoulders.

"Tessie, what's wrong? We had a delicious dinner, and then we had drinks bought for us by an almost-stranger, who also joined us for dinner. When is the last time a man bought us drinks?"

"Actually, he ended up paying for all of our dinner tonight, not just the drinks," Tess informed her sister.

"Of course he did. He's like some kind of upside-down hobo: he's riding the rails, but he's hot, single, and a successful author. Well, I guess we only have his word for the last two things." Ruth paused to wipe the tears off her sister's face. "Anyway, back to the questionable tears—what is wrong?"

"I made the mistake of calling Josh, and I guess each of us were still holding on to the belief that we were right. I wouldn't back down and Josh couldn't admit that he was in the wrong. I did apologize, hoping to just get us on track, but he took that to mean I agreed with him. How can Josh be the man of my dreams if he is trying to change me?"

"You know, Tess, I love Josh, too, and have known him almost as long as you have. I have seen you both change over the years, which is what you should do. But you need to make sure that you are changing to grow together, not apart. Have you tried calmly talking to Josh about how his attitude is making you feel? I know you think that he should understand about your weight and your mentality, but the truth is, it's different for men, and he hasn't been 'heavy' since college. Like when I met Sean, who has never had an issue with his weight, he couldn't understand some of my feelings about my own self-esteem and how my weight has played into it. We had to have some real 'come to Jesus' conversations about it, and I'm not going to lie—they were tough. Tough for him to hear and tough for me to admit. Sean says he has never seen my weight as an issue, he only sees it as a part of who he loves. This is what you need to get Josh to wrap his head around."

Tess sighed, "I know you're right, it's just you think he would get that already, having been a former fatty. I guess because his brain is so logical, he always has to find an answer for something. Well, that and he has always been very good at segmenting feelings and experiences, which is completely frustrating. When I look at Josh, I still see that sweet, shy boy who needed a friend, and I was there for him. I didn't feel judgment, only acceptance, but that's on me," Tess gave her sister a wobbly smile and said, "I think what I really need is some sleep."

"Yes! I can't believe I missed out on dessert with you guys. I had just gotten back to our room when Sean FaceTimed. He wanted to say goodnight to little peanut, and I was practically falling asleep on the phone, which isn't easy to hide in a video call."

Tess's phone pinged with a text from Josh. "Sorry I was being difficult. You are always my dream girl," Tess read out loud to her sister. She replied back to him "XOXOXOXO".

"Clearly I was being an overly dramatic head case. Sorry for waking you up, Sis. Now I can rest easy," she smiled at Ruth.

Ruth wasn't as easily taken in by Josh's text as her sister was, but it was too late to discuss further. "Love you, little sister."

"Back at you, big sister."

CHAPTER
Fifteen

Sam

Good god, who was calling him at this hour? Opening one eye, Sam looked toward the window and could barely make out a sliver of light underneath the shade. His phone trilled again, and now Sam squinted at his phone on the table next to his bed and saw that it read six forty-five AM. Who the hell calls this early? Sam had never been an early riser, and it was made worse when he was working on a book. Looking at the name, he saw that it was his agent, Brock. "Yes?" He brusquely answered the call.

"Wow, Sam, I am in shock, man, absolute shock. This is some of the best stuff I have ever read from you. I read it as soon as I checked my email. These first three chapters are like nothing you've done!" His agent, exclaimed. Wow. Morning people could be so annoying in their exuberance; it was almost like they went out of their way to get under the skin of people who preferred to sleep until the sun actually crested the horizon.

"Thanks, Brock. I wasn't exactly expecting to be awakened at the crack of dawn by you, though, however special my writing is," Sam grumpily replied.

"What do you mean 'crack of dawn'? It's almost eight here. You know I get up at four and work out before going into the city." Right, Sam had forgotten about the time difference. Having absolutely no idea where he was in the continental United States right now made time seem irrelevant. He dialed down his annoyance with Brock, who was not only an incredible agent but also someone he counted as a personal friend. Brock had taken a chance on him with his first novel, after he had gotten rejected by what seemed like a dozen other agents.

"Yeah, sorry, I'm an hour behind you, somewhere in the Midwest. Plus I was up until all hours writing. Whatever was blocking me has lifted," Sam proclaimed.

"Oh, hell, you're doing that train trip this week. I forgot—I guess maybe it's riding the rails that is inspiring you? I read some of the romantic development between your characters to my girlfriend and I kid you not, she was swooning. Powerful stuff. The publisher was right—this is exactly the shot in your arm your series needs! I can one hundred percent see you getting a wider audience with this, if my wife is an indication. Bigger audience equals bigger sales. And this third book could definitely even be a starting point for the new readers, but I'm guessing most will go read the first two books. How much longer are you traveling?"

"I have two full days yet on the train, and then I'm at Lake Tahoe."

"Great—I expect three more chapters by then. Excellent work, Sam. Absolutely brilliant."

And with that, Brock was gone. Sam had written until almost three in the morning, so driven with inspiration was he that he could not stop. His fingers were merely a conduit for his imagination, but he had to credit some help from Theresa; he'd never had a muse before, but all he knew was he had been absolutely stuck creatively until he met her, and last night he had to *force* himself to stop writing. Sam dragged a hand through his dark hair, knowing he probably looked all the worse for wear due to his late night. He had been so thrilled when he walked into the dining car last night and saw her there still eating. When he originally escorted her to the dining car and then had walked back to his room, he had sat down to write, but all he could think was that it would be nice to not eat dinner alone, and Sam had wanted to get to know Ruth a bit better, also, seeing as how Theresa and her sister were so close. So he had brushed his teeth and taken a very brief shower, and then tried as hard as he could to casually stroll back to the dining car.

Sam reclined back on the bed and shut his eyes. Was this fate? Him being on the train and then seeing Theresa through the window? Almost as if she'd been placed there by the powers that be, for him to see her struggle and then come to her aid. Not that she couldn't have handled it herself. Aside from his mother, he had never met a more competent woman. Everything about Theresa was just so full—her boisterous personality, her genuine satisfaction with her baking, the obvious love she had for her family. She was lush and rich and vibrant. Whatever this was, though, he wondered if he needed to pull back just a little. For all he knew, she could have someone in Brooklyn. It dawned on him last night that they had not really discussed anything too personal, but he HAD only met her yesterday. Thinking of Theresa then made him consider his ex-wife, Amanda. Although they were still on friendly terms, as he'd told his mother, he still felt a pang of loss when he thought of the end of their marriage. Could he have done more? Was the failure a barometer for future relationships?

Before he could talk himself out of it, he was ringing the one person who could potentially talk him out of falling for someone he had only met yesterday.

"What went wrong with us?" He asked as soon as Amanda answered.

"Sam? Oh my god, is everything okay? Are you okay?" Amanda replied huskily.

"What? No. I mean, yes, I'm okay, I just needed to know what went wrong with us."

"You're calling me up before it's even light here and asking why we got divorced? You do realize I live in California now, where it is still technically nighttime. Not to mention I am in bed with my fiancé." Amanda always could be counted on to put things in perspective.

Sam was stunned, and elated, to hear the news Amanda was engaged. "Wow, mazel tov, Amanda, to you and Steve."

"Thank you, but what's the emergency? What couldn't wait until the sun is up?"

"Sorry, I'm an ass. Brock just called and woke me up to talk about the new book I'm working on, so it has me thinking about relationships. I've been sitting here wondering why exactly we ended. I mean, I know I was a selfish prick who went on my book tour and didn't try to make it coincide with your schedule. And I never put your needs first. Am I on the right track?" Is it concerning he was relying on his ex-wife for guidance on a potential future relationship?

Amanda sighed, "Wow, okay, we're going deep before dawn. I get it. Just bear with me, I'm going into the bathroom so I don't wake up Steve." She paused, and he could hear a door shut. "Okay. First of all, we both agreed that we never should have gotten married in the first place. We knew it the day after; hell, if we were honest, we knew it the day before. I was on the rebound, and you said that you fell head over heels instantly. We should have taken more time to get to know each other—to make sure that we truly jelled, you know? Don't misunderstand me, Sam, I fell and I fell hard, but I think so much of it was surface. It wasn't your book tour that tore us apart—it was the fact that you didn't consider my work or needs as important as yours. And I was just as guilty about that as you. I was so resentful, and it burned up my love."

Sam sighed, and feelings of guilt once again surfaced. "I'm so sorry I didn't treat you fairly or value our relationship. Even if everything has worked out, probably as it should have all along, I still feel remorse and even guilt. Honestly, I've had such writer's block with this recent book, but have finally had a breakthrough. When I think about when I wrote the other two books, that segues into remembering my first book tour. Plus I talked to my mom yesterday, and she brought up our divorce, so thoughts have been circling."

Amanda laughed—she and his mom had not had a close relationship, probably because his mom had known something was off about the speed at which they had gotten married; Amanda was never good with pushback of any kind. "I bet she did. One of the happiest days of Jane's life was when we signed those divorce papers, and I don't blame her for that one bit," Amanda laughed ruefully. "Now let's talk good stuff—you're working on your third book in the series? That's wonderful. Those first two were fantastic, you know."

"Yeah, and you'll never believe this, but speaking of relationships—I'm throwing in a romantic subplot. I've resisted going on this path, and had some doubts in the romance area, but my publisher was putting on the pressure. I'm really into it, though; I needed the challenge of this, and have been very inspired the last couple of days," Sam paused, then said, "Listen, Amanda, thanks for answering this call. I don't regret us, but I'm glad we owned our mistake and didn't flog our marriage. I wish you the best, and I honestly hope we can remain friends, in whatever form that takes."

When Amanda replied, Sam thought he could hear her holding back tears. "You'll always have a place in my heart as a friend, and one who was there for me at a very dark time, and I love you for that. Bye, Sweetie."

"Take care," Sam replied. Whew—he was so relieved to have taken care of that. He truly believed that one of his causes of his writer's block was how he had felt his rise in the book world had led to the demise of his marriage. The guilt crippled his creative process. Between meeting Theresa and this call of atonement, he realized he no longer had any barriers.

Chapter
Sixteen

Tess

Tess awoke to the sound of her sister speaking, but after glancing at Ruth's bed, she saw that it was empty. Where was Ruth, and who was she talking to? "Ruthie?" She called out. Silence. Tess kicked off her blankets, reached for her glasses on her side table, and swung her legs off the bed. "Ruthie?" She called out again as she slid on her glasses.

Suddenly the door to their cabin flew open, "Oh, hey, Sis, I was trying not to wake you. You will never believe what was just delivered to our room!" And then Ruth came through the door, pulling a rolling cart that appeared to be laden with all kinds of covered trays. The porter came through the door last, having helped Ruth with the cart. "I also have these," he said, and Tess saw him procure a bouquet of flowers.

"What in the world?" She exclaimed. "Ruth, what is all this?"

Ruth laughed and said, "Well, I know Sean is a romantic; or he is when he wants to be anyway, but I highly doubt this is for me! Look, here's a card," and Ruth handed her a card from the table.

Tess tore open the envelope, and pulled out the card, "My dearest Tessa," she read, "please know I am always thinking of you and miss you terribly. I arranged your favorite breakfast items to be delivered to your room this morning, and I know these flowers will match you in their beauty. All my love, Josh."

"I'm speechless; I hope he at least ordered some of *my* breakfast favorites," Ruth said dryly.

Tess looked shocked. "This is so very thoughtful; I can't believe Josh arranged this. I mean, it's all so sweet, but that is not Josh on the card. Do you think he had someone else write that, or did he google it and then write it?"

"Umm, Tessie, I think you're missing the big picture—just go back to it being thoughtful, okay? It shows Josh is trying, especially after the rough road you guys had yesterday. Don't overthink it."

"Right, but on the other hand, he would have had to have arranged this in advance, so I highly doubt it has anything to do with our communications yesterday." Tess shook her head. "No, you're right, I'm looking for flaws, when I should just be pleased. So—what's for breakfast, Sis?"

"Let's see," Ruth lifted one of the lids, "looks like scrambled eggs and ham in this one." She put that lid down and lifted another, "Yummy—sausages in this one. Plus there are croissants, yogurt and berries. And the coffee smells divine. Oh, and it looks like Josh made sure to tell them 'extra cream' for you. Wow, he really did think of everything."

"Sis, you forgot to lift the last lid," Tess told her, while lifting it up, "and now for bacon! My favorite! Well, all of this is looks delectable, and I'm sure little Ruth junior is extremely hungry this morning."

"Haha. I bet she is, if she's anything like her mama and her aunt." Ruth picked up a croissant, split it open and loaded it up with eggs, bacon, and sausage. "Can we talk a bit about last night? Are you feeling more like my confidant little sister again? I hate that you are even having any of these doubts where your body image is concerned. Wait—is it cool to talk about body image while I'm eating three meats on a croissant? Anyway, where is it coming from—do you really feel like Josh is trying to change you?"

Tess took a bite of her yogurt and berry concoction, using a chuck of croissant like a spoon. "Oh, this is a nice combo; Ruthie, you should try it." She took a breath and then another bite. "Yes. No. I don't know," she tried to answer her sister's question. "If I'm being honest, for just a hot second, I will admit that I have been bothered by how long it took us to get engaged. I was of the understanding that once he was done with med school, he was going to propose, and then he didn't. Instead, he waited almost five years. And now we've been engaged more than three years. Anytime I wanted to set a date for the wedding, he would say that it wasn't the right time, and he always had a reason that sounded valid, enough, I guess, but looking back I just question if he actually was trying to buy time?"

Ruth nodded, and said, "I'm not agreeing that I think Josh was trying to buy time, but I did think both timelines took ages—like, you've known each other FOREVER and aside from that little blip after he graduated college, you've been a couple the whole time. At this point, everyone expects you to be married, so what's the hold up? Isn't it really a formality? I mean, Sean and I have only known each other six years, but in that time, we got engaged, hitched, and now knocked up."

"Exactly! I couldn't rush Josh for any of this, even though it's what I have always wanted. I will not be that desperate woman begging her man for a ring or coercing him to propose. Besides—Josh does not respond well to ultimatums, as you know. While I am halfway venting here, can I also add that the older we get, or maybe it's the longer we are together, every decision has to be made by Josh. I will try to make a decision, but he hems and haws or says 'no' outright, and then he will counter with his decision, and that is that. Done deal. Even with me having my own store front bakery, he puts the brakes on anything that will move it forward. I just get so frustrated with him sometimes," Tess sighed.

Ruth had now moved onto the yogurt and berries, along with her second croissant, and as she followed Tess's example, she asked her sister, "You still have half of that money that Grandma and Grandpa Bergen left us, right?" The Bergens, their mother's parents, had made some very wise investments in their day, and when they had each passed, Tess and Ruth had inherited what amounted to a small fortune in their eyes. Since their mom had been an only child, they had been beloved and cherished granddaughters of doting and loving grandparents.

"Yes, but Josh says the market isn't good for a bakery storefront, especially in the neighborhood where I want to open it."

"But isn't that neighborhood the one you're currently living in?" Ruth looked flabbergasted.

"Yes, but Josh says if we want to move in the next five years, what will I do with the store?"

"No offense, Sis, but if you say 'Josh says' one more time I will dump this yogurt over your head. This is your money, and your dream, and why would you be moving in five years? You always sound like you guys are loving life in Brooklyn."

"We are, we are, but what happens if Josh gets a job offer at a different hospital after he finished his residency? Like in another city?"

"Okay, so you're supposed to put your career, and your dreams, on hold in case he gets a job offer? That kind of sounds like ultimatum bullshit to me. Despite him arranging breakfast in bed for us, I am vibing him some bad juju right now." Ruth saw a look of angst on her sister's face, so she held up a hand. "Don't worry, it's nothing that will last forever, but just like some twenty-four-hour bad juju."

Tess laughed, as Ruth had hoped she might. "That's better, Tessie. Now, let's talk about something else. You are looking mighty fine this morning—the tousled hair, the glasses. You know I have always thought glasses suited your face so well. Why don't you wear them more often?"

"Josh says—oh god, not the yogurt, please!" Tess exclaimed as her sister held up the yogurt bowl in a slightly threatening way. "He prefers me in my contacts; he says my eyes sparkle more. Besides, you have a glasses fetish, even if it applies to your sister."

Ruth snorted out a laugh. "Too true, little sister." Ruth paused, and said, "Listen, I meant to tell you last night that I had a major look around the room for your ring when I came back. Looked under the beds and the chairs, behind the toilet, too. Still no sign; I'm sorry."

"That's okay. Thanks for checking again. That reminds me: I forgot to show you—I thought this was my ring," and Tess went and got the keychain from her pants pocket. "Look, it's the same size and shape. How funny is that?"

"Yeah—minus the rock, it definitely feels like a wedding band. So where did you find this?"

"Oh, yesterday, when Sam was in the room. I had dropped my phone and when I leaned over to pick it up, my hand brushed against this under that chair over there. So it's kind of funny that you checked under that chair last night, huh? Anyway, when I picked it up, I just put it in my pocket before Sam walked me down to the dining car. I checked it then before I saw you for dinner last night. Funny, right?"

Ruth studied Tess. "Huh," Ruth wondered. "So you thought you had found your ring, but instead of putting it on, you put it in your pocket? Why didn't you just look at it when you picked it up? Why'd you hide it in your pocket?"

Tess flushed. "I wasn't exactly 'hiding' it. I guess I didn't want to make a big deal about it, so I put it in my pocket. Plus Sam was here, and it just seemed awkward."

"Look, Babe, I'm certainly not judging you here, but that makes like zero sense. Didn't want to make a big deal out of what? Having a ring? Being engaged?" Ruth let out a huge gasp, "Oh. My. God. Sam doesn't know you're engaged, right? How could he? Unless he noticed your hand when he helped you with your luggage, or when we briefly saw him at breakfast yesterday. After that, you weren't wearing your it. Theresa Lydia Lefferts. What are you up to?"

Now would be a great time for a bout of that famous morning sickness, Tess thought to herself. Gathering her gumption, she finally refuted, "I'm not up to anything Ruth Ellen Lefferts Mills. What motive would I have? I'm an engaged woman, riding a train with my pregnant sister, heading to my bachelorette weekend. Do you know I have always hated that term— bachelorette? Sounds so trashy." Tess took a breath, lifted her glasses, and rubbed her eyes. "I don't know. I guess from the moment I met Sam, I got to be someone else. You know, leaving out the whole engaged thing, I'm still me, but it's a different me. Just me—not the 'Tessa' who is tied to Josh. I have never even really flirted with another man, and I don't think that's what I'm doing with Sam, but our interactions have been nice. He doesn't know my past, or insecurities; hell, he doesn't even know my name. Since I am in full confession mode here, I introduced myself as 'Theresa' yesterday, not Tess, I guess for all of those reasons I just announced. He just sees the confident and put-together…well, for the most part confident and put-together, woman he knows as Theresa."

Ruth looked at her sister knowingly, "Oh, the missing piece of this puzzle has just been put into place. I thought it was a bit weird last night when you cut me off after I started introducing myself to him, but I thought maybe I had imagined it. Look, I get it. The whole point of this train ride is to relax and enjoy yourself. Frankly, it could do you good for you to discover who you are without having Josh be a part of it. After all, you DO have six months until your wedding-"

Tess cut off her sister, "I'm not planning on anything with Sam, or anyone else, if that's what you're inferring. This is about me, and my journey to myself."

"Well, Sis, that part is true—you will have the journey to yourself on this train. As for Sam, from everything I've seen, he definitely likes what he has found so far on his journey." And with that, Ruth helped herself to more bacon.

CHAPTER
Seventeen

Sam

After Sam had hung up the phone with Amanda, he had taken a shower, and then powered through another chapter; he had also gone back to the beginning of the book to write a prologue. Even with his first book, when he was bursting anew with ideas and possibilities, he still had to force himself to write; he looked at writing prompts online and had a circle of writers he would meet with monthly to discuss plots, characters, or settings they were working on. Still, nothing had been as seamless as his writing had been for the past two days. Was it the train, was it the woman, or was it both? He pondered.

The advantage of being awakened so early meant he had also been able to watch the sunrise from his room, and it had been spectacular seeing the landscapes change along with the horizon. He had hoped the large window in his smaller room would afford him such a view, but truthfully he hadn't expected to be fully awake for it. Thank you, Brock, Sam thought to himself.

Sam stretched out his arms above his head, rubbed his belly, and looked at the time. Just after eight in the morning. Seemed like a good time for breakfast, so he changed out of his shorts and day-old T-shirt. His mother had drilled into him to never go out in a public place in shorts, and it was one of his mom's "rules" that he still adhered to—some were better than others, and he and his brothers, now that they were adults, were able to pick and choose from these as they wished; as kids, though, his mom had ruled her roost with what she had hoped was an iron fist (although her husband would beg to differ). The truth was that his parents had definitely been fantastic parents to him and his four brothers; they had both worked full time and money was tight when he was growing up, but they had eaten dinner together as a family every night, cooked by either his mom or his dad. Sam would watch his dad take his mom in his arms while the boys cleared the table, and he would dance her around the kitchen while the dishwasher was being loaded, or fold her into his arms for a hug and kiss while their sons washed the pots and pans. Although his dad could come across as rough around the edges, he had never refrained from showing the world how much he loved his wife. Watching his parents express their love for each other frequently and openly had instilled in him the belief that true love existed and was attainable. A romantic at heart, Sam was slightly embarrassed that it had taken the urging of his publisher for him to incorporate a love story into his third book. However, he had fought against being labeled as a romantic writer after the publication of his poetry, and had in fact pointedly focused his first novel as hard hitting science fiction. He supposed this was all part of his evolution not only as a writer, but also a human.

Sam walked through his car, passed through the lounge car, then a run-of-the-mill passenger car, before finally getting to the dining car. He chose a small table near a window on the other side of the car, smiling at the waitress that came over. She introduced herself as Carol, and he ordered a pot of coffee, two eggs over medium, sourdough toast, and a side of bacon and sausage. Opening up his email, he read through a few from his writer's group, and with the exception of one other writer, each member was really digging the new chapters. The one holdout was a proud "realist" and he generally loathed anything that had too much emotion in it. He was from Maine, and had once confessed to the group that no member of his immediate family had ever said "I love you" to each other—the group could at times almost be a stand-in for a therapy session.

"Mind if I sit down?" Sam looked up and saw that Ruth was standing at his table. "I hate to drink alone, and I've just ordered a latte from Carol, with an extra shot of espresso, because I love to be bad," she said, rubbing her belly, and before Sam could react in any way, Ruth had taken the seat across from his.

Sam laughed, "A woman who knows her own mind is one to be not just valued, but appreciated." Sam looked to the doors, hoping to see Theresa in her sister's wake, but had no luck, so maybe she was joining her later. "How are you this morning, Ruth?"

"I'm wonderful, thanks. My sister and I had room service this morning, and then she started belting out Trisha Yearwood songs, which I took as my cue to give her some privacy. She loves to sign Trisha in the shower, and she also has the hot water blasting, so our room is like a karaoke club in a sauna right now. One thing about Tes-Theresa: she doesn't do half measures. Not sure if you've heard her laugh yet, but anyone within a ten-mile radius can hear my sister laugh. Used to get us in all kinds of trouble as kids. Oh, look, this must be your breakfast," Ruth said, nodding to the incoming plate.

"And your latte, it looks like," Sam told Ruth. "Thanks, Carol," and Carol smiled at him and addressed him as "Hun". "I've never been happier to see a plate of eggs. Man, am I famished."

"So, Sam, you look bright-eyed, and bushy-tailed this morning—did you go for a jog around the train or something? I desperately need to get some exercise today. Thinking about walking the length of the train a few times. I had too many cookies last night when I was talking to my husband."

"No, no jog, but I have been up for a few hours. Talked to a couple people on the phone and then spent the rest of the time working. I did walk a few cars to get here, though. My room is on the opposite end of the train. I assume the cookies you had were some of Theresa's cookies? Those are truly the best cookies I've ever had. Sorry if I have depleted your stash."

"Yes, she got the gift of baking—from both of our grandmas. I can bake a bit, but my strength is in cooking, not baking, so much; I'm more of a 'dash of this, pinch of that' kind of cook. Much to my husband's cha-grin," Ruth joked.

"I think your sister mentioned you live in Philadelphia? How do you like it?"

"LOVE it. I don't know if you know this, but we grew up in the Mid-west, and I have always loved the history of Philly. My husband, Sean, and I, moved there when I got a job with the school district, almost five years ago." Taking a sip of her latte, Ruth studied Sam over the top. "Where are you from, Sam?"

"Boston, born and raised. My parents still live in the house I grew up in, and all of my brothers live in a five-mile radius. I have a condo down by the Charles River. Luckily my books have afforded me a great view when I'm at home. We didn't have much when I was growing up, so having the luxury of a downtown view is one I do not take for granted."

"Brothers, huh? How many do you have?" Ruth questioned Sam.

"Four brothers, all younger than me. You mentioned your sister's laugh, and I have definitely noticed it—it's almost musical, and reminds me of being at home: boisterous with a side of mischief."

"Mischief? My sister? Haha, she is one of the most strait-laced people you will ever meet, and I mean that in the most loving way. She loves lists, and checking off her lists, and rules, and making sure she is always follow-ing those rules. I used to try to get her in trouble when we were growing up, but she hated disappointing our parents in any way."

"I can see that, now that you mention it. That explains why she was so flustered when I helped her with her baggage yesterday; she seemed very out of sorts. I was afraid she was going to take out the whole train at one point." Ruth laughed while Sam thought fondly of that moment—coming to her aid, giving her relief. His parents had drilled chivalry into him and his brothers, and Sam had never taken more pleasure in being chivalrous than he did yesterday. Thinking of Theresa made him shift in his seat, and without even realizing it, he found himself looking around the car for her. No sign of her, but Carol was heading to his table with a coffee refill.

"Can I get you folks anything else?" Carol asked.

"I'll take another latte, when you have time. I have to say that we had Todd as our waiter yesterday, and he was so great, but clearly Amtrak only hires amazing people. Everyone here is so accommodating; even the delivery to our room was impeccable." Ruth praised.

"We aim to make the ride an enjoyable once for all who take the train—even the ones riding in the regular cars. I will get you that latte right away," and then Carol was off, after smiling warmly at both Sam and Ruth.

"Is Theresa joining you down here, by any chance?" Sam asked as casually as he could muster.

Ruth shook her head, "I highly doubt it. She loves to lather on all her potions and lotions, and beauty takes time, you know?"

Sam smiled appreciatively, loving the image he now had of Theresa rubbing on lotion to every inch of her delectable body, and then said, "You ladies definitely are riding in style—made me a little bit jealous to see your room yesterday. I have a sleeping room, but it is a bit more basic. Perfect for just me, though."

"Yeah, our room was courtesy of our parents, who gifted us the opportunity to ride in style. Not sure what we would have done otherwise—probably just scaled back to a basic room. Maybe one day my husband and I can do this trip together," Ruth paused, and rubbed her baby bump, "on the other hand, it will be a few years before we have that option again," she laughed.

"May I ask when your little one is due? One of my brothers and his wife just had a baby a few months ago, and they had to change their lifestyle pretty drastically, but I'd say the payoff seems to be well worth it; especially for me, since I get to spoil my niece rotten."

"I'm about halfway along, so junior here is due in about five months. My first, and we are both terrified, if I'm being honest. Sean is great, though, and comes from a big family like you, except he has three older sisters, so we have been practicing with their kids for a while. Hard to believe sometimes that we have been married for five years and now will be parents. Sometimes life passes faster the older you get, right? Oh, here's my drink," Ruth observed as Carol placed the drink down the table. Ruth's phone pinged, and she looked down at it. "Well, Sam, it's been nice chatting with you. I better get back to the room and see what my sister is up to."

Sam quickly stood, and pulled out Ruth's chair, then helped her up by her elbow. "Please give my regards to your sister, and let her know I look forward to seeing her later."

Ruth stared up at Sam, studying him intently. "I shall relay your message. Oh, before I forget, thanks so much for that list of reading materials for my students. I appreciate it," and Ruth took his hands and squeezed them, before grabbing her drink, turning around and heading toward the exit.

CHAPTER
Eighteen

Tess

Considering that Tess was currently belting out "Wrong Side of Memphis", also known as her go-to karaoke song, she was surprised to still be able to hear her phone ring from outside the bathroom. Tess preferred to listen to her music on her "old school" iPod, and she had carried along a small set of speakers so she and her sister could jam out properly. After she tightened the belt on the fluffy white robe provided by AMTRAK, Tess stepped out of the steamy room, turned the music down, and padded over to her bed. To her delight, Josh was Face-Timing, so she answered on the next ring. "Hi, Babe."

"Good morning, beautiful," Josh began, and then started laughing, "is that a robe you're wearing?"

"Yes—you like?" She asked, as she slid her hand suggestively down the front opening. The flirtatious move was a wasted one, though, as Josh wasn't even looking at his phone. Her face was currently frozen onscreen, which meant he was multi-tasking while on the phone with her. "Hello? Earth to Josh?"

Suddenly he reappeared on the screen, "Sorry, I just got a text from Fitz. Evidently he talked to his ex this morning. Remember I told you how he had that quickie wedding a few years ago that lasted maybe a year? He just texted that his ex is engaged. Wow. She wasted no time."

Tess sighed, wondering why the moment can never be just about them. "So you interrupted our phone call—no our FaceTime—to answer a text from 'Fitz'?"

"Well, no, I didn't answer him, I just read it."

"Josh, that's even more annoying. I thought this was our time to re-connect. You can answer your texts when you're off the phone with me," Tess scolded.

Josh looked up at his screen, and she finally made some sort of eye contact with him. "You're right. Why am I getting it so wrong these past couple of days? You know I'm not good on the phone: too many chances for miscommunications."

Now Tess was sorry she'd said anything; the last thing she wanted were any more ill feelings before their respective weekends with friends. "Let's start over," Tess smiled brightly to her phone. "Good morning, Josh,"

Josh chuckled, "Good morning, Gorgeous. Your hair is really curly—you must have just showered? Oh, are those flowers behind you the ones that came with your breakfast delivery?"

"Yes! Oh my gosh, I was so surprised when everything was delivered this morning; you are so thoughtful! All of my favorites, and we still have some left for lunch later."

"Tessa, you can send the leftovers back; you don't need to snack on them all day. All of those carbs and fatty meats? Not to mention that your activity level can't be very high while traveling. Don't overindulge now because you have a big weekend coming up, too."

"I swear to god, Josh, can you please give it a rest? For your informa-tion, we have been fairly active on board, considering our sleeping car is at one end of the train and the two food cars are somewhere in the middle. You know, we also have to pass through the regular passenger cars to get to the actual dining car, so there's been a great amount of walking on board."

"Okay, okay, I'm sorry. I know this is a sensitive subject. Just know I love you, right?" Looking at his face, Tess did see genuine sincerity.

"Always. Anyway, I haven't had a chance to tell you about the train. There are two different sleeping cars—one for first class, and the other seems to be mixed depending on what sleeping needs a passenger has. I'm not actually sure how many passenger cars there are, but those are the ones for people who maybe are only traveling for the day. Then there is the lounge-slash-cafe car, and there's a separate dining car, for formal meals. It is such a cool experience; we definitely need to do this at some point again. Maybe for our honeymoon? Speaking of, when can we talk about the honeymoon? We should start making serious plans about where we're going. My passport is totally up-to-date, if we're thinking overseas. But I'm also good with continental US. What about a road trip, like doing Route 66? When Ruth and I were younger, our parents took us to some of the sights left from it, and all the Midwest stuff is pretty amazing. Or speaking of the train, we could do one of the coastal routes, like in California. What do you think?"

"Whoa—lots of ideas for future vacations, definitely, but now that I have a chance to respond, I was honestly thinking maybe we should wait a year before doing a honeymoon? I mean, I'm just starting this residency, and it seems a little abrupt to suddenly leave for a big trip."

Tess was silent, and her hopes for a honeymoon were flitting away one by one. She feared that if they didn't take a honeymoon immediately, they would never do it, especially as Josh worked longer at the hospital, and taking a honeymoon after a year of being married? That was a first anniversary trip! As a child, Tess believed in the fantasy of weddings, and she would buy bridal magazines and clip out which bridesmaids dresses she would choose, and what type of honeymoon she wanted. Granted, her tastes were all over the place, but certain details always remained the same: big, formal wedding, with several attendants, all of them outfitted in matching gowns, perhaps the maid-of-honor varying slightly in either color or style. The men in formal tuxes, Tess wearing her hair loose around her shoulders; the music, the colors. The one traditional detail she DID NOT want was a June wedding, which she considered passé, but any other time of year was up for grabs—well, not really at all during the summer, if she was being honest (and lucky for her, her wedding to Josh was a winter one). As mentioned, that was the only tradition she was bucking; however, the honeymoon was most assuredly not on that list.

"But, Josh, you already asked for the time off when you started, right? Or at least, that's what you told me. We've been planning this for two years. Or at least, I've been TRYING to plan it for two years. I distinctly remember you saying that you told them you'd need two weeks off for the wedding, and they agreed." Tess was trying her damndest to not look or sound annoyed, but wasn't sure she was succeeding; she could tell by the look on Josh's face that whatever he had to say, she wasn't going to like it.

"Look, Tessa, yes I told them I'd need two weeks off for our wedding, but as I was saying it to them, it sounded extreme. I mean, who takes off two weeks for a wedding?" Josh seemed to be under the false impression that if he spoke slowly to her, she'd be calmer about this. He was wrong.

"People who want to take a honeymoon!!" She yelled into her phone.

"As I was saying, I told them two weeks; unfortunately, about a month ago, this chance for a fellowship came up for my department, and that would be huge for me, so after speaking with the head of surgery, I ended up scaling my time off for the wedding back to five days. So we can still do a mini honeymoon, if you want."

Tess was in shock. "I can't believe what I'm hearing right now. You did all of this without talking to me first? You kibosh my plans for my bakery, but are willing to put your own career over me? Do you have any idea how this makes me feel? You know I've been wanting a real honeymoon, and now you're offering me a mini honeymoon? So, what, like a night in Vegas? Or how about a trip to Times Square—after all, it is just a subway ride away. Then, you can ditch me and I'll make my way home alone while you go to the hospital—sounds brilliant! And just how much time for the actual wedding were you allowing? You know I want to do it ourselves: put all the decorations up, help set up, all of that. Were you expecting just to breeze in for the vows, and that was it?" Tess was well aware she was on the verge of tears and nearing hysteria; one more "surprise" from Josh would definitely push her over the edge, but she couldn't stop herself from adding, "And what do you mean 'if I want'? None of this is what I want!"

"Tessa, please, I'm begging you to PLEASE understand this from my point of view. My career is just unfolding, and it would be too precarious for me to be so haphazard with time off right now, especially considering this fellowship. If I receive it, I could be set here for years to come." To be fair, Josh looked as upset as Tess felt, but she had a feeling he was only concerned about his precious career.

"And I'm begging you, Josh, to acknowledge my feelings. Everything, from me moving to Brooklyn, to me patiently waiting for you to propose, and then you not agreeing to a wedding date for years—you're acting like a relationship dictator, and I would appreciate both of us discussing our future without you blindly planning for it." Tess heard a noise at the door, which meant Ruth was back. "I've got to go, and I'm sure you have something else you'd rather be doing. Thanks for the flowers and the breakfast. Love you."

Ruth came bursting through the door, hell on wheels. "Sis, I could hear you out in the hall—what in the hell is going on?" Ruth asked as Tess, once again, burst into tears. "Okay, I am the one who is supposed to be hormonal. Tessie, what happened? We were having a lovely morning but now I'm guessing that Josh ruined it?"

Tess collapsed on the bed, with her sister's arm around her shoulders, and told her in detail about her FaceTime with Josh. Ruth just let her talk it all out, and held her sister while she cried. "This sucks. I can't believe I am heading to my pre-wedding party and I am so annoyed with my fiancé. Why is he acting like this? I guess some of this I have just overlooked for so long, and now me being passive has led to this? No say in any major decisions affecting our future together."

"Okay, wipe those eyes. I have a nice afternoon planned for us, but I can't have you all mopey. Look, Josh is a damn idiot sometimes, despite what a genius brain he may have. He's had to work hard for where he is now and what he has, you know that, and he's NEVER been great at communication. Now, I am going to step out for a few minutes, and when I get back, I want you dressed and ready for some fun. Okay?" Tess nodded her head in agreement, blew her nose, and stood up to hug her sister.

Ruth strode for the door, on a mission, and then she was gone. Tess turned around and started walking to the bathroom when she heard her sister at the door again. Pulling open the door, Tess felt her robe slip off her left shoulder. Laughing, she said, "Ruthie, you haven't given me any time to get dressed."

"I was bringing this by for Ruth," said Sam, holding out a coffee cup. "Carol wanted her to have one on the house."

CHAPTER
Nineteen

Sam has the sudden urge to blind himself, because as far as he was concerned, nothing else he would ever see in his life would measure up to Theresa, standing before him in this white robe. From her bare feet all the way up to her red curls framing her stunning face, he was nothing short of dumbstruck. He had to look away, or he was going to implode on the spot. Well, that was useless, because his eyes slid over again and began to track up shapely legs, to the robe that fell mid-thigh; and then up where she had cinched the belt to the curve of her waist, and just above her could make out the swell of her breasts. And then seeing that her robe had slipped off of one silky looking shoulder was driving him to madness. He had never wanted to put his hands on anyone more in his thirty-six years. The coffee he was holding for her sister was a blessing, as it was keeping him from making an absolute ass out of himself. He cleared his throat, and said, "This is for your sister," and held out the coffee cup.

Tess felt lightheaded and knew she was probably blushing. How humiliating to be caught in this robe, by a virtual stranger. Suddenly she realized her robe had fallen off her shoulder and quickly put it in place. Why could she never keep it together when Sam was around? What in the world was he doing, anyway, showing up at her door yet again? With a coffee for her sister? "I'm sorry, what?"

Sam explained, "Ruth was just down in the dining car while I was eating breakfast and she sat with me and had a latte. Well, two lattes, actually, and there's a new server today: Carol, her name is. Very friendly. So when I finished my breakfast, she brought over another latte and told me it was for my friend. I'm sorry—I'm babbling, and have clearly interrupted you. I'll just put this on the table and be out of your way." He took the few steps to the table he knew to be by Ruth's bed, put the coffee down and turned, just at the moment that Tess turned back to him after shutting the door. The impact of their bodies colliding made Sam reach out and he grasped Theresa by her arms, locking his legs to brace both of them, which incidentally brought her body flush with his. He could feel every curve she had pressed against him, and then she brought her hands up and put them on his chest. Sam stared down at the top of her head, willing her to look up at him. She was so soft, so lush, and he was aching to put his hands all over her, unwrap the robe from her body and lick every inch of her pink skin.

Tess was mortified—Sam must think she is fondling him or something at this point, since it felt like hours when they had essentially crashed into each other. She tipped her head back and looked up into those dark eyes— so dark she could not see where the irises stopped and the pupils began. Completely overtaken by the moment, she slid her hands up to his shoulders, while he pulled her closer to him, if that was even possible. She could feel the strength of his thighs as he braced them, and the power in his chest as he was holding her. Her breasts were crushed against his chest, and heat radiated from his body. How could they both be emanating so much heat and not have incinerated yet? She watched as his gaze lowered from her face down to her throat, and then to the deep V of her robe. Tess inhaled deeply and slowly exhaled, and Sam's breathing was in sync with hers, and she tasted the mint on his breath.

They continued to be completely caught up in each other, and slowly Sam was lowering his head down to hers, desperate to have his mouth on her. He'd start with her plump lips, so wet and red, and he would take all the time he needed drawing his tongue down her throat, still dewy from her shower. He envisioned ever so carefully opening her robe, and touching any exposed skin, sure that it would be the silkiest and pinkest flesh he had ever had his hands on. He brought his hand up to her face, alarmed when her phone began ringing.

Tess pulled away from him (reluctantly? regretfully?) and with the spell broken, she looked over at her phone on her bedside table. She groaned—it was her mother. Well, she would call her back, sure that Ruth had already filled her in on what had happened between her and Josh.

Clutching her robe shut, Tess looked once again at Sam, mortified at her own behavior. "Sorry about that, Sam. I guess you must think I am a total klutz at this point. And presumptuous, to answer the door in my robe. Ruth had just left the room and I thought she was back, which makes this the second time we've had this happen—me mistaking you for my sister." All Tess could do was laugh.

Sam was sure he must be drunk, because no way in hell did he feel sober right now, standing in Theresa's room, with so little space between them, even though she had stepped back from him. So little space, so little air, and *so little clothing*. Why was he here again? He asked himself—oh, right: coffee. "I just wanted to bring the coffee by, but you're clearly in the middle of something so I will just head out-"

"No," Tess stopped him, "you don't need to go. Just give me a minute to put some clothes on." Tess felt like she wasn't ready for Sam to walk out that door just yet, not when every nerve in her body was on fire.

"Sure, I'll be right here," his voice sounding an octave lower than normal, and he watched her sway into the bathroom, saying an internal good-bye to that delicious robe. He has never been as close to losing his mind as two minutes ago when she was in his arms. She was soft and supple, so damn sexy, and when she had looked up at him with her emerald-green eyes, all the blood had drained from his head. He'd been on the verge of kissing her, hell, he'd been damn close to tossing her on the nearest bed, when her phone had rung. He made a note now to turn his phone on silent, because the last damn thing he needed was to be interrupted by anyone calling him when he was with Theresa.

Trying desperately to clear his mind from all primal thoughts, he thought back to earlier after Ruth had left him to his breakfast when he'd gotten a text from Josh, Sam had the sense that since they had spoken yesterday, Josh was reaching out today just keep in contact until their guys' weekend. Since Josh had met Amanda a couple of times, once when they were in New York City, and the second time when Josh had been in Boston for a conference, he had spread the good news of her engagement, while also hinting that it was a blessing to Sam in more ways than one.

Okay, mental diversion was not working for him, so he ran his hands through his hair, and then dropped into one of the chairs by the window, and rested is head against the window frame. Think, he told himself, trying to bring down his own body temperature. "Umm, Ruth had mentioned you would be listening to Trisha Yearwood. She's one of my favorites, too," Sam remarked to Theresa through the closed door.

Tess slumped against the back of the bathroom door, running her hand down the front of her robe, and desperately tried not to imagine Sam's hand there instead. "Oh, really? I am in love with her so much—I've gotten to see her perform live a few times, and I also adore her cooking show. Have you ever seen that?" Tess walked over to the faucet and put some water in her hands and splashed herself with the cold liquid.

"No," Sam answered, "honestly, I'm not much of a cook, although I do make a mean clam chowder. The secret is the right amount of bacon and potatoes—you don't want them to overwhelm the clams, just to bring some fun the party." Yes, Sam, he told himself, more talk of food, less thinking of pale fleshly thighs.

Tess twisted her red curls into a loose knot on top of her head, and decided to just wear her glasses today and not fuss with her contacts. She was considerably too shaken up to put anything in her eyes, anyway. Today was an excellent day for one of the dresses she'd brought along, she had decided earlier today, so it was already hanging in the bathroom. Wraparound navy blue, it was sleeveless, and the length came to just above her knee. Hopefully once she was fully dressed, she would feel like she had her armor on and not feel weak in the knees when Sam looked at her. She took a deep breath. "Clam chowder is one of my all-time faves," Tess replied, as she came out of the bathroom.

"How do you do that?" Sam asked, rising out of his seat.

Tess was confused, "Do what?"

"Leave me speechless every time I see you," he whispered to her, as he took a step closer. Laying a hand on her shoulder, he said, "Do you know how amazing you are?" And he pushed an errant curl behind her ear.

Tess was a flutter with a mix of emotions, and had to pull gently away for her own sanity. "I think you might need your glasses adjusted. I'm just trying to do my best to keep it all together, in case you hadn't noticed," she replied lightly. Desperately needing a distraction, she said, "So, are you a country music fan in general?"

Sam felt maybe he had crossed a line with Theresa, and the last thing he wanted to do was make her uncomfortable. On second thought, maybe that wasn't the case? He carefully studied her twisting the belt to her stunning dress. It was just the two of them, still together in this intimate room. She could have busted his ass out of here if she had been so inclined, yet she seemed to want to spend time with him, too. He reminded himself that he wanted to take it slow with her, no matter what. Back to her question, "I love country music—we grew up on it. I'm not wild about a lot of the 'bro country' that is so popular today, but give me some classic Willie, Waylon, Haggard, and line it up with '90s country, and we have ourselves a party!"

Tess laughed, "I've never felt more seen than right now!" She indicated he should take a seat, and then also sat down. "That's how I feel. I do love me some rock, but country speaks to my soul," and she held her hand to her heart.

"My brothers and I went to see that big Garth Brooks tour that he did a few years ago—did you see that?" Sam was thrilled they had musical tastes in common.

"Yes! Ruth and I saw him in Camden, which is right outside Philly, essentially."

"I think I've seen a few shows there," Sam said. "One of my brothers is a Dead Head, and he has dragged me to shows all up and down the Northeast corridor."

Tess made a face; she had never been able to get into the Grateful Dead. Sam laughed when he saw her expression. "I know, they're not everyone's cup of tea; hell, they're not mine normally, either, but sometimes a brother's gotta do what a brother's gotta do for his brother."

"Right, Ruth went through this phase when we were younger where she loved Britney Spears, and the two of us were able to see her a couple of times, along with some other friends. I thought it was cool going with my big sister, but between you and me? I wasn't sad she didn't come around to our neck of the woods often," Tess whispered.

Sam chuckled, knowing the feeling well of doing something just to please a sibling. "You and your sister seem close, like my brothers and I are."

"We are, very close, sometimes too close, I guess. She can be a bit… how shall I say it? Overprotective? She's always been that way. If anyone dares to wrong me, Ruth will hunt them down and make them regret knowing her. Fortunately, I haven't been wronged that often. You know, teenage drama in high school, that kind of thing. She's two years older than me, so she was always making it a point to stick her nose in my business, but she has also always been my best friend. I know I tried her patience on more than one occasion, but she always let me tag along with her friends, and then when she got her driver's license, she'd take my friends and me to the movies or the mall if we went to the big city." Tess found herself smiling over at Sam, wanting to hear more about his family. "You mentioned you had brothers? How many?"

So Sam filled her in on his family, and they compared notes on how their childhoods were similar. While they were talking, she started drinking the latte meant for her sister, and forced herself to choke it down. "God, this is terrible—what is it? Let me guess—she ordered an extra shot in her drink? Why does she always do that? I imagine this is what gasoline tastes like. I try telling her that coffee was invented so humans could drink cream without looking insane." Tess looked at Sam and said, "You seem like one of those black coffee kind of guys—am I right?"

From his pocket, Sam felt his phone vibrate, so he pulled it out and looked at the name. Damn, he had no choice but to take this now, and said remorsefully to Theresa, "It's my editor; I'm so sorry, I have to take this. I talked to my agent this morning, so this could be important. I'll catch up with you later, Theresa," and he answered the call as the room door closed behind him. Ruth was right—it was fun to watch him go.

CHAPTER
Twenty

Ruth

"What the fuck, Josh? Where in the actual fuck is your mind? Do you realize how upset you are making my sister, your fiancée, on the days leading up to her bachelorette party? Why the fuck can't you control yourself? See, now you're making me swear in front of my baby—what kind of life will she have if the first word out of her mouth is the f-bomb?" Ruth took a breath, and tried to remember the last time she had fully cussed someone out like this. Since she was well known for such behavior, however, she figured it had probably only been a few days. Who better than Josh, the current tormentor of her sister's, to bear the brunt of all the fucks, then.

"Ruth, what are you talking about? I just talked to Tessa less than an hour ago and I thought we had an okay call—I mean, I had to cut it short because I got an urgent message, but she told me she loved me before hanging up."

"As I live and breathe, Josh, I will never understand how you can be such a genius when it comes to science or math, or better yet, cutting someone open to remove an organ, but when it comes to the woman you profess to love, the woman you are engaged to be married to, you can be on the other side of this phone in complete LaLa land. I mean, seriously, was like a section of your brain removed at some point—like the part that is reasonable and rational? I've known you for almost twenty years and I know you to be a fairly sympathetic person. Would you agree with that?" No answer from Josh, which only served to further annoy the hell out of her. "JOSH—would you agree that you are a sympathetic person?"

"Oh, is this my time to speak? I finally caught on that this is one of Ruth Lefferts's ass chewing talks, so I wanted to make sure that I respond in the designated sections of my ass chewing. Just tell me what I did, so I can tell her I'm sorry." So now he was going to take a tone with her? Not on my watch, Ruth thought.

"I'm not telling you one damn thing until you answer my question—are you a sympathetic person?"

Josh sighed heavily, and then said, finally, "Yes, I believe myself to be sympathetic. Now, what did I do? Is this about the honeymoon, because in retrospect, I am sure Tessa will look back and agree that this is for the benefit of our future."

Ding ding ding—there was life in his brain after all! "Okay, maybe we're getting somewhere now that you're realizing where you fucked up earlier. And what is this bullshit about always being on her about her weight? You know how sensitive she is about it; but here you are, having had two phone calls with her and you just had to bring it up both times?"

"We have actually had three phone calls-" and now he was correcting her? He always was a slow learner, Ruth mused.

"I'm not sure that was an answer to my queries, son. You correcting me is not how this conversation is going to go. Do you understand how lucky you are that my gorgeous, creative, intelligent sister even deigns to talk to you, let alone agree to marry you? While she may believe that you are the only man who will ever love her, I know, and you know, that is far from the truth. She is stuck on this idea of the two of you from high school as destined to be together, and no offense, but I have tried to convince her otherwise over the years. Especially after you dumped her like a cold plate of cheese fries when you graduated from college. Remember that, Josh? You broke up with her, claiming, what? You needed to find yourself? I called bullshit on that then, but everyone said 'No, Josh was confused; Josh was starting his life.' Or how about the first time she came to see you at college, and she was so out of her element, but you did nothing to help her; left her there floundering on her own, for your little frat brothers to mock and ridicule? I told her to dump YOUR ass then. Instead you wait until you're graduated and then break up with her."

Ruth paused to take a breath, giving Josh the chance to jump in, "Don't blame all of this on me. Yes, I broke things off with her when I graduated, but she said she wanted space also; that she wanted to concentrate on her culinary degree. It was understood that we would stay in touch—it's not like I abandoned her."

"Josh, you started dating someone pretty quickly after breaking up with her—what was she supposed to think? She has had that in the back of her head, about you finding someone else. So I want you to do me a favor and stop with these head games, whether intentional or not. You have this preposterous habit of making her jump through hoops, and it's completely bogus."

Josh sighed heavily, "You are giving me too much credit for being some kind of manipulative control freak, Ruth; you've known me as long as I've known Tessa. Everything I have done for Tessa has been out of love. Yes, I dated a couple of women when we broke up, but she is the only woman I have ever loved, and she knows that. I admit it was an egregious mistake on my part, but I do think that it made us stronger when we got back together."

"Look, Josh, just let it rest while she is on vacation, okay? No more dropping information bombs on her, no asking her how much sugar she has eaten, no anything that could potentially upset my sister! You have no call to even DISCUSS the wedding dress: am I being heard?" Ruth asked insistently.

"I do hear you, Ruth, I do. I will call her now and-"

"Absolutely not!" Ruth interrupted. "You are going to give her space and if she wants to speak with you, she can call you. Mind you, if she DOES call you, you had better damn well answer. Other than that, just send a text to her in an hour or so telling her that you love her. That's it.

Now, I will end our chat on a high note, and say that breakfast was much appreciated and the flowers were beautiful. Bye, Josh, I'm hanging up."

Ruth lightly hit herself in the head with her phone, wishing her head was Josh, and that she could really let loose. Good lord, he could be so exasperating. Details were his best friend, and unless he could align all the tiny minutiae of life, he wasn't happy. Tess wasn't wrong—he WAS an absolute control freak, but he also had one of the biggest hearts of anyone she had ever met. Throughout their relationship, though, Ruth had often wondered what would happen if Tess could have met someone else, and how much of Josh and Tess being together had to do with her sister being afraid of being alone. No, it was more than that, though, she thought, shaking her blonde head. She was fine being alone—she just wanted to be loved, and Tess was terrified only Josh could love her for herself. Ruth knew it was bullshit, but making someone else see themselves through your eyes was impossible.

Ruth's phone lit up; speaking of love, she answered, "Hey, Sweets, how did you know I needed you right now?"

Her husband, Sean, laughed, "I can always tell, especially from across the miles, when you need me. Seriously, I was just lying in bed, naked, of course, and longing for my wife. When are you home? God, I miss you."

Ruth loved it when Sean seduced her over the phone, but she would be able to enjoy it more if she wasn't in a public place. "Down, boy, save it for when I am alone again in the room," she laughed throatily. "I had to come out to one of the passenger cars to call my nitwit almost-brother-in-law."

"Oh, Josh, what did you do now?" Sean asked, trying to feel Josh's pain.

Ruth could always count on Sean to protect her sister as much as she did. It helped to marry a man with sisters, or it did in her case. His empathy for women, particularly those he was close to, was off the charts, and it was what made her fall hard and fast for him, and why she fell in love with him more every day. Ruth relayed what led up to her calling Josh, and then regaled him with the actual phone call, but she left out the swearing she had done. Sean was adamant their little bean would not hear any foul language until said bean was a teenager, which was funny since one of the things he loved about her was her creativity when it comes to cussing.

"Does Josh want to get married, or is he trying to get Tess to call the wedding off? I know he can be a bit obtuse at times, but this is out of control nuts for him. Is he coming off the rails the closer the wedding is? Now I really wish I was going to be at the bachelor weekend—I do love a good drama," Sean replied.

"In an interesting turn of events, since you brought up Tess calling off the wedding, I do have a little bit of a secret. Tess has kind of 'met' someone on the train." Ruth hinted.

"What? Like another passenger? How?" Her husband loved an intrigue as much as she did, bless him.

"Evidently he helped her with her bags when she boarded In New York, but we have been bumping into him in other cars on the train, and he is VERY into my sister. As in, the heat is off the charts when I see him with her."

Sean whistled, "Wow—how does Tess feel about him?"

"Oh, you know Tess, basically clueless when it comes to men, but he is pretty fine, so I'm sure she has noticed that. He's also super nice and seems smart; oh, and he's an author."

"Now that should intrigue your sister—I know how much she loves books. So question: how do you feel about her possibly being attracted to a man when she's engaged to our friend Josh?" Leave it to Sean to ask the difficult question.

"I think it's good for Tess to realize her worth and how other people see her as desirable. Listen, you and I have talked about their relationship. It's not that I want Josh to be hurt, but I think my sister deserves more than he gives her, and frankly, I think this is all he has to give. She needs fire and desire and some hot-blooded man to sweep her off her feet."

"Settle down, mama," Sean laughed.

"I know, I know. I'll mind my own business and let things play out as they will over the next two days, but you'll never believe when I tell you this…" And Ruth proceeded to tell Sean something only she knew, for now at least.

Tess

After Sam left her room, Tess had put her hand on her heart, willing it to slow down. What was wrong with her? She was an engaged woman, she chastised herself, and she loved Josh. She did. But when was the last time she could feel desire emanating from Josh with only a single glance? When was the last time his touch had set her skin on fire? Thinking back, Tess admitted to herself that she had a difficult time recalling when exactly they had last had sex, and that was a problem: maybe not that it had clearly been a while, but that she could not even remember. More importantly, she pondered when the last time was Josh had asked her any questions about what **she** was interested in, or shown that he valued her? Doubts had been simmering for quite some time in their relationship, but Tess had firmly put them to rest, or so she thought.

Now that her heartbeat had returned to pre-Sam levels, she packed up a small bag of her snacks, a bottle of water, and her book, and left in search of the car she had been wanting to see since she got on the train, but had eluded her yesterday—the viewing car. According to the online reviews, it was a magnificent addition to this route on the train, with a double-decker car that had windows lining the sides and all the way up to the top. She had been so caught up in just being on the train the prior day, and then the Josh drama occurred, that she had gotten sidetracked; today she was determined to check it out. Tess wondered about her sister's location and what she was up to, but also craved a little time alone, to just decompress and read. Although she and Ruth had always been very close, and Tess also had several friends she counted in her tight circle, at her core Tess was an introvert who loved and needed time alone. Where some of her friends had to have constant companionship, Tess had no problem going out alone for lunch or dinner in New York City when Josh had a long shift, or even taking in a Broadway show on her own. As long as she had a book with her, Tess was never bored, and most certainly never alone.

Tess had to pass through the dining car on the way to the viewing car, and she couldn't help but look around to see if Sam was there. Finally admitting to herself that they were connecting on some level was one thing, but she wasn't sure how deeply she wanted to think about it after that. When he had first approached her to help her with her luggage, all it took was a single glance at him to register how attractive he was; it was her experience that men who looked like Sam always knew how attractive they were, yet she had to be honest and acknowledge that he hadn't come across as someone too into himself. The more time they spent together, the harder it became to deny a flicker of attraction on her part. Maybe that was why she was so upset with Josh, she wondered. Could it be that she had been feeling guilty about Sam? Perhaps she was blowing all of this out of proportion to make it okay for her to flirt with another man. Tess shook her head, and willed herself to just stop overthinking; it was one of her fatal flaws. Not seeing Sam in the car was both a relief and a disappointment; she walked through a passenger car, and then finally made it to the viewing car.

Gasping as soon as she opened the door and stepped through, Tess was taken aback by the brilliant blue sky atop the glass ceiling. She could feel the warmth of the sun penetrating the windows, and all around were swaying amber waves of grain. Although Tess and her family had lived on a farm for years, they were not 'farmers', so they weren't emotionally tied to the land, as so many of the kids she had grown up with were—generations of families who have raised crops and livestock, who passed down the farm to their children, and then their children's children. Tess had friends from childhood whose families had lived on the same land for multiple generations. Her father's ancestors had actually started out in Brooklyn, almost three hundred years ago, and the Lefferts name was widely recognized there, so it was a bit of a full-circle moment now that she was living there. During some ancestral research, Tess had discovered that they had headed west about one hundred years after setting in Brooklyn, first living in Pennsylvania for a few generations, and then Ohio, and they just kept moving further west, ever so gradually, until her paternal grandparents had landed in South Dakota, and that seemed to stick with them. Her grandfather Lefferts was a pharmacist, and her dad became a vet. They were a family not tied to their land, but to their community.

Tess found the perfect seat by a window, in an aisle by herself, which was the way she preferred it. She sat down, opened up her bag of Chex mix, and placed her book on the table. She had only read the first few chapters so far, and was anxious to get into it; Tess smiled as she opened it up to the next chapter. Both Tess and Ruth were avid readers, a gift handed down to them from their mom. From the time the girls were babies, Ellen had read faithfully to them every nap time, every bed time, or during moments where she felt they just needed to settle down. Their mother was a wonderful narrator, and she had voices for all of the different characters she would read to her daughters. Trips to the library were their version of a trip to the mall for other kids. Tess, along with her sister, had had a library card at the public library once she turned twelve, and she felt like she had read every book in both her school library and the town library. A trip out of town always consisted of a trip to the bookstore; some girls bought makeup or clothes, but for Tess, her money was always spent on books, and she prided herself on building her own home library every chance she got, sometimes much to Josh's chagrin. He often grumbled that they were running out of room at their apartment, to which Tess would respond that meant they needed a bigger place!

After reading for about an hour, Tess took her phone out and saw that she had a missed call from her sister nearly half an hour ago, and just as she was going to call her back, Ruth rang her.

"Yo, Tessie, where are you? I got back to the room and you were gone, which is no big deal, so I took a shower and you still weren't here. Then, I called you, which you didn't answer, so I laid down and took a tiny nap, and still no Tessie!"

Tess laughed at her sister, knowing she would understand, but still felt guilty she hadn't kept in touch with her. "Sorry, I needed some me time. I'm in the viewing car. You need to get over here—the views are absolutely stunning!"

"Are you sure? I can just do my own thing if you want need more time."

"Yes, get your tush here!" Tess insisted. "I'm saving you a seat. I do have a bottle of water and the Chex mix, though, if you're up for some snacking."

"Perfect—actually, I'll bring this cup of coffee with me that's in the room. For the life of me, I'm perplexed as to how it got here in the first place. I can't wait to hear THAT story." Ruth hung up, and Tess couldn't wait to tell her sister what had transpired earlier.

Thinking about Sam wasn't what she should be doing, especially since she and Josh were having this disconnect, and it didn't feel right to start comparing him to Josh. She and Josh had started so young, as friends, gradually beginning a relationship. In some ways, now it was about comfort: having that person who knows you so well. He knew her favorite color, what food she craved when she was hormonal, the song to play if she was in the dumps. Tess liked being comfortable, and loathed uncertainty.

But Sam: she couldn't stop herself from remembering the feel of him pressed up against her body, with only her robe covering her. She had felt tingly all over since she'd been in his arms, and never had she felt an electric attraction to someone. Sam was the opposite of comfort, yet there was no denying his embrace felt so right. God, what was she doing? This wasn't Tess—she despised betrayal, so why didn't any of this feel like betrayal? Truthfully, she felt guilty only because she BELIEVED she should feel guilty. Was it wrong to appreciate being desired by Sam? Sex with Josh was good, but Tess bit her lip imagining sex with Sam. Her hand traveled the line of her cheek that he had stroked earlier, and her flesh was warm. If only she had leaned up, stretched up on her tip toes, her mouth could have met his. There, right there, was her truth—she had wanted him to kiss her, wouldn't have minded if her robe had parted just slightly more, giving him a glimpse of more skin underneath. His fingers had felt rough against the softness of her cheek, his touch had been ever so gentle, yet determined. No doubt he desired her, and despite all of the romance novels she had read during her formative years, and her own personal beliefs insisting she remain true to Josh—her one true love—she craved it: his attention, his touch, his body.

"Tess? Tess? EARTH TO TESS!"

"What the hell? Jesus, Ruth, scare me half to death, why don't you?" She glared at her sister for interrupting her Sam haze.

"Okay, what is going on? I have been sitting here for like a minute, and you were somewhere else. Good thing I had the view to keep me entertained."

Ruth looked at her sister, and before she could question her further, Tess blurted out, "Sam was in the room before."

Ruth held up the coffee cup, waving it slightly in front of Tess, "and is that where this came from? Just the way I like it, by the way. I stopped by the dining car and they warmed it up for me."

"Yes, evidently you two had breakfast together—or he had breakfast and you had coffee? Should you really be having that much caffeine? It can't be good for the baby!" Ruth waved her on, so she continued, "I guess that the waitress bought you a coffee on the house, and Sam dropped by to deliver it, because he is so thoughtful." Too damn thoughtful.

"Carol," Ruth supplied.

"What?"

"Carol—that's the waitress. Lovely woman; not as gregarious as Todd, but I liked her. And I'll bet Sam could not wait to bring me that coffee, especially after I told him you were in the shower." Ruth wiggled her eyebrows at Tess, "So, what were you wearing?" She asked suggestively. "And may I add that you are looking super fine in that dress—isn't that the dress you brought to wear on Saturday?"

"Well, I do love this dress and it seemed a shame to only wear it once on the trip. You know how I don't get a chance to wear dressy clothes every day. Baking and dresses do not go hand in hand. The comfier the clothes, the better. Besides, you know how messy I can be-"

Ruth cut her sister off, "Yeah, mess, comfy, big deal—tell me about Sam!" Tess blushed, and Ruth's eyes widened. "Ooh, if you're blushing before you even give me any details, I know this'll be good. Where's that water you mentioned? I might have to hose myself down."

"Stop, stop, you are WAY too dramatic! So as you know, Josh had called-"

"Nope, skip the Josh part. The last thing I want is to relive that daymare this morning. I would actually rather have morning sickness than talk about Josh right now. Go on," Ruth prompted.

"ANYWAY, he called, you came and then left, so I was heading back to the bathroom and I heard a noise at the door, thought it was you again, so I opened it up, and-"

"And it was Sam? Sneaky little devil, isn't he, always pretending to be me at our cabin door. Funny how he always shows up right after I've left; he has some sense of timing, for sure." Ruth stared at her sister, widening her eyes even more, her mouth opening up into a noiseless gasp, "O-M-G—tell me you were still in your robe! Hot damn, you were wearing your robe." Ruth began fanning herself with both hands. "Water—I need that water NOW!"

Tess laughed, and took her book to lightly thump Ruth in the arm. "Would you please calm down? Yes, I was wearing the robe, but like I said, I thought it was YOU! I had been heading back to the bathroom to get dressed, for your information! But then Sam was there, delivering your coffee like the hottest Uber eats guy I've ever seen."

"So you admit you think he's hot? FINALLY!"

"What? Of course I think he's hot—I do have eyes; I just don't go around objectifying the opposite sex like my beloved sister does, apparently."

"Enough about me—please continue."

"There's not much more to it: he came into the room, I turned around to get something at the same time he turned to me, and we ended up, like, bumping into each other? He reached out to steady me, I guess so I didn't mow him down or something, and.." Tess took a deep breath, unsure about sharing the next bit. Part of her wanted to keep it to herself, this sexy secret almost-kiss.

"And…and what? Wait, let me get a visual," and Ruth closed her eyes, imagining the scene. Suddenly her eyes popped open, and she grinned a wicked grin. "I got it, Babe. You're standing there in that tiny little robe, probably with your cleavage teasing poor Sam to death, and he's bracing you, or whatever you want to call it, but you two red blooded adults are now pressed body to body." Ruth gasped, "Did you have sex? I will die right now if you tell me that you had sex with Sam."

"Seriously, would you please lower your voice. For god's sake, no, we didn't have sex. Do you even know me at all?" Tess questioned her sister, and then paused to clear her throat. "Admittedly, there was a moment, though. Like a very tiny, minuscule, flash-in-the-pan moment where we were just kind of staring at each other, and it seemed like his face was coming closer, and then my phone rang, and it was over."

Ruth was gulping down her coffee, trying to ignore her burning throat. "This is making me hot—the coffee and this story. Obviously I was kidding about the sex stuff, but wow—you almost kissed Sam. Good for you," she grinned at Tess.

"Well, I mean, I can only say how it felt on my side, and yes, if it hadn't been for Mom calling, I maybe would have kissed him." Tess groaned, "UGH, Ruthie, what is going on with me? Why am I feeling this way? If I'm being totally honest, I should feel way worse about it than I do," Tess confessed.

"At the risk of repeating myself: just relax. You haven't done anything wrong. Your feelings for Josh have never been tested before, so maybe that's what all of this is about. Honestly, I think you should just be a leaf and go where the wind takes you the next couple of days. Spend time with Sam, or don't; you have always done the 'right' thing, and you have more integrity than anyone I know. Can we go back to how it felt to be pressed up to Sam, though? And pass me some of that snack mix."

CHAPTER

Twenty-Two

Sam

S am hung up the phone after talking with his editor. She had sent
some notes on the chapters he had submitted; they worked well as
a team, and Jenna, Sam's editor, usually had some insight into his
work that enhanced it. Sam preferred to make any changes or corrections
sooner, rather than later, so they communicated frequently during his writing process. True to form, Jenna had a few very specific ideas on how to
enhance his female character even more, which made Josh eager to start
writing this afternoon. Once he quit obsessing over this morning's encounter with the very luscious Theresa, that is.

He raked a hand through his hair, grabbed his keyboard and iPad and
sat at the table in his room. Closing his eyes, he leaned back in the chair
just to get another look into his memory of Theresa standing before him
in that robe. At the first sight of her, all breath had left his body. Their
fortuitous crash into each other was what his dreams were currently made
of, and he had been so close to kissing her. He could still feel the warmth

of her breath drifting up to him, how silky her cheek felt under his hand, the swell of her hips under his other hand. His feelings were more than the electric desire he had for her body, though. The connections they were making concerning random likes and dislikes; he loved learning about her, and was intrigued to know more. If he could make this train trip last an eternity, he would, until he could discover every layer of Theresa; he was afraid when he left this train, he would never see her again. Was it irony that only this morning he had been telling himself to take it slow, and now he was imagining knowing her forever? Or was it stupidity? Maybe both?

His phone ringing brought him out of his stupor—it was his brother, Chris. "Hey, Chris, what's up?"

Chris was a lawyer, and the two of them lived in the same apartment building. "Thought I would let you know that Huckleberry and Sawyer are two well fed cats this morning. Man, those two can eat! I did pop in yesterday afternoon, but they were in hiding, I guess, so I left some food out for them. This morning they were front and center, though, and slightly annoyed at my late appearance," Chris laughed. Sam had adopted the bonded pair three years ago, after passing by a pet store hosting an adoption event a few blocks away from his condo. He and his brothers had grown up with a variety of animals that one of them had usually plucked from some form of near death. His mom was a born nurturer and would never turn away a soul in need, and her sons took full advantage of this when it came to strays.

"I was hoping to get a proof of life shot at some point, so I do appreciate the call. How's the case you're working on?" Chris often did pro bono work on the side, and when he wasn't working, could be found at home reading the latest law journal. Chris was someone in desperate need of a social life, for sure.

"Tough stuff, this one. Any way I come at it, I don't imagine a happy ending. I need some uplifting news right now, so I figured I would call you and pump you for info on this lovely lady I'm hearing about?" Forget about women gossiping—his brothers spread word faster than TMZ.

"I won't even ask how you found out about her. Chris, I don't even know what to say—in some ways it feels like fate, but then it feels ridiculous. I'm trying to balance working on this book now with getting to know a woman I met under completely random circumstances, while also trying to NOT lose my head. Taking the train was supposed to be about both my comfort and working on my deadline, and I can't lose focus on that; however, she has inspired some of my current storyline."

"That's great, big bro—listen, I called for a second reason. I know Mom called you yesterday, but it wasn't totally out of the blue," Chris paused. He was the second youngest in the line of brothers, and known for being the most pragmatic.

"What is it—is it Dad?" Sam asked in a panic. Last year their dad had a minor heart attack; it didn't require open heart surgery, thankfully, but it had set them all on edge. When you are young, you expect your parents to live forever, but then it seemed when you hit your thirties, it dawned on you, as friends started losing their parents, that you will eventually experience that same loss.

"No, it's not Dad," Chris reassured his older brother, "but it is Mom. I don't know if you knew, but she had a mammogram a couple of weeks ago? Well, it seems they've found something-"

"Something? What something? Like a lump? Had she felt it before?" Sam stood up from his chair, and began to pace his room.

"No, she hadn't felt it, and it is extremely minuscule, the doctor said, so whatever it is, it is early stages. She's going to have a biopsy done tomorrow. She wanted you to know, but when she called, she didn't want to bring you bad news, especially while you were traveling. She said you sounded the happiest she's heard you in a long time," and with that he thought he heard Chris's voice break.

"Okay, I'm going to get off at our next stop. I haven't even been cognizant as to where we have been making stops, but I will find out. Then I'll fly home from there." Sam felt frantic, and suddenly claustrophobic.

Chris said adamantly, "No, absolutely not. Mom knew this would be your reaction. She wants you to stay on, keep doing what you're doing, go to your weekend party, and then she will see you when you come home. It's a small procedure, on the grand scale of things, and the rest of us will be there. I'll keep you posted with every finite detail, and text every five minutes. You know Mom—she would hate it if you came back for this."

He did know his Mom; he can remember, in his earliest memories, shortly after his brother Bobby was born. He was not yet three, and Jamie was two, but his mom had made sure to give them special attention so they wouldn't feel jealous about the baby. Jane and Sam would go on little mother/son dates every month, while one of his grandmothers cared for baby Bobby and toddler Jamie. She was so thoughtful and considerate, and the rock of their family; he knew his dad would come undone without her.

Sam took a deep breath, in and out, then replied to Chris, "You're right. Me coming back would probably be a compete clusterfuck anyway. Who knows where I would fly out of, and when I could even get a flight home. I'll call her when I get off the phone with you."

"No, don't—she'll know that you know, and you know her and that Catholic guilt. The way you sound now, you won't be able to hide from her the fact that you heard the news. Okay, I have to go. Love you, Bro, and I'll be in touch."

"Love you, too, and thanks for letting me know."

Although he knew his brother was right, that his mother would be suspicious of a phone call the day after she had called him, Sam still felt that he should reach out to her in some way. He was suddenly struck with an idea—maybe he wouldn't call her, but communicate in another way. She loved getting texts and photos. Sam would often send her a selfie when he was out jogging along the Charles in Boston, or if he was at the farmer's market trying to pick the freshest produce, he would snap a pic, asking her advice on which batch of strawberries to get, or which apples were crunchier. He looked around the room for photographic inspiration, but came up short—she'd hardly appreciate a picture of the pile of dirty laundry in the corner, or the evidence of his midday snacking piling up on the table. Taking out the brochure of the train he had snagged before boarding, he looked at the page for the viewing car, which he had yet to see. Perfect. His clothes, unfortunately, would not do, at least his shirt. "Why are you wearing a T-shirt in a nice place?" She'd ask, so in deference to her, he changed into a collared, long-sleeved shirt he had brought along for any "nice" event out in Lake Tahoe.

He changed clothes, also putting on his nicer pair of jeans, and checked his hair in the mirror. He rubbed the stubble on his chin, but didn't want to make a mess out of the shower. Plus, he had to give his mother SOME-THING to gripe about: he was a very considerate son, after all.

CHAPTER
Twenty-Three

Tess

Ruth had begun feeling nauseous in the viewing car, so she had elected to return to their room for some soda and perhaps a nap; before leaving, she had encouraged her sister to stay in the viewing car and read. Tess hugged her sister, promising her she would keep her posted if she went anywhere else—Ruth had serious issues with FOMO.

Instead of opening her book again, Tess reached into her bag and procured a pad of paper and pen. She had been considering some new baked goods she'd wanted to try for her clients. Although her dream was to have her own bakery, she genuinely loved what she did now, and her customers. One in particular was a small coffee shop on the corner of the block she and Josh lived. They had lived there for about five years, having found the apartment together. After Tess had graduated from culinary school, she had worked a couple of years in Napa Valley, until she and Josh had come across each other seemingly out of nowhere. At this point, they had been broken up for about four years. She remembered well the day he broke up with her. She had been planning to travel to NYC for his college graduation; in fact, her flight out was the next day. He had texted her, asking her to call him when she had time so they could have a "much needed conversation". Bewildered, she called him back. It had been their agreement that he was going to travel back to California with her after his graduation so they could spend the summer together before he began med school in the fall. Tess had thought maybe he was going to tell her he had to delay coming to California—possibly, he'd tell her that he would come at a later date instead of flying back with her. Instead, he informed her that spending the summer "bumming around" California with her wasn't "the best decision" for his long-term career. Instead, he had made plans to get an apartment with Fitz, and use the summer to read up on medical journals and surgical procedures. "Fitz really had the best idea" he said during that phone call. "So what is this?" Tess had asked Josh, "are you breaking up with me?" No, he had assured her, but maybe the break would be good for them for the time being. So Tess had gone along with it, even agreed it was best that she not attend his graduation. Disappointed to spend the summer without Josh, she had consoled herself by thinking once the new term came, they would get back together. She cringed now at her naïveté—why she had ever deluded herself in believing that while they couldn't be together for the SUMMER, but once school began, they could? Of course, Josh had let her believe it, never once correcting her the couple of times she called him over the summer (always her calling, never him).

During that horrendous summer, she had made a trip home back to South Dakota about a month before her term began, for the South Dakota State Fair. Growing up in the heartland, the state fair was an annual ritual that Tess and her family never strayed from. Her parents had a motor home that they would park on the fairgrounds, and Tess and Ruth would spend the five days of the fair as part of a community—one that honored agriculture, amusements, entertainment, and food. The sisters would get a fair pass which meant they could ride endlessly every day and long into the night, while their parents enjoyed all of the exhibits. The South Dakota State Fair was where Tess and Ruth saw their first concert. The girls would meet up with friends from their hometown, and "fair" friends they had made over the years. For Tess, being at the fair had always been a time of immense happiness that she anticipated recreating every August.

However, the August before her first year in college ended up being a time of overwhelming heartbreak. While she and Ruth were walking the fairgrounds and eating corn dogs, they had crossed paths with Josh, with his arm around a woman neither one of them had ever seen before. Awkward introductions were made, along with a late-night phone call from Josh to Tess, that she let go straight to voicemail. "I'm sorry" and "I never meant to hurt you" were expected, but "we've only been dating a few weeks" wasn't. It was the ultimate betrayal to Tess, and the fact that Josh hadn't been honest with her, that he hadn't done her the courtesy of giving her the truth she deserved, was what hurt the most. This all led back to her beef with Fitz; despite Josh's denials, it was easier to take their separation as being more Fitz's fault than Josh's, and it certainly made the transition smoother for them when they did reconnect four years later, ironically enough at the South Dakota State Fair again.

When they saw each other those four years later, Tess had been taken aback by how Josh had changed—more driven, but clearly regretful. Tess had been considering a life change, away from California, but not truly committed to moving back to South Dakota. She and Josh had spent the next week together at the fair, riding the carousel, eating popcorn and fried cheese curds, and drinking tart lemonade. He had won her a few stuffed animals from some carnival games, and the two had later donated his winnings to a children's hospital. Slowly during that time, they had begun to rebuild their relationship, now fully adults, and both aware of the hurt that had come from their breakup. Tess hadn't been entirely sure she could ever trust Josh again, so they had parted after that week as "more than friends", but not as a couple. Once she was back in California, Josh had begun calling, at first every few days, and then daily. Finally he admitted that he still loved her, had indeed always loved her, and wanted them to give their romance another try, but only if she was willing to move to New York City. Since her life was in limbo already, Tess had figured why the hell not? If you're making a change, make a big one! She put in her two-week notice, packed up her meager belongings, loaded up her car and moved into an apartment with Josh, on the Lower East Side, where they lived for three years before moving to Brooklyn.

Tess tapped her pen against her mouth, a move that brought her out of the past and back to the present. Turning her thoughts back to her baking, Tess was thinking that what was missing in her local eateries were some Midwest favorites with a NYC-spin, maybe chocolate caramel rolls, like a babka meets cinnamon roll, or mashup of coffee cake and crumb cake: both sounded like delicious ideas. She still marveled that so many of the dishes she grew up eating were unheard of in Brooklyn, but that was part of the joy living there, when she could merge her "then and there" with "here and now".

Tess's phone lit up, first with a text from Ruth, telling her that she was feeling better after some ginger ale, and then an incoming call from her mom. "Hi, Mom," she answered.

"Hi, Tessie, I just wanted to check in on my girls and see how the trip is going?"

"It's fantastic! We love our room, and I am currently in the viewing car, and Mom, you would love it, both you and Dad! The sights are breathtaking. I'm kicking myself that I didn't make it here yesterday, but I am making up for lost time today! How are you and Dad?"

"Oh, Honey, same as yesterday—madly in love and too stupid to deny it," Ellen laughed. Tess's mom was a big fan of self-deprecating humor. "We went to a couple of open houses today for some condos, so that was a bit jarring. I can't imagine downsizing, but really, do we need all this space?"

"I suppose not, Mom, but what happens when we come to visit? And now, with Ruth having a baby? I'm still on board with whatever you and Dad want to do, obviously, but just want to make sure you have thought it all through?"

"I think it will be good for us, to kind of have this fresh start with a new place. Create memories going forward, and not looking back. We love you girls so much." Her mom took a moment to blow her nose, clearly emotional. "So I have to be honest that Ruth did call a bit ago, and filled me in on your issues with Josh—how are you feeling about everything? I'm so mad at him right now, I'll have you know. And so is your father—wants to give him a good talking to! You know how stern your dad can be, especially when it comes to you girls."

Tess chuckled to herself, because her dad's idea of stern was a fierce frown and nothing else. The man was an utter teddy bear, and he was quite fond of Josh, as he had been since the day he was introduced to him. Josh and John had bonded over their love of science, often comparing notes about veterinary medicine and human medicine.

"Mom, I just think we are having a disconnect right now, and it is being made more difficult since we are physically apart. Josh has never been great on the phone, and communication isn't his strong suit in the first place. He just can be so frustrating. Did you have problems like this with Dad? I just hate feeling like I have no say in our relationship."

"Well, Tess, I hate to use that old saying that 'things were different in my day', but it's true, for the most part. However, you also know your father is not great with making decisions, which is part of what drove us apart. It drove me crazy having to decide everything—what to have for dinner, where to put the sofa in the living room, what car to buy; these decisions didn't matter to him. Me, you girls, and his animal patients are what he preferred to focus on. I guess in a way, with Josh focused on his career, he and your dad are alike."

"Except I don't seem to make his radar, unlike the other side of Dad's concerns. Ugh; I need to move on from dwelling about it, Mom. I will have plenty of time when I'm back in Brooklyn to deal with reality. I appreciate you reaching out, but Josh and I will be all right. Anyway, I should check in with Ruth and see what she's up to, maybe go to the lounge car for a drink."

"Okay, Sweetie, love to you, and give love to your sister." She heard her mom blowing kisses over the phone, an Ellen Lefferts trademark.

"Will do. Love you, Mom." And Tess blew her mom kisses back.

Tess gathered her items, intending to head back to her room; as she stood up, she glanced around the car. A flash of black curls caught her attention, so she grabbed her bag from the seat, walked down the aisle, and back to where she had seen Sam. It would be rude not to go say hi, she told herself. Wouldn't it?

CHAPTER
Twenty-Four

Tess and Sam

As Tess got to Sam's row, he was still staring pensively out his window. She cleared her throat, and said tentatively, "Fancy meeting you here, huh?"

He looked up at her, but she could tell his thoughts were miles away. "Oh, god, that was stupid. I'm sorry. Sometimes I try to make a joke and it falls flatter than a pancake. Ruth is so much better at it than I am-"

Sam stood up suddenly, laughing, and shaking his head. No, no, sorry, I was out of it." That was the only reason he could think that he wasn't aware of Theresa standing over him, since every fiber of his being seemed to be so finely attuned to her since meeting her. He gestured for her to take a seat beside him, then turned to face her. After just staring at her for longer than was entirely appropriate, he leaned in and said, "Did I mention this morning how bright your eyes are, even in glasses? You are just what I needed to brighten up my afternoon."

Tess smiled shakily, grateful she was sitting down—she wasn't convinced she could stand when he looked at her like that. She had never been exactly comfortable with compliments, so she did what she usually does: change the subject. "How did your call go with your editor? Is that what you were thinking about? Plot points and dialogue?" Tess asked.

"I wish—my book is actually really coming along. No, my brother Chris called with some unfortunate news about my mom." Sam watched her eyes widen with concern.

"What is it? Never mind—you don't have to share anything with a perfect stranger. My curiosity can be a little excessive at times. Forget I asked."

Sam's brown eyes stared deep into Tess's own green eyes. "I know we only met yesterday, but you feel like anything but a stranger to me." He took a deep breath, and continued, "Evidently my mom had a mammogram, and they found something suspicious. She called me yesterday and never mentioned that any of this was going on."

Tess reached over and grabbed his hand, "Oh, Sam, I'm sorry. It's so hard when something happens to our parents. How is she doing?" Tess was absentmindedly stroking the top of his hand with her fingers.

Sam had never held anything softer in his hands than Tess right now at this moment. Her touch was so gentle, so reassuring, and he found himself finally being centered after thrown for a loop earlier.

"I think she's doing okay—they're going to do a biopsy. I haven't spoken with her; Chris said she didn't want to upset my trip. The good news is apparently whatever it is, it's small, which means they found it early? Oh wait—this is her now." Sam looked down at his phone, and smiled. "I came to this car to take a selfie to send it to my mom." He showed Theresa his phone, and his mom's text read "My handsome son".

"She certainly is right about that, isn't she?" She teased.

Sam looked at her, and said "Oh, really? You think I'm handsome? All right: the truth is finally out!"

Tess blushed, she could feel it from her head to her toes. "I mean, I, um, well, I was just agreeing with your mom. It would really be rude not to," and as she was speaking, her voice was getting softer and softer, until she found herself whispering, and as she did so, he was moving closer to her. It dawned on her that they were still holding hands, but could not make herself let go of him.

Sam glanced down at their hands, and he laced his fingers through hers, stroking his thumb across the tops of her knuckles. He saw her shiver in response, and he leaned over to her, and tucked a loose red curl behind her ear. He brought his lips up to her ear and said, "I have thought about you all day and am so happy that you are sitting here next to me now," and he ran a finger from her ear, sliding it down the side her neck, across her bare collarbone, and over to her shoulder. "I've thought about touching you like this since I saw you in this dress this morning, so bold and beautiful."

Tess was entranced, by his low tones and his words, by his touch and his searing gaze. "I sometimes feel like I never want this train ride to end," she confessed. "It's wrong and I shouldn't feel that way, but I can't help it."

Sam was speechless, having just had those same thoughts earlier in the day. "It's not wrong—I'm feeling the same way. I think what we need to do at this moment is take each second we are given, in the here and now." Sam ran his fingers up her neck to her ear, and then cupped the back of her head with his hand, and brought his mouth down to hers; that was his intention, anyway, until—

Tess's phone pinged with a message, and startled her into unintentionally pulling out of his grasp. She groaned, "Why are our phones always blowing up? Oh, it's Ruth. She is wondering about meeting up for dinner?" Tess stared at Sam, biting her lip and then rushed forward, "Do you want to join us?"

Sam reluctantly shook his head. "I would love to, but I don't want to interrupt your sister time—I know how important it is for you to be here with her. I should do some more writing, anyway." He then lifted her hand to his mouth, turned it palm up, kissed her in its center, and delighted in the shiver that rocked her body. He offered instead, "How about the two of us go to the lounge car now, have a drink, and then you and Ruth can have dinner? Afterward, you can swing by my room for a night cap?"

You really should NOT do any of this, Tess advised herself. No drink now, no nightcap later. Especially alone. In Sam's room. For the first time in her life, Tess chose to ignore her good sense, and instead, she found herself nodding and smiling, "I love this idea; I'll text Ruth back now." Finally disentangling her hand from his, she texted her sister to meet her in the dining room in an hour. Ruth promptly responded her agreement.

Sam proceeded to stand up and offered Theresa his hands, gently pulling her up to him, letting go of one of her hands while still tightly holding the other one, he moved them to the aisle, hand in hand. It felt natural for the two of them to walk holding each other, through the viewing car, then a passenger car, until they were at the lounge car. It seemed the "cafe" portion of the lounge car was ending, with most riders choosing to eat meals in their rooms or in the dining car. There was a bar in one of the corners, with seating either there or at the cafe tables.

Sam led Tess over to the bar, only just then having released her hand. "What would you like, Theresa?" And motioned for her to sit on the barstool at the end of the bar. Sam remained standing.

Sliding onto a barstool, Tess selected a glass of white wine, and Sam chose to join her in the selection, so he ordered a bottle for them to share. The bartender opened the wine and poured two glasses for them, and as he did so, Tess started swaying in her seat to the music that was playing, the notes of "Brown-Eyed Girl" filling the train. Watching her begin to sing along, Sam smiled. "Van Morrison fan?" He guessed.

Tess opened her eyes, "Definitely—how can you be a human and NOT be a Van Morrison fan? I have broad tastes, despite painting myself into a country corner this morning," she laughed.

"I have no doubt that you, Theresa, have many, many tastes that I can't wait to experience," Sam said suggestively, bending low to whisper in her ear. "Now, what should we toast to?"

"Let's stay in this moment and make a toast to our wide musical tastes," she said.

"To Van," Sam proffered.

"To Van," Tess agreed, and they clinked glasses. "Ooh, this is nice. Very crisp and refreshing. So, Sam, considering Van Morrison, I'm guessing you are an *Astral Weeks* man."

"One hundred percent correct. A few years ago, my parents, and all of my brothers and I went to see the fiftieth anniversary of the album; Van played it in its entirety. Life changing. We grew up listening to my parents play all of his stuff. What about you?"

"Love that album, but my absolute favorite is *Moondance*: so poetic and haunting. If I'm happy it can make me cry, and if I'm sad it can make me smile."

Sam nodded, "I get it. That's the Irish for you—always hovering between happy and sad. I say that with much experience," Sam laughed. "All of my grandparents are from Ireland, actually, and both of my parents still have family over there; we went as a family like twenty years ago, and I've been dying to get back since. Have you ever been to Ireland?"

"Yes, once, about ten years ago. My mom's family is Irish, through my grandmother." She and Ruth had taken a trip there, after Tess had graduated from culinary school, and spent a week exploring castles, the remains of medieval churches, and family folklore. "It was one of the most beautiful places I've ever been. It's funny because I always heard that no place was as green as Ireland, and it was unbelievable how true that was. So many greens, it took my breath away."

Sam watched her circle a finger around the top of her wine glass, and that small action was hell on him, so he lifted his eyes to her face. "I can see green that takes my breath away now."

He had chosen not to sit, and the width of his shoulders was blocking the rest of the car from view, giving her a feeling of intimacy. The scent of the soap he had used filled her nose, and it was intoxicating. With their eyes locked, she reached a hand up to his face, unable or unwilling to stop herself, and stroked his stubble on his cheek. "It looks like it would be rough, but it's so soft."

Sam reached out and took her hand, lifting it to his lips; again, he turned it over, kissed the palm of her hand, and this time ever-so-lightly licked her lifeline in the center of her palm, an action that sent all the blood out of her head, leaving her dizzy. He then took her hand, and placed it over his heart; she could feel the pounding rhythm beating through his shirt. "This is what you do to me, Theresa. Make no mistake I am mad about you."

Bringing her wine glass up to her mouth with her other hand trembling, she took a large drink of wine, put the glass back on the counter, and then stood up to be closer to Sam. Tess stroked her other hand up his arm, until she came to his shoulder, and brought her body closer to his, with her hand still on his heart.

"Holy hell, Tessie, I thought you were meeting me in the dining car. Good thing I have to walk through here or I never would have found y—"

Ruth's eyes were huge by the time she reached them, having only seen them from behind. "Well, am I interrupting?"

CHAPTER
Twenty-Five

Tess

Tess and Ruth took their seats in the dining car. Tess had managed to sidestep any questions from her sister so far, but knew she would not hold her off much longer. Before she and Sam had parted, he had leaned down and whispered his room number into her ear, with the action sending shivers down her spine. Goosebumps on her arms were still raised, and her head swam with the time she had just spent with him.

After Carol had given them their menus, Ruth studied her sister, not sure what to make of this new Tess that was unfolding over the course of two days. She had always believed her sister deserved to be swept away by love, not stuck in a relationship that seemed to be held together by time and comfort. Tess had a strong moral compass, and Ruth knew better than to question any of her actions or motives.

"I must say, Sis, when you go off the rails, you go full steam ahead. What I walked in on back there was off the charts—I could feel the heat coming from you two from the other side of the car. So what exactly did I interrupt?"

"Wow, Ruthie, only the one question? I have to say I was expecting to be peppered with them, and unable to answer any of them. Like 'What were you thinking?' And 'why were you doing it?' Although they would, I am sure, be more eloquently phrased than that."

"Uh huh, and now you're pulling a Tess and evading the one question I have asked! Frankly, I find it fascinating that you and Sam keep running into each other; almost like you're orbiting planets. So PLEASE give me some details or I am going to lose my shit right here. You don't want your sister, mother of your future niece or nephew, lifelong best friend, to lose her shit, do you?" Ruth jokingly begged.

Tess took a breath, still relishing the time she had just spent with Sam. Although it should feel like betrayal, she admitted to herself that no one had ever made her feel the way Sam did—both about herself and about another person. Her body, her mind, her soul—all came alive with his look, with his touch, with his words, and she was shaken by it, but refreshingly so. She was discovering parts of herself she hadn't known existed before this trip, an awakening almost.

"Ruth, I can't explain what is happening, not really. When Sam looks at me, the outside world ceases to exist. I never expected to meet anyone on this trip, let alone a man. I mean, what am I doing? You know me—I'm logical, I like things to make sense, and not much of this makes sense to me, but for the first time in my life, I don't care. I don't care about what I should or shouldn't do, and honestly, it's refreshing. Maybe it's because I have been so disappointed by Josh, from the moment he broke things off between us; yet, here I am, still with him, unable to give up on the life I always thought we were creating together. Then there's this little voice in my head, when I see Sam, that voice is telling me that maybe there IS something bigger out there for me. And then what? I let something happen with Sam, and I still go to my bachelorette weekend? Still have a wedding in six months? It's insanity—I don't even know his last name, for crying out loud. Ugh, so I just turn off the logical part of my brain when I'm with him and let myself FEEL." Tess covered her face with her hands, lifting her glasses off her nose. "I'm such a trollop," she moaned.

"Stop right there," Ruth admonished her sister. "You deserve to discover who you are, regardless of the situation. You know how they say drug addicts, once they start doing a drug, their brains stop maturing? Your brain is like that, and Josh is your drug. You met when you were babies, a couple of little idiot teenagers. Your brains weren't fully formed. He had his chance to spread his wings, if you'll recall, and where did that leave you? You didn't even DATE when he broke up with you. You focused on your degree, and you travelled some, and you worked, but you never opened up to anyone and let yourself have those experiences, or allow yourself to trust anyone." Ruth reached over and took her sister's hand into hers. "You are allowed to feel any way you want to right now. Just get through this trip, this train. This train can be your Vegas, and what happens on the train stays on the train. If it's meant to be with Sam, you will get all his pertinent information, and then can make further decisions. And I thought we had an unspoken agreement that we weren't calling it the 'bachelorette' weekend, but a general 'girls' weekend? No extra labels. Some of these women you haven't seen in years, and I'm looking forward to seeing everyone and meeting a couple of new people. Each and every one who will be there loves you and knows how amazing you are."

"So you're saying I'm a Josh addict? Sis, that doesn't seem right," Tess replied, trying to lighten the mood.

Ruth burst out laughing, "That's my girl! Oh, here's Carol. What are you having?"

Tess ordered the pan roasted chicken breast, and Ruth the salmon. Carol asked, "will your gentleman friend be joining you ladies?"

"No," Tess replied, "just us sisters."

Carol then said, "You know, when I saw him in here this morning with you," indicating Ruth, "I didn't think you two looked like a couple—way too casual. But then I was walking through the lounge car on my way here, and I saw you with him," she nodded at Tess, "and that made more sense. You two looked very much in love."

Tess stared at Carol as she walked away, certain she was wrong. In lust, yes, but not in love. She didn't even know Sam well enough to be in love.

"Actually," Tess started, "not to put a damper on things, but poor Sam did get some upsetting news today: his mom has to have a biopsy. He got a call from his brother saying she found a lump in her breast. I felt so bad for him because he was clearly devastated. I had come across him when I was leaving the viewing car to come back to our room." Tess didn't feel it was imperative to admit that she had actually gone to Sam, instead of leaving out of the door on the opposite end of the car.

Ruth gasped, "That's terrible. He was probably relieved to see you and have a friend to talk to. For what it's worth, we had a very nice conversation this morning at breakfast. You two do seem very compatible, not to mention electric, which brings us back to the lounge car—what did I stumble on?"

Tess flushed from head to toe. "We decided to grab a drink before you and I had dinner, and ended up ordering a bottle of wine-"

"Wow, you guys went from a 'drink' to a bottle of wine? Sam, Sam, Sam," Ruth said, "you continue to impress me. Okay, so you got a bottle of wine, and?"

"If I could finish without being interrupted, you know you'd get your details much more quickly? Well, when we sat down, or rather I sat down, and Sam stood against the bar. Van Morrison was playing on the speakers, and we got to chatting about him, and our favorite album, and then kind of just sat there, staring at each other. Turns out I can't keep my hands off of him, though, because first I" Tess stopped suddenly.

Ruth was leaning over the table just as Carol delivered their food to them, "Here you are, ladies, enjoy."

"Thanks, Carol," they said in unison.

"What? Because you what?" Prompted Ruth as soon as Carol had walked away.

"Well, when he told me about his mom, in the viewing car, I wanted to give him some comfort, so I kind of started holding his hand."

"Sure, sure, makes sense. I mean, if you really wanted to comfort him, you have those nice breasts, remember, and they are looking fine in that dress. I'm sure Sam would appreciate maybe pillowing his head right between" Ruth was cut off as Tess took a piece of bread roll and threw it at her. "Sorry, I don't know how serious to be with all of this: like super serious or lighten the mood with some jokes?"

"You and me both. I guess I don't want to take anything too seriously, just enjoy the moments." Tess ate some of her chicken, then told her sister, "when we were in the lounge car, he was standing, and I was sitting, but on the bar stool, you know, and all I could see was Sam, and he smelled all woodsy and manly, and his shoulders and chest seemed to be surrounding me, and I reached up and," Tess's cheeks were flaming.

Ruth stopped with a bite of her salmon halfway to her mouth, "My god, did you fondle him? Did you lay hands on Sam?" She put her fork down, picked up a napkin, and proceeded to fan herself. "Water, I need some water," she ordered, to no one in particular.

Tess put her face in her hands, with her shoulders shaking, and cried out, "I told you I had no sense left. What is WRONG with me?" She looked at her sister, with tears of laughter streaming down her face.

"Sis, I'd say absolutely NOTHING is wrong with you. You are living in the moment, on this train, with me and we have tonight and tomorrow left."

"Have I mentioned that I'm going to Sam's room for a nightcap after dinner?"

Ruth looked around the car and said, "Okay, please, can someone bring me that water?"

CHAPTER

Twenty-Six

Sam

Sam had gone back to his room after leaving the lounge car and ordered a burger from room service, wishing he had gone to dinner with Ruth and Theresa, but the last thing he wanted was for Theresa's sister to think he was horning in on their time together. He also made a mental note to get her cell phone number, not wanting to leave it at the last minute. He had straightened up his room, making sure that any dirty laundry was tucked well out of sight. When he had left the lounge car, he had also brought the remaining bottle of wine with him. He'd had the sense to add a bottle of champagne to his room service order, along with some chocolate mousse and strawberries. He was thinking of this night as maybe their first "date", and he couldn't think of a time he was more nervous.

Wanting to put his mind at ease in other areas, he made the decision to call his mom, but much to his surprise, his dad picked up. "Hello?"

"Hey, Dad, I was just giving Mom a call—is everything okay?"

"Yes, we are just getting back from a movie. We saw that new Liam Neeson movie down at that fancy theatre that serves food and drinks now: you know the one?"

"Yeah, there's actually a small chain of them in the Boston area, and one close to my building." Sam paused to think of what he wanted to say next. His dad, although loving, was of strong Northeast stock, and not known for wanting to discuss his feelings. He didn't consider it unmanly, he just thought people spent too much time thinking of their feelings, and then wanting to talk about their feelings. Drove his mom crazy, because she definitely felt any emotion you threw her way, but he supposed that was their give-and-take manner, their yin-and-yang. His mom had commented more than once that it was a blessing in disguise that they had only had sons, because daughters would have wrung the life out of poor Scott. "So Chris called me earlier and told me about Mom. How's she doing?"

Sam could imagine the aggrieved look on his dad's face, for he felt the same: unfair that this was happening to his mother, a woman who kissed their skinned knees growing up, who baked them cakes on their birthdays, who learned to play baseball because all of her sons, from Sam on down to Eric, wanted to play. Where his dad could be reserved in the affection department, Jane was a self-described hugger, and if you ever went out in public with her, you would realize pretty quickly that she never met a stranger. This trait alone should have been his first hint that something was off in his marriage to Amanda—his mom didn't care for her, and to a fault she loved almost everyone: not my cup of tea, she would say about Amanda.

"She's your mom—taking care of everyone else and ignoring herself. She was going to wait even with the biopsy because she didn't want to worry you while you were on your trip, and then it was until you had your book finished, or Bobby had his week off from the firehouse, or Chris was done with his case. She had a reason for not disrupting the schedule of any of you boys. Ridiculous. 'Who's going to care about any of this if you're not around anyway?' I asked her. Then she started crying, and we were both a mess."

"Do you think I should come back for the biopsy? Honestly, Dad. I will get out at the next major city and get a flight home."

"I am absolutely certain that she would not want that. The biopsy will be a quick and fairly painless procedure—she'll be in and out, takes like an hour, they said. Hopefully she won't even have to get general anesthesia, just the local kind." And then in the background Sam could hear his mom.

"Is that Sam? Tell him how much I loved that picture he sent me before."

"Here, you tell him yourself," and his dad handed his mom her phone.

"Sam, you were so handsome in that shirt you were wearing. Dressed so fancy for the train, I see. Or are you dressing up for that woman you told me about? Oh, I was talking to Chris and he said she just sounds lovely. Do you suppose when you get back, we could all meet her? You looked so happy; you know that's all I ever want for any of my boys."

"Ma, I don't even know her last name at this point, or have any contact info. Let me get through this train ride and we will see what happens after that," Sam laughed. "I need to make sure she can handle me, let alone my crazy family." Although Sam knew for certain that Theresa could more than handle him, and in all the right ways.

"Well, we will all be here when the time is right. I meant to also say that the view from that car was stunning. Maybe your dad and I should take a train trip like that for our fortieth anniversary? We have been tossing around some ideas; he'd have to take time off from work, god forbid, and you know what a pill he can be about that. Like there are no plumbers other than Scott Charles in the Boston area. How I have put up with him for so long, it is sometimes a wonder."

"Your sense of adventure has always been one of your best qualities, or so I've heard from your own siblings. Listen, I heard about your procedure—can you please let me know how everything goes tomorrow? I will be thinking of you all morning, and then I'll be back in a week. Remember, I'm taking the train back."

"Of course, Sam, of course. I'm sure all of your brothers will be in touch at some point. Eric is coming up from New York tonight and is staying the night."

Sam was dumbfounded. "So everyone will be there but me? Mom, I don't like the sound of this. I really feel like I should come back-"

"No way. Eric is going back right after the procedure. He was planning on coming up at some point to get some old playbills he has here, anyway. I don't want you making a fuss about me. It is a simple procedure, according to my doctor. In and out. Routine. Done every day."

"Okay, enough with the hospital taglines. I get it—I'll stay put and think of you from afar. Love you, Mom."

"Love you, too, my angel."

Hanging up from his mother, Sam realized he had a secret weapon in his back pocket—Josh. He shook his head, wondering why it hadn't occurred to him before to reach out to him once he heard about his mom. Sam brought up Josh's number, hoping it wasn't too late to call.

"Hey, Fitz, didn't I just talk to you yesterday?" He heard Josh laugh.

"Yeah, you know how it is—can't get me enough Josh sometimes."

"That's what my fiancée says, too, I hope. Although Tessa can be a little more exacting than some of my buddies. Actually, I'm glad you called, because there's something I should have told you, like YEARS ago, and now that the wedding is getting closer, it could be an issue for you. And for me, I guess."

"Okay, this is out of nowhere—what is it?"

"Well, the only reason I bring it up now is I think Tessa might be holding a grudge against you, and now that you're in the wedding, I don't want things to be weird. I should have told you yesterday when we spoke, since the wedding is top of mind lately. Remember when I was getting ready to graduate from university, and you had come back for an alumni weekend: I was supposed to be joining Tessa in California for the summer? After talking with you, I ended up breaking up with Tessa, and you and I spent the summer renting that apartment and hiking the Catskills?"

"I knew you guys had broken up, obviously, but you said that you wanted to give her the chance to have her freedom in California, and you also needed some space. I recall we wanted to spend the summer hiking in the Catskills, but then you met that girl from—was it New Jersey? I went back to Boston instead."

"I guess those were the details—anyway, after Tessa and I got back together, I may have inferred to her that us breaking up was kind of your fault."

Sam was speechless—he had always felt like there was something more behind Tessa avoiding him whenever he came to New York than their failed first time meeting. He got the sense that she went out of her way to not see him, ever, and even once she had joined Josh on his trip to Boston, but then didn't come with him when they were all supposed to meet up (this was when he was still married). Now he has the missing piece of the puzzle: where he had thought it was maybe embarrassment over the frat house, it was in truth her belief that he had been responsible for Josh breaking up with her.

"What do you mean she thinks it was 'kind of my fault'?"

"Fitz, when I first broke up with her, I did tell her that we needed to work on ourselves, to mature and have our own experiences, but she was devastated. And then when I ran into her later that summer at the state fair and I was with—god, I don't even remember her name, but yes, I guess she was from New Jersey—she looked so upset, and then I didn't hear from her for years. So four years later, when I ran into her again, I felt like an ass, because I knew I had made the biggest mistake; I wanted her back, but I had broken her heart, I knew that. I knew that you guys had that run in at the frat house, so I just played on that. I didn't think that you would mind, especially since you had already thought she blamed you anyway."

"Goddamnit, Josh, sure, I don't mind," Sam said sarcastically, "but your fiancée hates me, and has hated me for years, evidently, and now I'm supposed to be in a wedding where the bride hates your groomsman? How did she even okay that?"

"Tessa has a very forgiving nature, and I told her you had matured. Look, I'm sorry I never told you. I just needed her to forgive me, and I was sorry I had ever broken up with her: she is the best thing that has ever happened to me."

"What I don't hear you saying is that you're sorry you weren't just honest with her. Yeah, I thought she blamed me because she had to blame someone, but I didn't know it was because *YOU* had actually blamed me! Of course, I'm glad for you that she forgave you and you guys got back together, but the last thing I want is to cause any awkwardness at the wedding. Maybe I should just be a guest? Not an attendant?"

"No, I swear I will talk to her before the wedding. She has been planning this wedding for years, and everything needs to be perfect."

Sam sighed, and realized he needed to just let this go; it wasn't up to him to be relationship counselor to Josh, and this was one more reason for him to doubt this soon-to-be marriage, but people had to make their own choices. "Fine, whatever you need to do for you guys, but I do think you should be honest."

"I know, I know. Oh, listen, buddy, I'm getting another call. See you this weekend." And he was off.

Sam rubbed the bridge of his nose, and put Josh out of his mind. He was slightly disappointed that he didn't get a chance to ask Josh about the biopsy for his mom, but he was irritated with him now, and frankly didn't want to be on the phone any longer as it was. Besides, he had more tantalizing things to ponder, and that brought a smile to his face: Theresa should be showing up soon, and he wanted to finish getting everything ready for their night.

Chapter

Twenty-Seven

Tess and Sam

After Tess and Ruth had finished dinner, they had gone back to their room, with Tess wanting to freshen up a bit before going to Sam. She had had a difficult time concentrating, because she kept mentally repeating his room number to herself; Tess had the worst short-term memory sometimes, and definitely did NOT want to forget his room number. Ruth had assured her she still looked fantastic in the dress she had worn all day, but Tess still wanted to go over the clothes she had brought. Instead, her sister had pulled out one of the dresses she had brought. Ruth was a couple of inches taller than Tess, and normally a few sizes smaller; however, Ruth procured one of her maternity dresses that was form fitting across her bust, and flared out over her hips, so it accentuated her good bits and camouflaged what Tess considered to be her not-so-good bits. The color was a bright scarlet on top, and a marbled pink, red, and white on the bottom. Some redheads couldn't pull off any shade of red, but Tess had always loved how she looked in the color—plus red made her feel daring; since that seemed to be the theme of her evening, she was going with it. Ruth had also convinced her to wear her hair down, but she couldn't talk her into putting on makeup: that was too much. For a fraction of a second, Tess thought about her misplaced ring, wondering where it had gone to, but not bothered enough by it, evidently, to think of it before now; so, she put the ring completely out of her mind once again.

"Okay, Sis, I'm going to head over to Sam's. I'm sure I won't be long—just enough time for a glass of wine, okay?" She stopped and studied herself in the mirror, pondering this brazen woman and where she had come from. She turned back to her sister, "Is this stupid? Am I an idiot?"

Ruth strode over to her sister and took her face in her hands. "From the time you were born: wait—I guess, I don't really know, but from my first memory of you, you have always been so steady, and so thoughtful, always wanting to do the right thing, and never wanting to hurt anyone. For once, just take tonight to only think about you, and consider what could be true happiness, and not what you THINK should be happiness. I am so proud to be your big sister. Now get the hell out of here before Sam shows up wanting to carry you back to his room, like 'An Officer and a Gentleman'. Oh god, remember how hot we thought Richard Gere was? I mean, he is still pretty hot, and that man at his finest-" and with that, Tess walked out the door.

Walking through the various cars to Sam's room, it occurred to Tess that she should feel nervous, but nothing had ever felt more natural. She had grown to love this train over the last two days, and she smiled and waved at the workers and various riders she become accustomed to seeing since yesterday. Only one more car to pass through, and she would be to Sam. She had some butterflies popping up now—was she really going to do this? She shook her head then, and reminded herself it was all completely innocent. Sure, she was an engaged woman wearing no ring (that she hadn't even thought of since yesterday), and she also happened to be wildly attracted to, for all intents and purposes, a stranger. This was like the plot of a steamy novel—sad woman meets hot man on a train heading across the country. Nobody would ever believe it could be happening to her—particularly anyone who knew her. Tess Lefferts was not the sort of woman to inspire lust in a sexy stranger. The truth was, there were times she felt she didn't inspire lust in her own fiancé, and had been doubting her own sex appeal for years.

Here she was: the other car for sleeping rooms. With her hand on the door to the car, she took a deep breath, shook her head, and opened the door. Walking into the car, she was struck by how dark it seemed compared to her own car. Was the lighting better in first class, or was she imagining things? It seemed to fit the atmosphere better, this dark car. It suited the slightly illicit feeling she had. Tess counted down the numbers, and finally came to Sam's door. Tess fought up her hand to knock on the door, when it suddenly flew open, and there was Sam, looking supremely gorgeous. Those brown eyes of his locked onto hers, and he smiled. "How did you know I was here?" She asked.

Sam chuckled, feeling slightly embarrassed. "I've been looking down the hallway every five minutes, waiting for you. If you hadn't shown up now, I was going to go to your room and sweep you off your feet to bring you back here," and with that, he reached out to her, and gently led her into the room. "You know, like Richard Gere in-"

"*An Officer and a Gentleman*," Tess finished, laughing. "So this is your room, huh? I've wondered what it looked like."

"Oh, yeah, is that something you've done—thought about where I'm sleeping, maybe what I'm wearing. If you have, you're not alone," and he reached over her to push the door shut, with the action bringing his body into contact with hers. "You smell amazing, you know. I could hold you this close and always find something new to fantasize about."

Tess's knees started trembling, and her hands reached up to clasp Sam's forearms for support, and she felt the strength in them. One drink, she reminded herself. Then she would go back to her room.

He brought his arm down to her waist, and led her to the small table by the window. As they crossed the room, she tuned into the music that was playing. "Do you have on *Moondance*?" She realized the title track was playing, and she stopped and stared up at him.

"I thought you would like it. Come over here—look what I have," and he held up the strawberries and champagne he had waiting for her. "Care for a glass?"

Tess was stunned, unused to having anyone go to any trouble for her—she was the planner, the list-maker, the one who sorted out events. She whispered, "I'd love one."

Sam prepared a glass of champagne with strawberries sinking to the bottom, and handed it to her, and then made himself one. "Now, what shall we toast to—sorry, I can't help myself. I come from a big line of toasters," and they both laughed.

"To Amtrak," Tess offered, trying to keep things light, and Sam clinked his glass to hers. "I wasn't expecting champagne," she confessed.

"No? What were you thinking? Maybe a Dr. Pepper and some ginger ale?" Already it seemed they had made memories together on this train.

Tess giggled, "Not exactly, but more along the lines of some of that wine we had earlier."

"Well, lovely Theresa, as a matter of fact, I did bring that back here, and I ordered in some of that chocolate mousse, also." Which Sam could not wait to share with her later—among other things, if he had his way.

"A man after my own heart," she sighed. Tess, this is not in ANY way keeping things light, she scolded herself. Undeniably, she was sinking faster and further into the fantasy in this room—Sam, champagne, strawberries, and chocolate. "Is this something you do every time you're on the train? Be charming? Lure unsuspecting women to your den of seduction?"

Sam looked into her eyes, putting every ounce of sincerity in his face, and brushed a hand over her hair, down her back. "If you believe nothing else, believe this: you are the only woman I have ever lured back to my room," he said, with a lopsided smile on his face, and received her stunning smile in return. He drank the last of his champagne, and then plucked the strawberry from the fluted glass, placed it at Theresa's mouth, and trembled as her mouth opened to take in the berry. She bit off half of it, and then he put the rest to his own mouth to eat it.

He turned the to the table and pulled the chair out for her to sit in, and then pulled the other chair over to her, close enough for his knee to brush up against hers, so he was somehow both beside her yet still facing her. He spooned some fluffy mousse into a dish, and topped it with large pillowy dollops of whipped cream, and took a spoon and brought it to Theresa's mouth.

Sam watched her taste her mousse, and when she rolled her eyes back in her head, he groaned, and she said, "So delicious. How is this not served after every meal?" She moaned then, with what could only be described as pure bliss.

"I love seeing you experience things—you seem to get joys out of even simple things. Have you always been like that?" Sam inquired, as he then took his own bite, and noticed how her pupils dilated as he licked whipped cream off their spoon.

Tess took a deep breath, and knew her plan to keep things innocent was sinking like the Titanic, especially as she saw the way his eyes dropped down to her chest and then rose up to intently look her in the eye, as if the answer to his question was all that mattered. "I think so. Ruth and I grew up in the country, and our parents worked, so we had to entertain ourselves, you know? I'm sure you had all those brothers to keep things interesting, right? We had our books and tv shows, of course, and then I started baking and trying different recipes out. My mom never knew what to expect for dinner," she smiled.

"How old were you when you started cooking?" Sam asked, after feeding them each another bite of mousse.

"Cooking or baking? Baking I was probably like ten, by myself. And cooking, I guess, like twelve? Mom would get home after six, and I saw how frazzled she seemed when she got home—she was tired and often hadn't planned on what to make, so I just started coking simple things, like soups or casseroles, hot dishes, pasta."

"Excuse me—hot dish? I need some clarification on that," Sam said.

"Oh, right, you're not a Midwest boy. A hot dish is like a casserole; we use the terms interchangeably." Tess took another bite of mousse, much larger than before for some inexplicable reason, and as she went to wipe the corners of her mouth, Sam reached over and wiped it with his finger, and dragged his finger across her lips. He watched her intently as her tongue darted out to lick her lips.

They finished their mousse, with "Into the Mystic" serenading them. "I was in Cape Cod once, and I put this song on, and it was magical. The fog had settled in, and all the lights were hazy, and for a moment, it felt like I'd always lived by the sea. It's a different world growing up in a land-locked place," Tess confessed.

"I can't imagine not living by the water. Looking out, seeing the rhythm of the water. When my brothers and I were younger, our parents would take us to Martha's Vineyard for a week, right in the middle of summer. I don't know how they afforded it, but we loved it. They'd rent a house a block from the beach. My parents seem like opposites, but they are perfect for each other." Sam paused, and then continued, "just so you know, I called my mom earlier, and she asked about you."

Tess widened her eyes, "What do you mean?"

"I was so taken yesterday when I first met you, and my mom called shortly after returned to my room; I happened to mention helping an incredibly beautiful woman with her luggage-" Sam stopped suddenly. "I'm sorry, I know I shouldn't talk like this. TMI, as the kids say," which made Tess laugh. "You truly have the most amazing laugh—matches your smile perfectly."

Tess reached over and took Sam's hand, "I've never had a man be so open with me before, and I have a hard time believing such sincerity is for me, if I'm honest with you."

Sam picked up her hand and brought it to his mouth, taking each finger and tenderly kissed each one, before turning her hand over and kissing her in the open palm, as he had done earlier, his eyes never leaving hers as he did so. He noticed the shiver that ran down her body, so he repeated the action with her other hand. Anything he could do to make this night last a lifetime, that's what he wanted. He stood up then to get the champagne in the champagne bucket, cursing himself for not having it at hand already.

Tess stood up, as Sam refilled her glass, with "Caravan" finishing playing. She took another sip of her champagne, and then turned to look out the window. "I like your room," she started, and then shut her eyes as "Crazy Love" started to play.

She felt Sam come up behind her. "Dance with me, Theresa," he breathed into her ear. He folded her into his arms as he was still behind her, and sang into her ear, "and the heavens open every time she smiles." He then turned her to face him. As they swayed to the song, the electricity sparked in the air surrounding them.

"And when I come to her, that's where I belong," Sam sang. Tess marveled at his beautiful, deep voice, and Sam slid his hands from her waist, up her back, and into her hair. He took her head in his hand, and tipped her head back. "Can I kiss you, Theresa? I've thought of nothing else since I first saw you out on that platform, and—" Tess broke him off, "Yes, please," and then she reached up, took her glasses off and put them on the table and repeated the action with his glasses; she then placed both of her hands on his cheeks and pulled his face down to hers. Their lips met and both of them exploded inside. For Tess, this kiss was the most electric, sensual experience she'd ever had in her thirty-two years. She thought of nothing else, only Sam, and how sexy and desirable she felt in his arms and in his eyes.

Sam was rocked to his core: her lips were plump and soft, god help him, like the rest of her body. He was drowning in emotion, right here in this train cabin. In his arms, he was holding everything good in the world, and he knew that it was what he had always needed. His hands were still in her hair—those luscious red waves tumbling down her back and all over his arms. When he opened the door to her earlier, his heart had dropped to the floor, seeing her there with her hair down, and in that sexy dress; he couldn't believe she was here for him. His hands now slowly drifted down her body, pulling her closer still, so they were flush with each other, no air in between: he felt her pressed against his body, and deep in his heart.

Breaking slowly apart, ever so slightly, Tess and Sam gazed at one another, seeing reflections of their desire, their longing. Lips bruised from kissing, cheeks pink with the heat they gave off. Van Morrison continued to play in the background: he was the soundtrack to their emotions.

Sam had dragged his hands from Tess's waist up to her face, cradling it in his hands, and then rubbing his thumbs over her lips to her ears. "I don't know how I will say goodbye to you when my ride is over, Theresa; it's been so long since I've felt this way about anyone, and I'm not sure I ever have."

"Shh," Tess put a finger to his lips, "let's not think about tomorrow, or anything past tonight. All we need is this moment right here, with only us: uncomplicated and pure." She stood up on her tiptoes and pressed him up against the wall, having decided that only a ferocious meeting of their mouths could transport them to a world that existed only for the two of them.

CHAPTER
Twenty-Eight

Ruth

Waking up to the sound of a ringing phone, Ruth looked around the sleeping cabin. Where the hell had she put her phone? Mentally retracing her steps brought her back to her late-night phone call with Sean, and, having the room all to herself, Ruth and her husband had traded sexy pillow talk with each other, until one of them switched to FaceTime (why hadn't they thought of that first, Ruth had teased Sean), and then their desire for each other had scorched even the cell towers, Ruth was sure. When she had finally fallen asleep, it had been with her phone in her hands. She tore back the comforter, and there was her phone. Yet, nothing on screen showed it was ringing, so where the hell was it coming from?

Getting into a sitting position was getting more difficult every day, she thought to herself, but once she was up, she followed the ringing. Persistent little bugger, whoever was calling. Reaching into her sister's suitcase, she found the phone under a stack of clothes. Well, this was interesting: so,

Tess didn't take her phone along last night? Wait—Tess! Ruth's curiosity was at one hundred out of a possible ten. No Tess, and it was six AM??? At that moment, Tess's phone rang again, and no surprise: Josh. Seeing four missed calls from Josh, and with no Tess here, Ruth decided her best course of action was to answer her sister's phone. She also knew she didn't have to be happy about it. Ruth picked up, "What? You realize it is barely dawn here?"

"Um, Ruth? Where's Tessa? I've been trying to call her. Why are you answering her phone?" Josh sounded way too perky this morning.

"I think the bigger question here is why the hell are you calling so damn early? You do realize I am pregnant and have been struggling with morning sickness? You think this is what I need—to start my morning early so I can then be sick? I would have thought after our chat yesterday that you would have some consideration for me, Josh, and for my sister. Who, by the way, is still sleeping."

"Well she must be awake now if you're yelling at me. I really need to speak with her, please. I have to go to the hospital in ten minutes, but I swear this is urgent."

"For your information, I am in the bathroom with the water running, so she can't hear me," said Ruth, from the middle of the room. "Sorry, Josh, no, she had a rough night last night, and is totally wiped. I will give her a message to call you when she is up."

Josh sighed, and said, "I guess that will have to do. Tell her I need to clear something up from years ago—it has to do with Sam?"

Ruth stilled, suddenly feeling unsure. "Sam? What do you mean, Sam?"

"I'm sure Tessa has mentioned him—one of my frat brothers from college? Sam Charles? Oh, she may have called him Fitz; you know, now that I'm thinking about it, I don't think she ever knew his real name."

"I'm still confused here—Fitz's name is Sam Charles?"

"Yeah, he's a big author now, I guess. He's going to be in our wedding, too, but I'm sure Tessa would have mentioned that."

"Yep, she sure did, oh, Josh, I've got to go—not feeling well. I'll tell her you called." And with that she hung up. It couldn't be—Fitz was Sam. She wasn't sure what the last name of Tess's Sam was, but it couldn't be a co-incidence that this Sam was an author, and Fitz was an author—or could it? Ruth plopped down on the bed. Oh shit, oh shit. What were the odds that they would be taking a train to get to their bachelorette party, and Sam could ALSO be taking the train to the bachelor party? He never did say why he was taking the train, but did he say where he was going? Sam was from Boston, she knew that because he had told her, and now that she is trying to make a connection, she recalls Tess saying that Fitz lives in Boston. Ruth put her head in her hands, unsure of what to do.

"Oh crap," she yells out loud. She knew one thing she must for sure do now, and she got back up and went to her purse. Pulling out Tess's engagement ring, Ruth put it in the pocket of the pair of jeans her sister wore the first day on the train. She had found the ring the night she had left Sam and Tess sharing dessert. She had liked seeing her sister regain whatever confidence she had lost, little by little, after so many years of being with Josh. She had been hoping that once Tess and Josh got married, Tess would not let him dominate so much of their lives, and she would get stronger and feistier, like she was after they had broken up those years ago. Tess had seen their breakup as devastating her, making her lose her confidence, but Ruth had seen things from a different perspective. Tess had been allowed to do whatever SHE had wanted, and she had travelled and experimented with recipes, tried out different cooking jobs. And then four years later, after seeing Josh again at the damn state fair, she had gone right back to Josh, and then all the old habits she had with him had come back, rearing their slightly ugly heads. After Tess met Sam, though (and it was clear he had the mega-hots for her sister) Ruth had been interested in seeing where it would go, and what Tess would do. So, Ruth had found the ring and decided it couldn't hurt to just let it be "lost" for a little while longer, and let her sister have this flirtation with a hot stranger. But now, if Sam WAS Fitz, what would that mean? She wasn't necessarily advocating for Tess to dump Josh, because what did they really know about Sam? And, Tess *did* have her wedding coming up in six months. However, with her sister still obviously with Sam, it was clear that things weren't as cut and dry in the Josh department. And it was telling that not only had she clearly left her phone behind deliberately but she had also HIDDEN it: girl clearly wanted no interruptions.

Hearing the door jingle, Ruth looked up, and hurriedly closed Tess's suitcase, and hopped over to her bed, sliding in just as her sister came through the door. Ruth yawned, and said as tiredly as she could, "Hey, Sis."

Wow—Ruth wasn't entirely sure what had happened to her sister last night: did Tess have the look of someone well-fucked, or just well-romanced? Ruth threw an arm over her face. When should she tell her Josh called? When should she tell her about Sam/Fitz? Too many major decisions looming this early in the morning!

"Hi, Ruthie, sorry did I wake you?"

"No, I had just gone to the bathroom." God, her sister was beaming, absolutely shining. When had she last seen her look this happy? With a dreamy expression, she watched as Tess slipped out of the dress she had worn, and into the robe she had on yesterday. The she came over to Ruth's bed and slid in beside her. Growing up, they had shared not only the same room, but the same bed until Ruth was ten, and then she had made the decision that she was too old to share a bed with her sister, so their parents had gotten them twin beds; then, when Ruth was twelve, their father's office had become Ruth's room, and his office had moved to an annex built onto the back of their farmhouse. Even though they had stopped sharing a bed over twenty years ago, there were times when the sisters needed the comfort of snuggling up to each other. So Ruth turned to Tess, and enfolded her into her arms.

"Sis, I need help," Tess implored Ruth. "Help me. I don't know what to do. I'm in, like, a haze. A Sam haze, and I never want it to lift. Why can't we just stay on the train forever?"

Ruth rubbed her sister's back, "I know, but wouldn't that just be weird at some point? The Lefferts sisters, raising a baby together on the train, not really going anywhere? And what about Sean? You know he's going to be a really kickass dad, right? And then there's Mom and Dad, so excited to be grandparents, plus they're getting married again-"

"Ugh, no wedding talk, even if it IS Mom and Dad's wedding." Tess rolled onto her back, and this time it was Tess tossing an arm over eyes. Ruth eyed Tess's face, neck, and throat, seeing the evidence of stubble burn all over her sister, not to mention what looked like well-placed love bites.

Ruth cleared her throat, "So, how was last night? And this morning? Am I allowed to ask? Clearly I should've given you a curfew: I was getting ready to send out an SOS. Come on, I'm starving for details and food—let's order some room service and then you can tell me anything you want to."

CHAPTER
Twenty-Nine

Sam

After he escorted Theresa to her room, Sam walked in a daze back to his, threw himself onto his disheveled bed and fell into a deep sleep. He awoke to the vibration of his phone, bouncing on his bedside table, and realized it was still on silent since yesterday. Glancing at the time, he saw it was eight a.m.—okay, so he'd only been sleeping for a couple of hours, but it felt like he'd had days of sleep, not remembering a time he had felt more at peace than he did now. Every fiber of his being was so completely satiated, and he wanted to keep the world at bay for a while longer yet. He turned over in bed and smelled Theresa in the folds of his sheets. Damn! He had forgotten to give her his cell number, once again. He made a mental note to do that as soon as he saw her today, but part of him appreciated their happenstance meetings and the impromptu-ness of their burgeoning relationship.

His eyes fell to his bedside table, and he noticed a pair of glasses; make that two pairs of glasses! He cast his memory back to the image of Theresa taking them off so he could kiss her, and what a kiss it was. Her mouth, so pliant and supple under his, made him want to kiss her for eternity, and it felt like he had done exactly that last night. The only time his mouth left hers was to slide down her body with it, leaving none of her delicate pink skin untouched. As far as he could tell, she was all he had dreamed of—every curve, every freckle he found, her intelligence, her humor, and that laugh—she was the undiscovered jewel that men search years for, in the hopes it will make them richer. Well, here she was, and he felt like he had won the lottery. She lived in Brooklyn; he lived in Boston—that's not a tough long-distance romance—they could do it! Hell, in one way it would be easier to live in New York City, since his publisher was on Broadway in Midtown. Sam relished the thought of watching her bake something she loved: she could open that bakery she had dreamed of. Maybe they could have a bakery/bookstore kind of thing. Hell, he could buy the building, and they could live on top of the store.

Okay, big guy, calm down, first things first, he said to himself as his phone rang again, but he continued to ignore it. He pondered Theresa, coming to his room last night, deliberately leaving her phone behind in her room. She had whispered this to him when they were lying in bed, face to face. She had wanted no interruptions, none of the outside world coming between them. She said it was enough that Ruth knew where she was, in case of emergencies. They had made a date for tonight, again, dinner in his room—their last night together. Early dinner, though, at five, giving them the entire evening for just them. She had agreed to let Sam arrange the entire meal, and her trust meant the world to him; yes, he realized it was just food, but that she would want to spend her last night on the train with him rocked his foundation. He was going to try (very hard) to stay out of the way during the morning and afternoon so she and Ruth could have their time, but he was a moth to her flame, and somehow they eventually ended up in the same places.

When he selected the soundtrack for their night last night, he knew *Moondance* was the only option; even if Theresa hadn't mentioned it earlier yesterday, it was a brilliant choice; Sam considered it to be one of, if not the, most romantic albums of all time. Seeing her eyes light up when the music hit her ears was magic. Logical Sam had never believed in love at first sight, but writer Sam always had, and here he was, completely and utterly smitten since the first moment he spied Theresa out the dining car window on that fateful platform.

He needed to get up and get some water—romance makes a man parched, he thought. As he walked to the table by the window, he saw his phone light up with another call. Well, I may as well check to see who's been trying to reach me, he mused.

Picking up his phone, he saw that three of his brothers had tried calling, leaving out only his baby brother, Eric, who only ever received calls: he rarely made them. What the hell was going on? While he was trying to decide which brother to call first, the phone rang, and it was Jamie, who had made the choice for him.

"Jamie, what's up?" He started, "I saw a call from you earlier, and then Bobby and Chris both called. What is it—news about the Red Sox?"

His brother took a breath, and blew it out slowly, "I wish it were that. Look, Sam, something happened this morning with Mom-"

"What do you mean with Mom?" He asked impatiently, "she had her biopsy, right? Did they already get the results? Is it…cancer?"

"Sorry, no, I mean, we don't know if it's cancer," Jamie paused again, "she was at the hospital for the procedure but before she went in, she had an episode, like a seizure. Then like an hour later she had what appeared to be another seizure. She's checked into the hospital and they've scheduled an MRI for this afternoon. Dad's a mess, but we're all here with her— Eric got here about an hour ago-" Jamie's voice broke off in a sob, and then he heard Jamie's wife, Tamzin, take the phone.

"Hey, Sam," she said softly, "everybody is pretty freaked out about your mom. We just wanted to let you know what was going on. I left the baby with my parents and am here with Jamie. She's conscious and everything now, just scared. She didn't want to bother you on your trip, but your dad insisted on calling you."

"Tam, what happened? She really had a seizure? Is this related to cancer at all?"

"No, Sam, nothing like that. First of all, they don't know definitively that it WAS a seizure—it could be a reaction to the medicine she's been given or something of that nature. That's what the MRI will tell us. and secondly, she didn't even get the biopsy done yet because of what happened, so we don't know anything about any cancer; aside from this, your mom has been in good spirits, and was fine even just this morning, before all of this."

"How is everyone else doing? How's my dad? My brothers?"

"Everyone is pretty rattled, honestly. Your dad was obviously shaken up by this, but he has been pretty torn up since her mammogram. Jamie is just coming back from the bathroom—oh, he wants to talk to you again. Okay, Sam, love you, and we will keep you posted."

"Hey, Sam, sorry about that: it's been an emotional morning. We were all ready to get this biopsy done, and now these seizures, or whatever they were, fucked it all up. How are you?"

"Honestly, I was flying pretty high until this news. Shit, I had a bad feeling about this yesterday, and was even going to ask Josh about it. I knew I should've come back—I'd be on my way there by now." Sam put his phone on speaker and proceeded to load a travel website on his phone. "Well, I'm looking at flights now. Looks like we will pull into Denver in about an hour, so I am scheduling a flight that leaves this afternoon from there that will get me back to Boston by ten tonight."

"Sorry, Sam, that this wrecks your weekend, but I know Mom will be so happy to hear you'll be here tonight. You know she likes all of her little chicks around her."

Sam smiled at the analogy, and it was true. "No worries about the weekend, because I already had the moment of a lifetime last night."

"Can't wait to hear about it—talk later, man. Love you."

"Love you, too, J."

Sam hung up the phone, hanging his head. He was terrified for his mom, but in all honesty, he could not feel guilty for staying on the train yesterday. His night with Theresa was more than he had ever hoped to have, and he knew she would understand about it all. The problem was, he didn't have time to seek her out. He had to pack and make sure he was ready to get off the train in less than an hour, and that meant canceling the rest of his journey to Reno.

Taking out a piece of paper, Sam wrote out a letter to Theresa explaining everything that had happened, and giving her his personal information, which included his cell number (FINALLY), address and his full name. He also was very explicit in how much last night had meant to him, speaking from his heart, not mincing any words, and how much he had been looking forward to tonight. He rang the porter to get him to deliver the message to Theresa, and notify him of the change in his travel plans.

Sam sealed the letter inside another piece of paper, using a trick of paper folding he had learned years ago in Boy Scouts. He wrote "Theresa" in big block letters on the front, and her room number of 123. The porter knocked on his door, and after a short conversation, he entrusted him with the envelope, and he watched as the porter headed down the hall.

CHAPTER
Thirty

Tess

Tess remembered her glasses after she had woken up in her room later that morning: how had she managed to leave his room without them? Without a doubt, seeing was the last thing on her mind, and she supposed it had helped that Sam had escorted her back to her room, so the need to see wasn't quite as pressing as it was when she opened her eyes to the blinding light streaming into her room. After she showered, she put her contacts in, and she and Ruth devoured the breakfast that Ruth had ordered. Funny how her night with Sam had stoked all kinds of appetites inside her, she mused.

"Sis, do you want to go back to the viewing car today again? I thought the sights were so stunning from it yesterday, and I think we're going to be in the mountains today." Tess was more awake now than she could recall having been in a long time.

"I am all in on that idea," Ruth answered. "Were you going to stop at Sam's and get your glasses?"

"I want to see him, but I also am enjoying the anticipation of seeing him later."

Ruth gave Tess a knowing smile. "You're into the longing, is that it?"

Tess smiled at her sister, "Something like that…"

The sisters gathered up their books, cookies, and snack mix (both of which had dwindled down drastically, according to Ruth), and headed out the door. They both watched as a porter carrying a note passed by their room, and headed down the hallway. They turned in the opposite direction and walked through the dining car.

"You know what? Maybe I will drop by Sam's room and get my glasses. That way I can wear them if I want to tonight. Meet you at the viewing car?"

"Yeah, sure," Ruth winked at her sister, "if this is the last time I see you again until San Francisco, just know I love you."

Tess laughed and turned in the other direction to go to Sam's room. She began feeling incrementally more tingly with each car she passed through to get to Sam's car. Upon reaching his car, she ran a hand down herself—she had chosen a pair of curve-hugging capris in a cornflower blue, and a sunny yellow sleeveless top, with a deep V at the neckline. Was she ridiculous in feeling so excited to see Sam again, after spending all night with him? Perhaps she SHOULD, but everything with him felt so right, and so natural. She had never expected to feel this way about anyone she had only known for two days, but here she was, and she knew she'd have decisions to make once back in Brooklyn.

Slowing down, she noticed a maid cart near Sam's room, and figured whoever was next door had departed—maybe driven out by the noises coming from their room last night? The thought made her smile, but as she got to his room, it was clear that the maid was actually in HIS room. What was going on? She wondered. Approaching the doorway, Tess spotted her glasses on the top of the cart; then, as she peered into Sam's room, she saw it was completely empty, except for the bedding and towels bundled up in a pile by the door.

"Excuse me?" She called inside the room to the maid, "Is something going on with this room?"

"Yes, the man who was staying here left this morning, so I am cleaning his room."

Tess felt her heart squeeze and her breath catch in her throat. "You mean he just changed rooms, right?" That could be the only explanation, she told herself—Sam would not have left the train without telling her first. No way.

"No, I do believe that he got out at Denver. Not sure what happened, because according to my room schedule, he was due to check out tomorrow. But he is gone. Did you need something else?"

Tess felt sick to her stomach, "These are mine—I left them in the room last night," she told the maid as she plucked her glasses from the cart, before turning and running down the hall, back through the train cars that only minutes ago had brought her such joy, and the butterflies that she'd been feeling indicating anticipation were now signaling dread, mixed with regret.

Fumbling with her key card, Tess stumbled through her doorway, and let the door shut on its own, just as she wanted to do with the entire world now. "Oh god, what have I done? What have I done," she moaned. How had she gotten it all wrong? Wait, calm yourself, she thought. This isn't the Sam she had come to know the past two days—he would not have just left, without telling her. And why would he leave? She was missing information here, and desperately needed to talk to her sister. Ruth was amazing in a crisis, and while Tess wasn't entirely sure this counted as a crisis, certainly nothing about it was good.

Heading to the viewing car now, she began to feel a bit calmer, although furious with herself for never getting any of Sam's info—particularly his cell number. Too caught up in the moments with him, and not wanting reality to enter in to any of it, and now she was screwed. If he had left, that meant her fantasy was over. It meant she had betrayed Josh, and for what—one night with a man she met on the train? Or was she simply feeling bereft that it was only the one night?

Upon entering the viewing car, she spotted Ruth immediately, and practically ran to her. Ruth looked up from her Linda Castillo novel, her mouth full of snack mix, and it was clear from her face that she knew something was wrong. Tess slumped down next to her, and told her what had just occurred. Ruth's expression was confused as she looked at her sister. "I don't understand—Sam just left? And you're sure he didn't leave a note or anything for you in his room? Nothing with the maid?" Ruth's calm tone was aiding in slowing Tess's pulse.

Tess shrugged, "It doesn't sound like the maid even saw him, and the only thing I saw on her cart were my glasses—no note or anything else. Why didn't we trade numbers? Damn it—I wanted to just live in the moment with him, and now I've got nothing. Nothing." Tess buried her head in her hands.

"Do you think he could have gotten news about his mom—you said she had to have a biopsy, right?" Ruth rubbed her sister's back, desperate for anything but Sam leaving without a trace. "Or maybe his agent or publisher had an issue with his book? And he had to head back immediately?"

Tess sniffed, "I didn't think about that—I guess that's a possibility. I had thought about his mom, though. I could see how maybe if he got some news, he would have to leave suddenly, and our flirtation would only be a blip on his radar." Tess's eyes began to well up with tears. "Sis, I wasn't ready to say goodbye. We were going to have one more night. Now he's gone," and Tess began to cry in earnest, not caring who was around her in the car.

"Oh, Tessie, I know you were beginning to care for him, and I saw the way he looked at you. Have you asked yourself yet what it was you wanted from all of this? I know I have been kind of urging you to live in the moment here on the train-"

"'Kind of'?" Tess interjected, "You all but said 'what happens on the train stays on the train'."

Ruth had the good grace to look chagrined. "You're right, and I have to own that. But, Tess, I have never seen you more confident, more fucking sexy, that you have looked the past two days on this trip. You have been so sure of yourself—I mean look at you right now. Dressed in a top that shows your cleavage? Usually you wear a tank underneath to 'preserve your modesty', and I love that Tess, but babe, you are, like, embracing your sexual side. And you brought it out because of how Sam was making you feel. Have you asked yourself AT ALL how this was going to end, though? I hate to even mention his name, but what about Josh? How are you feeling about it all? You are devastated over a man who isn't your fiancé, but who HAS treated you with more respect and dignity than Josh has in a long time."

"Right—except Sam also left without any word to me, any thought about me. I find it hard to believe he didn't have five minutes to leave me a note, or send one to me—he's been to our room several times. Room 132: he knows exactly where it is. It's not as if the man was lugging around a lot of excess baggage—he could have even passed by our room on his way out." Tess took a deep breath, and stopped to blow her nose. "I don't know how to feel: hurt and neglected? Forgotten? You know one of my fears is being forgotten—I meet people and then I will see them in random places, and they have no idea who I am. I'm just not memorable, Ruth, not like you." As her sister shook her head in denial, Tess forged on, "You're brash, and funny, and people remember you. Even if they've never met you, they have heard stories. But I'm just not like that. Too quiet—well, except for my laugh, I guess, that IS loud. And Sam forgot me. As for Josh, I'm not even ready to put him in this equation. He has let me down so much." Tess stopped to take a wobbly breath. "The truth is, maybe I wasn't meant for romance, and I need to lower my expectations. It's probably for the best that Sam left—where could it have gone anyway? We couldn't have maintained anything started here. Josh is who I was meant to be with—he is my past, my present, and he will be my future."

CHAPTER
Thirty-One

Ruth

Three months later

Ruth was driving from Philly to Brooklyn to spend the weekend with her sister, probably her last weekend away before the baby is born, she surmised. Sean had been hesitant to allow her to drive by herself, but as soon as he had tossed out the word "allow" at her, she had, in typical Ruth style, balked and dug her heels in even more. And Sean, in typical Sean style, had relented, because if there is anything he hated more than seeing his wife annoyed, it was knowing that HE was the cause of her annoyance. Ruth and Sean still had about two months to go before the birth of little junior, and she had no intention of becoming housebound until she was in active labor.

Driving to see her sister had been the only option in Ruth's mind, because the train was causing her much angst post-bachelorette trip. Although the actual bachelorette party had been a smashing success, and Tess looked and acted like she was having the time of her life about eighty-nine percent of the time in Napa Valley, Ruth was conscious that deep down she was reeling from her days with Sam, and the loss his abrupt departure had caused. Ruth had considered trying to reach out to Sam, but short of asking Josh (a non-starter) for his personal information, she was stymied. For a celebrated author, he didn't seem to have a personal social media presence; he had accounts for his books and other writings, but it seemed way too awkward to contact him that way. She felt a tremendous amount of personal responsibility for her sister's pain after he left. Normally Ruth was proud to bear the title of "Puppet Master", but she had never crashed and burned as hard as she did on that train ride. Ruth had, since childhood, really, seemed to think that she always knew what was best for Tess, so when she saw how attracted Sam was to her sister, and then witnessed her sister returning that attraction, how could she stop herself from removing the obstacles that would normally keep them apart? She had reasoned with herself that it wasn't HER who had lost Tess's ring— she had just found it, and then determined it was in Tess's best interest to just make sure the ring stayed "lost" for a bit longer. God, they had seemed so good together, in so many ways that Tess and Josh simply did not fit anymore (she wasn't sure they ever had) Tess and Sam worked. She had seen the glances, the slight touches, almost as if they were each without the power to control them. Tess deserved that kind of attention and attraction, and she was giving back as good as she was getting.

Approaching the Goethals Bridge that connected New Jersey to Staten Island made Ruth extra anxious to see Tess: she hadn't seen her since the trip, because Tess had been in full baking business mode for the rest of summer, and Tess and Josh had even taken a couple of weekend trips away, which Ruth supposed was Josh's way of trying to smooth over the shit storm he had created about the honeymoon. Ruth, of course, was back working the school year as a speech pathologist until her baby was born. The reason Ruth was going to Brooklyn now was to assist Tess and work on the wedding invitations and other essentials that could be done ahead of time, and also to gauge her sister's emotional and mental state. Tess had thrown herself into wedding details after they had flown back from California, almost in a manic way, and Ruth was positive it was her way of forgetting about Sam and convincing herself that Josh was still her "one true love". Tess had always been such a romantic, even from a young age.

She wanted, even craved, the picture-perfect love story: wedding, baby, happily-ever-after. If Tess could just take a step back, maybe put the wedding on pause (Ruth had gingerly brought the possibility up last month on the phone, and Tess practically went into hysterics) she could get her own mind straight about how she truly wanted to live her life. Well, it seemed Tess had firmly set her mind on Josh, so Ruth was going to support her sister as staunchly as she always did.

One thing that had bothered her about Sam's disappearance was his lack of communication: this was the type of shit Josh would pull, and perhaps that's why Tess had just collapsed in on herself emotionally. Had her sister convinced herself that this is all she could expect from any man? Ruth knew that wasn't the whole truth, and there had to be a missing piece of the Sam puzzle, she just didn't know what it could be. She, herself, had had a long heart-to-heart with him when he was having breakfast their second day on the train—he had come across as sincere and genuine, heartfelt, even, so why the Houdini act? No man who looked at a woman the way that Sam looked at Tess would ever just ghost her, but short of stalk the entire city of Boston, Ruth was out of ideas. Although she did know relatively where he lived—in a condo by the Charles River. Well, that narrowed it down, she thought sarcastically. Not sure how much information Tess would want their parents knowing, Ruth had been vague when questioned by her mother, who had noticed from halfway across the United States that Tess seemed a little too laser-focused on the wedding. Ruth did admit that Tess had several "flirtatious encounters" with a hot stranger on the train, and she also divulged that she knew the man's name. Her mom then reminisced about 'the good old days" when you could just call information in a certain city to get a listed phone number, since it was all landlines in her day. Ruth agreed that would make it easy to find someone, and she did try to look him up in the white pages on the internet, but to no avail.

Finally having crossed Staten Island and then the Verrazzano Bridge, Ruth had made it to Brooklyn, and was filled with excitement at the thought of seeing her sister again! Her cell buzzed in and broke her reverie with a call from Sean. She answered hands-free, "Hey, Babe, I just got to Brooklyn."

"Yeah, I have been tracking you on the phone finder thing. I miss you already," Sean said silkily.

"Down, boy; you missed me before I even left this morning," she laughed, and immediately reminisced about the reason she had left an hour later than she intended to. "I'm glad to get out of my own head, though, so thanks for the interruption."

"Thinking about Tess and Sam again?" Sean always knew Ruth's thoughts so well.

"Almost constantly, the closer I get. I just don't know if I did the right thing by not telling Tess that her Sam is Josh's Fitz. I mean, she detests Fitz so much: would that make her feel better or worse about Sam theoretically ditching her on the train?"

"Well, you know your sister, and she's going to take anything with Fitz super personally. I guess if you want her to hate the Sam she met on the train, you should tell her—but isn't Sam-slash-Fitz in the wedding?"

"Yes, and that's why I would like to talk to him before then. Can you imagine the look on her face if she's coming down the aisle and sees Sam standing there? I'm going to have to tell her if I don't find a way to contact him; I cannot let her go blind into that scenario. Between you and me, I guess I had hoped that Tessie would come to her good senses and cancel this wedding. She sounds way too hyper when she talks about it, and I know it's a façade to hide her desperation. She's clinging to the idea of Josh like she's Jack and he's the boat Rose is in—you know, from 'Titanic'?"

Sean laughed loudly on the other side of the phone, "Yes, Ruthie, I have caught on to all of your most-used movie metaphors. You're nuts, but I love you anyway."

"Hey, I thought me being nuts was WHY you loved me! Anyway, wise one, tell me what to do about this Sam business, please?"

Sean sighed, "Well, three months is still a long time where anything can happen yet, right? Why don't you give it another month or so, and just enjoy this weekend with your sister? You guys can go out and eat, watch movies, and craft for a wedding that you are secretly hoping will implode anyway."

CHAPTER
Thirty-Two

Josh

Entering the office he shared with Lana, another surgical resident, Josh felt some of the tension leave his shoulders. The morning's surgery had been particularly challenging, but that is one of the aspects Josh loved most about surgery—the challenge. The methodical path for a surgery was clear cut (no pun intended, especially for Josh) as long as he followed the procedures he had spent the last ten years studying. Unlike the change that had somehow taken place seemingly overnight in his fiancée, surgery could be counted on; it had always been reliable for him.

Taking a seat at his desk, he looked down and saw Lana had left him a muffin and a coffee from the insanely delicious coffee place two blocks away from the hospital that the two of them had discovered a year ago. Josh enjoyed sharing the space with Lana—she was thoughtful and mostly quiet, yet he had come to count on her for advice when he was faced with a confusing situation. It was Lana who had helped him see that taking two weeks for a honeymoon at this stage in his career was not feasible, and she had convinced him to apply for the fellowship instead. Not that he had needed much arm-twisting: he had been crystal clear with Tessa since college how important his career would be to him. His dad had been such a huge figure in his life, and his only parent after his mom had passed away when Josh was twelve; Josh had been witness to how his dad could always count on his work, no matter what life had thrown at him, and how much comfort it had seemed to bring him after Josh's mom died. So, Josh had chosen a high-pressure career that saved people's lives, and had committed to it entirely. He knew Tessa was displeased at times with just how committed to his career he was, but he also was aware of how reasonable she could be.

Lana suddenly strode into their office, taking Josh out of his head for a moment. "Good morning, Josh, and welcome back."

"Welcome back? I'm the one who has been back to work for four days, Lana—you're the one returning from time off," Josh reminded her.

"Trust me, it was NO vacation. Why does my mom insist on being so difficult? Anyway, how was your weekend away? This is the last weekend getaway before your wedding, right?" When Lana had seen how conflicted Josh had felt about calling off his honeymoon, Lana had suggested perhaps Tessa could be soothed with a few "weekends away" BEFORE the wedding, and Josh had to admit that once again, Lana was right. Tessa had been much happier with every little trip they took.

"Yep, from now on it's all work and no play until the wedding in three months. Sometimes I wish we had more time, but if I even suggest delaying it, Tessa will kill me." Frankly, Josh would have liked them to be engaged for a couple more years before a wedding—not that he was hesitant about marrying Tessa (it was, after all, the most reasonable thing to do) but all of this hoopla surrounding it was so complicated: invitations and save-the-dates (weren't they essentially the same thing?), cake-tasting (and with Tessa worried about her dress), decorations (which will be torn down and thrown away the day after the reception). He imagined if his mom were still alive, she would have taken pleasure in it all, but he just didn't see the point sometimes. And then there was the issue of his best man and groomsmen—how many did he HAVE to have? If it were up to him, he'd just have Liam, his cousin and best friend since childhood, stand up with him and that would be the end of things; but, Tessa had all these friends and her sister she purportedly needed preceding her down the aisle, and she insisted on his number of attendants matching hers. When his cousin, Aaron, and his wife got pregnant and their due date unfortunately coincided with his and Tessa's wedding date, then he had to find another groomsman—thankfully, he knew he could always count on Fitz to take some heat when he needed to, despite Tessa holding a grudge against him all these years.

As if he had summoned him, Josh's phone rang with Fitz calling, "Hey, Fitz, what's up? I was just thinking of you." Josh waved to Lana, who was heading out of the office.

"Oh, yeah—after that last bombshell you dropped on me, I get a little paranoid when you say that." Fitz sounded tense to Josh's ears, and he hoped he wasn't going to confront Josh about confessing to Tessa the real truth behind their break-up.

Josh laughed, nervously, "I promise—no bombshell this time."

"Speaking of: have you told Tessa yet about the whole college breakup thing?" Fitz's tone held a note of challenge to it, and Josh frantically tried to excuse his inaction.

"No, but her sister is here for the weekend, so it might be a good time to do it—she's always calmer with Ruth around."

"Okay, well there may not be any need to rock your boat. I may have to backslide and just be a guest at your wedding, Doc. My mom is having a bit of a struggle with the chemo for her cancer, and since she had those seizures, they are being extra cautious; so it looks like they are extending her treatments. I'm so sorry—with all of this, I can't even guarantee I will make it *to* the wedding, let alone commit to being *in* the wedding. Rest assured, I will bust my ass to get there for the wedding, though, if at all possible."

"Fitz, I'm so sorry about your mom—that can be tough to have additional medical issues when she's being treated for cancer, but all of the updates you have sent me have all been very promising. I totally understand, and do hope I see you at the wedding. Give my best to your family, okay?"

"Will do, Doc. Take care." And Fitz was gone. Rather than being upset by Fitz's announcement, Josh actually felt a huge amount of relief. He wouldn't have to confess anything now to Tessa. It had never bothered him to see Fitz on his own, either up in Boston or here in New York. Tessa had been quite uncomfortable with Fitz in their wedding, so she was sure to be relieved about him canceling, although Josh wasn't sure she'd be happy about their mismatched bridal party now. He hoped she would see that it was all for the best.

Josh wasn't entirely sure when Tessa had begun to seem discontent with their life plan, but more than anything he wanted her to be the agreeable Tessa he knew her to be. One of his greatest mistakes was breaking up with her back in college, and he knew how much he had hurt her. He was also aware that blaming it on Fitz was not his best move, but it had made Josh feel less guilty at the time of the breakup: he had been under too much pressure and had needed a break. The truth was that no one was a better match for him than Tessa: she complemented him perfectly, and she was a lifeline thrown out to him when he'd been seventeen and starting a new school, with no friends, a face full of acne, and too many days immobile on the sofa at home. When she had approached him at that library table, seeing her with her halo of red hair around her beautiful face, it was as if the sun was shining just for him. If she were honest with herself, she would realize that their breakup had benefitted her, too, by allowing her no distractions. She'd become a top-notch pastry chef; he was well aware that she was frustrated by having to put her dream of a bakery on hold, but how much chaos did one couple need? First the wedding, then his fellowship, and THEN her bakery.

"Everything okay in there?" Asked Lana, pointing at his head. Josh hadn't been aware that Lana had come back into their office.

"It will be now," he answered.

CHAPTER
Thirty-Three

Sam

After hanging up the phone from his call with Josh, Sam felt a niggling he couldn't identify: was it something Josh had said? Sam had been too distracted thinking about his mom and her medical issues while on the phone with Josh, but something about his conversation had given him pause, however very brief it had been. He had felt uneasy ever since Josh had confessed about using Sam as an excuse for Josh's break up with Tessa those many years ago, and Sam didn't feel right about standing up at a wedding in which the groom was beginning their married life together with a lie from their past. Sam didn't doubt the possibility that there were relationships in which he WAS the party responsible for the break-up, but he was confident he had also been in those relationships.

When he had departed the train in Denver, he had been frantic to get to his mom, but by the time he had gotten back to Boston the next day, she had actually been doing pretty good. Her biopsy confirmed that she did, indeed, have cancer, but it was early stages and had not spread, so everyone was relieved to hear that news. The difficult part were her seizures, and the current doctors treating her were doing their best to ensure they didn't happen again.

He had called Josh immediately and explained about not being able to attend his weekend bachelor party, and that's when Josh had lent his knowledge and support to Sam, and he had been generous about going over everything the doctors were telling them; it was a huge relief for Sam to have that second opinion always at his beck and call, even if Josh's specialty was surgery, and not oncology.

Aside from his mother, Sam had been caught up in finishing his novel, and it was due to be published in a couple of months, which was a quicker turnaround than normal, but his audience was salivating for the third book; it was already getting some fantastic reviews by some early readers, with some saying it was his best work yet. Sam had never intended to be a best-selling author—he had just wanted to be creative and write something that somebody, somewhere, would be able to relate to, but he couldn't deny that job security felt pretty damn good.

Now he let his mind drift to Theresa, and how much he regretted having to leave the train without at first speaking to her. It had taken all of his willpower to focus his energy on packing and getting ready to leave, when all he wanted to do was go and find her, touch her, kiss her, look into those spellbinding green eyes, and tell her how he hadn't been able to stop thinking of her since he had met her, which was part of the reason he had chosen to not seek her out, but to write her a note. He had been fearful of rushing things, and maybe scaring her or putting her off with his intensity. Although caught up as he was in his emotions, he was also cognizant enough to realize that whatever decisions were to be made about him and Theresa, they both needed to be at the same place emotionally. Over the past three months, however, he had come to regret being so cautious that last day. He had given all the power to her by leaving his name, number, and address, and now he was left without any way to contact her. Why had she not reached out? Was he a fling to her, a mere dalliance on the train? Granted, he was the one who had pursued her, but then that made him paranoid that maybe she had begun to question his intentions. He knew she could be vulnerable, and he hated that maybe Theresa had been hurt by his abrupt departure.

Sam wasn't sure which scenario he preferred: that she got the note and had just decided it was easier to move on from their two days together, or that maybe something had happened and she DIDN'T get the note and thought he had rejected her. His mom always said "If it's meant to be, it will be" and Sam guessed there was nothing he could do now other than repeat her mantra, and hope that somehow he would cross paths with Theresa again.

His brother Eric's name flashed on his phone screen, "Hey, Eric, I am on the train now and get into Penn Station at noon—do you still have time to meet up for a bit?"

"Of course, for my big brother, I shall make the time. Sam, thanks so much for coming down for opening night—I know how much you have going on."

"Stop right there—I am thrilled for a weekend in New York, plus to be at the opening night of *The Big Lebowski*? Bonus! How has no one done a Broadway show of this before? Huge oversight."

"Haha, well the producers certainly think so. The previews went well, and it's getting some great buzz."

"Well, I wanted to surprise you: not only do I have tickets for tonight that you got for me, BUT I also am seeing it tomorrow, so this dude will abide in the theater all weekend."

"Most excellent! What about Josh—will you be seeing him like you usually do when you're in the city? And what about his fiancée? I mean, don't you have their wedding coming up? Wasn't there some strange history between you two?"

"I just talked to him, and he has to work all weekend, I guess—typical Josh. And the wedding deal is a long story. I actually just reneged on being a groomsman. Too much other shit. I just want to go to the wedding and keep it all as drama-free as I can. His fiancée isn't fond of me, but it turns out it's mainly Josh's fault after all." Sam sighed heavily, "But, if I tell her the truth, then that could create problems with them, and I don't need anyone breaking up to be my fault, you know?"

"I know you have more class than that, Sam, and it's one of the things I admire about you. Hey, not to change the subject from Josh's questionable morals, but I was thinking we could trek over to Brooklyn and go for a walk in that cemetery, Green-Wood, I was telling you about? A couple of the people in the musical rave about it, and since you'll be here by noon, we could head over there and check it out, before I have to be back in the city later this afternoon?" His baby brother was always coming up with an impromptu adventure.

"Sounds great—I packed light, so I can meet you there or do you want to meet up at the train station when I get in?"

Sam made plans with Eric to meet at the station when he arrived; he was looking forward to spending some quality time with is baby brother. About ten years was between them, but Eric had always had a maturity about him that had impressed the whole family. He was a talented actor and dancer, and had been living in New York City (technically Queens) for six years, and it was only a matter of time before he had his big break.

Sam lifted his glasses and rubbed his eyes. Damn, he wished he knew where Theresa lived in Brooklyn; he can't believe he will be so physically close to her and not have any idea where she is. He tracked his memory back to every word she had ever spoken to him, trying to remember if she had mentioned anything, like any of the cafes or delis she baked for, or at least a neighborhood, but he came up with nothing. If he had her info, he could have taken her as his date to one or both shows. Encouraged her to wear one of those dresses she'd worn on the train, each one making him weak in the knees.

His phone rang again, this time it was his agent. "Hey, Brock, any news on my book tour?"

"Sam, that's why I'm calling. Get your Sharpies ready, because you are going to do a Christmas book tour in the Northeast. Boston, New York, Philadelphia, DC. Who doesn't want a new book for Christmas? You had perfect timing getting it done and edited in time for the holiday market. We may even be able to book you on some morning shows."

Sam was actually looking forward to his book tour this time. Maybe Theresa would hear about his book and search him out? Make the connection that the Sam she met on the train is in truth Sam Charles, soon-to-be famous author.

An hour later, Sam and Amtrak pulled into Penn Station, and Sam grabbed his backpack, and strode to the doors. Stepping down on the platform, he looked around, remembering that this was the location he had first seen Theresa. He closed his eyes briefly, wanting to feel the warmth from her gaze, and the huskiness of her laugh as she had found humor in her own situation. He opened his eyes, checked his cell and saw a text from Eric saying that he was already outside the station up on Seventh Avenue. Sam flew up countless stairs and escalators, and finally saw his brother on the sidewalk.

The two brothers greeted each there with a hug, and then they were off to Sixth Avenue to catch the train to Brooklyn.

CHAPTER
Thirty-Four

Tess

"So he just called up and said he wasn't going to be in the wedding? I'm sorry, Josh, but that's just rude. Now the pairings will be off for the attendants—I will have an extra bridesmaid! Ugh—I knew it was a mistake having him in the wedding. Fitz has always been so selfish." Like she needed this added drama for the wedding? Tess thought to herself, cursing Fitz, and then cursing Josh for being friends with Fitz anyway.

Tess could hear the clicking of the keyboard, so she knew Josh was working while also trying to discuss their wedding with her. "Look on the bright side—now he won't be in our wedding photos, right? Anyway, things with Fitz aren't exactly what you think they are, and he is going through a lot of family stuff."

"Umm, okay, wow, thanks for clearing that up, Josh," Tess sighed out of frustration. "Well, I guess you are right about the photos; I will just pair up Heather and Siobhan with Brad. Word around town is he likes a three-some anyway," Tess said, derisively.

"Wow, Tessa, that was a little crass, wasn't it?" Josh admonished.

"My god, Josh, I was only kidding—your friend just called and can-celed on being in our wedding, which he has known about for MONTHS, so I should be able to be crass if I want to be crass." Tess was out on the street, having walked home from her last delivery of the day, and saw her sister's car parked in front of her building. "Listen, I'm just getting to our apartment, and I see Ruth out front. Are you joining us for dinner tonight?"

"No, sorry, I can't—Lana is going to help me go over some details con-cerning my fellowship application. Anyway, please be more relaxed about Fitz—his mom is battling cancer right now, so he is dealing with that. Even if he isn't in the wedding, he says he is still going to come to the wedding."

"So now I have to feel sorry for Fitz?" Maybe not, but now shitty, thought Tess. "I am sorry about his mom, though, and now I feel guilty about being so salty."

"Just giving you perspective, Tessa. Oh, Lana is waiting on me. Give Ruth my love," and Josh was done.

"Ruthie! Thank god you're here! You'll never believe what just hap-pened!" Tess hugged her sister, squealing with delight, and felt her worries begin to lift.

"First, I need a toilet desperately, then I need food! I am starving!" Ruth followed Tess into her building. Tess and Josh lived in a two-fami-ly house, and their apartment was, luckily for Ruth, on the bottom floor, known as the "garden apartment".

Tess held out the bag in her hands, "I picked up some ham and cheese croissants and chocolate croissants!"

"Bless you, my child," Ruth responded as they walked into the apart-ment. "Who is this?" Ruth asked of the cat laying on the sofa, "You didn't tell me you got a kitty!"

"I wanted to surprise you! Josh only agreed to foster, but I have already decided I am keeping her. She followed me from the cemetery last week. I named her Rapunzel—I mean, check out that fur!"

"I'm so jealous! I scold Sean all the time for being allergic to cats. She's gorgeous." Ruth fell into a slight trance petting Rapunzel, and then blurted out, "Oh, hell, I almost forgot my surprise! Sean scored us two tickets tomorrow night to the opening weekend of what is sure to be the greatest Broadway show of all-time: *The Big Lebowski*!"

"What!? I have seen ads for that, but it was sold out when I looked for tickets last week. How did Sean manage that?" In fact, Tess had mentioned it to Josh a month ago, and he had promised to look into getting tickets, but had not followed through.

"Oh, you know Sean—he always has some tricks up his sleeves! He texted me when I pulled up out front. Little devil can keep a surprise, though. I talked to him on my way here and he didn't say anything—he said he didn't want to hear my screams from the highway."

Tess laughed, "That sounds like Sean. Aww, that's so sweet of him. I'll bake him a babka his weekend to send back."

"Ooh, I love a gift for someone else that makes me happy, too," Ruth yelled from the bathroom. "Now—what just happened? You were going to tell me something but we got sidetracked..." she reminded her sister.

"Oh, right, Josh called and told me that Fitz pulled out of the wedding," Tess told Ruth as they walked into the kitchen and Tess pulled out the croissants from the warming oven, and poured them each a cup of coffee. "Oh, sorry, Sis, this is not decaf—is that okay?"

Ruth collapsed in her chair, "Oh, god, I'm starving, and yes, full throttle coffee is excellent. So you were saying that Fitz isn't going to be in the wedding? Did Josh say why?"

Tess was rifling through her cupboards, and pulling out silverware, plates, sugar, cream, and anything else the two could need for their lunch. "Well, and this I DO feel bad about: his mom has cancer."

Ruth gasped in response, "Oh, poor S-Fitz."

Tess whipped her head around, "What did you say?"

"Poor Fitz. I said poor Fitz." Ruth cleared her throat, and then admitted, "I guess it made me think of Sam—remember he thought his mom might have cancer?"

Tess stiffened, "Of course I remember Sam's mom had cancer. I also remember that he left me without a word on the train, after all his talk about how much he was feeling for me, and how attracted he was to me, how much he thought about me, and then he played Van Morrison, and I spent the night with him—I remember it all."

Tess was well aware that her voice was rising, and she felt herself turning red. When she had discovered that Sam had left, it had felt like abandonment. It had taken everything in her to not feel his rejection personally; after all, it wasn't like they had made any commitments to each other, or professed undying love. She had wanted him as much as he had professed to want her. Tess had only ever been with Josh, and being with Sam had been completely different: she had felt a certain freedom with Sam, almost a sense of discovery. She was grateful to him for that, for allowing her to open up and be honest with the Tess she had always known herself to be. Since she had returned from her bachelorette trip, Tess had been showing Josh more of a backbone than she had since they had gotten engaged, and there were times it clearly took him aback. She refused to backslide into "Yes, Josh" Tess, and she was still pissed off about the honeymoon, but part of her actually didn't even care anymore about it, either. She just wanted this wedding to be here and over, and then to move on with their lives. During the times she allowed herself to think of Sam, she did wonder how his mom was doing, how he was coping, maybe even if he ever thought of her?

"You know that feeling when you are trying to find the right word for something, or like, you meant to say something and then it just slips out of your mind before you can grasp it? That's how my time with Sam is to me—as if we were so close to having something: happiness, love, I don't know. But we came close, and then it slipped away. He was gone," Tess whispered to Ruth. "I think about all the times I wanted to give him my number, but I didn't, or get his info. Instead I played games, with him and myself: really tapping into that "what happens on the train, stays on the train" mentality. Why did I do that? He doesn't even know I was engaged, because I misplaced my ring, and then when I thought I found it, I still hid it! Hell, for that matter, he thinks I go by 'Theresa'! That's not me! And now look: I cry in the shower over a man who isn't my fiancé. I long for a man who I'm not marrying in three months. So I did my best to move forward, to have a good time at my party; then I came home, got my wedding dress fitted, arranged our ceremony, tasted cupcakes. But deep inside of my head, there's a tiny little voice asking me if any of this matters? And I don't even honestly care if it does. But you know me, Ruth—I'm not a quitter. And it's not like I don't love Josh; I do. I just wish I didn't now know that what I felt for Sam is so much more. I hate even comparing them."

Ruth was holding her sister's hand. "Oh, Sis, I wish you had told me all of this before—it must have been eating you up for three months. I had a feeling you were struggling, but I didn't want to press you and possibly upset you even more." Ruth took a deep breath, and said, "Since we're baring our souls here, I have to confess something."

CHAPTER
Thirty-Five

Sam

Sam had, once again, woken to the sound of his phone making noises, and this time it was buzzing—he had put his phone on theatre mode last night for the show, and he surmised he had forgotten to change it back. After the show last night, he had gone out for drinks with Eric and some of the cast and crew in celebration of opening night. Eric had been spectacular; really the whole production was amazing, but his brother was on the way to something big. What may have started as a supporting role was now bringing rave reviews. Sam looked at his phone and saw that it was his brother Chris calling.

"Yo, man, why are you calling so early?" Sam chastised his brother.

Chris guffawed, "I thought authors liked to get up early and write?"

"Maybe when they are LOOKING to write. I was out late boozing it up with our brother and his cast mates last night. I need my beauty sleep."

"No doubt, bro. You know out of all of us brothers, I have always considered you the least attractive."

"That's not what your high school girlfriend thought," retorted Sam.

"What did she know? She had the hots for older men, and you were in college. Anyway, you know that woman from the third floor?"

"Oh, Niamh, right? The one you are always too chicken to talk to in the elevator? When did you get weak? Where is the Chris Charles swagger that I have come to love AND hate?" Teased Sam.

"Damn, you are spunky in the morning! Well, I finally got my groove back and asked her out for tonight; unfortunately, she had plans, so instead we went out last night. Sam, seriously, I think I'm in love."

Falling in love almost immediately was evidently a Charles fate, it seemed. When their dad let them see any vulnerability, it was always about how at the first moment he had met their mom, he knew it was love. Same had happened with their brother Jamie when he met Tamzin, and again with Bobby and his fiancée Lorelei. Of course, it was only Sam who had done it poorly the first time, with Amanda. He had felt so sure with Theresa, but then fate got in the way, he supposed.

"I've had a few conversations with her in the lobby and laundry room, and she does seem like a good match for you, but doesn't she work for the district attorney? Isn't that a conflict of interest?"

"Nah," Chris scoffed, "love always finds a way." Oh boy, Sam thought, if Chris was already using love proverbs, he was head over heels. Chris was the one brother who the rest of the family definitely considered as playboy material: he loved women of all colors, shades, and sizes, and was an inveterate flirt. "The big news is, I was telling Niamh about Eric and the play-"

"Musical," Sam corrected.

Chris huffed, he hated being corrected, "Musical, whatever. Anyway, we went online last night and she found a ticket for resale and I bought it, and am almost to Manhattan! What hotel are you staying in? Oh, and don't worry, she said she'd look in on Huckleberry and Sawyer—see how perfect she is?"

"Great, I have a virtual stranger taking care of my cats?"

"One minute ago you were singing her praises!" Chris said defensively.

"I hardly think me telling you that I've had a few conversations with her is 'singing her praises'."

"Focus, big bro—hotel!" Demanded Chris.

Sam gave him the name of his hotel, knowing that now he would now be sharing a room with his fastidious brother. "What time does your train get in?"

After Chris stopped laughing, he answered, "I am driving, like a normal person does. Be there in twenty minutes, according to GPS."

Sam groaned: he was thrilled to have his brother to hang out with in Manhattan, but he was annoying as hell when it came to rooming with him. Always reprimanding Sam about hanging up his clothes, or properly folding them and putting them in the dresser—who actually unpacks their suitcase for A NIGHT in a hotel and uses the dresser? Chris Charles, that's who. Well, no sense in waiting for the king of clean to arrive—he'd better shower before Chris showed up. On the plus side, Sam had been entranced by the cemetery he and Eric had briefly visited yesterday, and was interested in seeing it again; Chris was the perfect companion for trekking over to Brooklyn with him. Eric was not available to hang out to due to having a matinée performance this afternoon.

Sam was toweling off when he heard a knock on his door—right on time, as always. He opened it up and greeted Chris, "Welcome to New York, it's been waiting for you."

"Man, you know I love a Taylor Swift reference. Thank you, thank you. I'm glad you got all dressed up for my arrival," Chris teased.

"So tell me all about your date with Niamh last night."

While Chris entertained Sam with his escapades the previous night, Sam got dressed in his favorite pair of jeans and a navy-blue button-down shirt with yellow stripes. "You will not believe this musical, Chris. It's unbelievable no one thought of this before. 'El Duderino' brings down the house, it's so good! And Eric has backing vocals, no less!"

"I can't wait to see it. So—what are our plans until then?"

Sam led Chris down the hall and then into the elevator to the lobby. Stepping out, they walked the four blocks over to Sixth Avenue and caught the subway near Washington Square Park, taking the D train to Brooklyn. As soon as they got on the train, Sam looked around the car, hoping maybe this time he would happen to see Theresa on the subway with him. All day yesterday, while in Brooklyn, he had wished for a sighting of her. He once again couldn't stop berating himself for not at least asking her which neighborhood she lived in, or of any local markers near her apartment.

"How does it feel to be in New York City?" Chris asked him.

"What? Why? Feels fantastic, as always," Sam replied.

"I just was thinking of Theresa, as I'm sure you have been—probably hoping you'll happen to run into her. That's what I'd be doing," Chris admitted.

"Everything makes me think of her—anytime I see a woman with red hair, or hear a loud laugh. God, I was pathetic last night, hanging out at the bar, until they play those little bells that signal the beginning of the show. I thought maybe there was a chance she could be there—you never know, right."

"I agree with you—you're right: you never know. Sam, the mere fact that you two met at all on that train is a minor miracle. Why couldn't you two buck the odds and meet again?"

Sam sighed, "Sometimes I just feel like an ass. I had two women approach me last night at the show, when I was hanging out near the bar, and then a couple more at the bar everyone went to afterwards, and I turned them all away. I have absolutely zero interest in meeting anyone else. How long can I go on like this? Not even meeting anyone, on the off chance I will see her again someday? I should be ecstatic that my book is coming out soon and I have a huge tour planned, and I am, to a large degree, but part of me is just kind of disappointed that I won't have Theresa possibly by my side," Sam sighed, and then admitted, "Also Mom's cancer is just a major bummer, too. How can I be happy when she is going through so much? The cancer, the treatment, and then the fear of another seizure. How do you think she is handling it all?"

"Mom? Oh, you know Mom—it's Dad I'm more concerned about. Have you noticed how much weight he has lost?" Chris asked worriedly.

"Yeah, I know. I was thinking we should get one of those meal subscription services, and take the pressure off either one cooking."

Chris nodded in agreement, "That's a great idea—we could find one where all you really do is throw the ingredients together. So—which stop is ours?"

"Actually, we get off here." And the brothers hopped off the train, shot up the stairs and out into the Brooklyn sunshine.

CHAPTER
Thirty-Six

Tess

Tess had gotten up normally at four am to do her baking for the weekend. All of her customers needed to be fully stocked for both Saturday and Sunday, with muffins, and sweet rolls for their breakfast customers, and then various pies, brownies, cookies, and cupcakes for any desserts they needed later in the day. Saturday was a huge day for most of her clients, but three businesses were always closed on Sunday, so Tess had decided she would be closed, too. Her baking didn't feel like work to her, because it was her passion. She also had a Brooklyn Blackout cake to make for her favorite coffeeshop, along with a lemon meringue pie and a chocolate cream pie, all of which would last in their cold cases for days. Ruth had come to her commercial kitchen after she had woken up, as it was only around the block from her apartment. She had actually picked up two coffees and a couple of breakfast sandwiches from Big Larry's Coffeeshop for herself and Tess. The sandwiches were made on bialys, and were a quintessential New York specialty.

When Ruth had confessed to her last night about finding her ring back on the train, Tess had little time to react, as their parents had FaceTimed the sisters, wanting to show them views from their new apartment. They had moved in last week, taking only what was necessary from the farmhouse for now. Since Ellen and John had only moved ten miles from their old home, it was simple enough for them to go back and fill in what they needed for their shiny new place; likewise, they were leaving any of their daughters' items until each one could properly go through what they needed or wanted as a keepsake. Both John and Ellen were planning on going to Ruth's after the baby was born to stay with her for a month, and then they'd come to New York leading up to the wedding—they had rented an Air B&B that was close to Tess's apartment. After they got off the phone with their parents, Sean had called Ruth to check in on her, and then Josh had come home to surprise Ruth and Tess for dinner out at their favorite Italian restaurant in Brooklyn. Of course he had to make it an early dinner, and then he was back to the office until late that night. It was concerning how much time he spent at his office, even when he wasn't scheduled.

Now that Tess was done working for the day, she and Ruth were taking a walk around the neighborhood before going back to the apartment—Tess had planned for them to sort out the invitations today before they went into the city for the musical. "So Ruthie, I don't understand why you didn't just tell me you had found the ring when we were back on the train?"

Ruth responded, shaking her head, "I guess I was feeding off of the energy that you were exuding. At first, you were frantic to find the ring, but then the longer you went not having found it, frankly, I didn't think you were that bothered by it. If I'm being perfectly honest, I was curious to see where things would go with you and Sam, and I thought, mistakenly so, if you had the ring, you'd feel compelled to put it on. I know, you had THOUGHT you found it, but I didn't know that until the next morning, and by then you and Sam had shared dessert that night, and you were floating. I know talking about Sam brings some pain, but, Sis, I truly have never seen you happier when you were on that train. Actually, scratch 'happy'—you were blissed out, ecstatic, on cloud nine. I'm not trying to put a damper on your wedding or Josh, but on some level do you think there's any chance you're settling with Josh?" Ruth had stopped walking now and turned to look at her sister.

"What's wrong with settling?" Tess asked defensively. "People settle in for a good nap. Families went west and settled on land to build new lives. Those are all positive things! Even if I AM settling, and I'm not saying that I am, isn't that my choice to make? Maybe I don't need a big, romantic story like you and Sean have, or like Mom and dad are having for the second time. I enjoy comfort; I like the predictable: look at all the lists I make! Why can't my life be like one of those lists? Boyfriend? Check. Fiancé? Check. Career? Check. Wedding? Almost check."

"Well, in the hopes of you not biting my head off, is your career really a 'check'? You want to have an actual bakery, and keep delaying it. No—not yet. No argument yet," Ruth warned her sister, as she watched her take a deep breath. "I am not in any way saying comfort is a bad thing, but all I want to know is that you will be truly fulfilled here," and Ruth placed her hand on her sister's heart.

Tess took Ruth's hand between both of hers, and assured her, "I will, Ruth. I can count on Josh, and we agree on the same things. I don't need big declarations or grand gestures. Wait—remember the breakfast he sent to our room on the train? That was a grand gesture! See—he can be romantic!"

Ruth sighed and said, "Well, little sis, then it's time to go and start on those invitations, I guess." She smiled at Tess, and Tess grinned back, relieved at having held her sister at bay again. As long as she could keep putting up this front, she would make it to the wedding. And then when she finally had the wedding behind her, her life could begin again. She understood where Ruth was coming from, but who's to say that life with Sam would have been romantic and complete? How was she to know that in the end she wouldn't eventually have been settling with Sam? Yes, he had looked at her with desire and she had felt every longing glance deep into her bones, but that kind of fire fades, right? No couple can maintain that level of heat, she told herself. While she appreciated Ruth's sisterly concern, she simply wished she would also stop bringing up Sam. The truth was, they didn't know why he left the train without leaving her any word—she had known he was concerned about his mom's biopsy, but that was a scheduled procedure and didn't seem to warrant a medical emergency that should have caused his abrupt departure. No matter what the truth was, Sam was now part of her past, and all she could do was treasure her time with him, have no regrets, and look to her future with the man who was steadfastly, and currently, in her life.

The sisters had gone back to the apartment, with the sun streaming into the windows facing the back garden. Tess got out the invitations and her list of invitees, keeping her list separate from Josh's. "I'm going to work on my list, in case I happened to miss anyone, but here is Josh's list," she told Ruth, handing her his handwritten list. Josh had balked at having to write it by hand, but Tess firmly believed more mistakes were made when something was digital. Josh had gone over the list several times, so Tess was confident his was complete. "We can work on these for a couple of hours, and then get ready for the show tonight."

"Sounds good, Sis. Oh, did I tell you some of the names Sean and I are considering for little junior?"

"Does this mean you know the sex of the baby? PLEASE tell me whether I'm having a niece or nephew!"

Ruth laughed, "No, still a secret. There's no way Sean could keep a secret, especially from me, and I wanted to have the gender be a surprise! I love that we have painted the nursery in all kinds of colors, and what few clothes we have bought are neutral. I want to welcome this baby without any expectations. Oh god, here come the waterworks!" And Ruth started crying, but failed to get out of the kitchen chair, so Tess hopped up and grabbed the box of tissues from the bathroom.

"It's usually my job for the tears lately—you're stealing my thunder, Ruthie."

"I know—usually I'm so stoic, but I just am so anxious for Mom and Dad to come, to see their grandchild, and it makes me miss our grandparents. I know Grandma Lydia is still with us, but it pains me to only see her a few times a year. And I've been kind of bummed that Mom and Dad will be so far away while junior is growing up. All those weekends growing up where we would spend either with Grandma and Grandpa Bergen or Nana and Papa Lefferts? We would get spoiled rotten—that time was so special. I hope I appreciated it all when it was happening, you know? But I want the same for my baby," Ruth took a deep breath, and then rushed on, "which is why Sean and I are thinking about moving to South Dakota, to be closer to Mom and Dad, somewhere not more than a couple of hours away."

Tess looked up, feeling crushed, "What? No, Ruth, I love having you live so close. Don't leave me," and then she, too began crying.

"I'm so sorry to tell you this now. Sean is the one who first brought it up. He has talked to his mom, and since she is now living adjacent to his oldest sister, he feels like the time is right for us. He can move his practice to wherever we are—pediatricians are especially needed in smaller areas."

"When would you move? What about your career? Your house in Philly?"

"We will stay in Philly until June. No sense moving until after the baby is here, and we wouldn't want to leave before your wedding or Christmas; I'm on maternity leave, anyway, through February. I thought I would stay those final months in the school district. And then, who knows? I already know it's going to kill me to go back to work after the baby, but Mom said she will come to help out, and Sean's mom will also help take care of the baby those few months. I don't want to miss any time seeing junior roll over or crawl or walk. I have plenty of time to consider any and all options. As for the house, since we did all of those renovations the first couple of years after we moved in, it will have no problem getting sold."

"Wow—I can't say I'm THAT surprised, but I do understand. I'm happy that you two will be able to find something together. Aww, Ruthie, I will miss you," Tess said, before getting up to hug her sister.

Ruth and Tess then spent the next two hours, at least, addressing envelopes and then carefully inserting an invitation into each one. Tess had designed them herself, and found a local printer who could do the work in the style she wanted. Josh had initially been difficult to convince, asking why they couldn't just go with a preprinted design. Tess had stood her ground, though, and after showing him her ideas, he warmed up to it. She had considered sending out "save-the-date" announcements, but Josh felt they were a waste of money, so the couple compromised and thought if they sent the invitations out early enough, people would then save their date from those.

By this time, it was late afternoon, and Tess had made dinner reservations in the theatre district for her and Ruth for two hours before the show began. Tess rose from her chair, stretching her arms above her head, "Well, I am going to get ready for tonight. Thanks so much for helping address those invitations. Now tomorrow I can put stamps on them and get them in the mail on Monday. Do you want to see the dress I am wearing tonight?"

"Definitely. I'll stay here and you can bring it out and show me?" Ruth asked, and as Tess turned and went into her room, Ruth took the invitation from the bottom of the pile she had worked on and slid it into her bag that was on the floor at her feet.

CHAPTER
Thirty-Seven

Sam

Sam and Chris had made it back to Manhattan following their afternoon in Brooklyn. After touring around the cemetery again, he and his brother had headed over to Brooklyn Heights Promenade and strolled the length of it while taking in the view of lower Manhattan and the East River. Then, they had enjoyed a late afternoon lunch at Junior's, which was always a treat, and walked off their pastrami and cheesecake by walking over the Brooklyn Bridge and back to the hotel. After changing their clothes, they had decided to walk up to the theatre, which was only a couple of miles from the hotel. Sam had put on a pair of gray pants, and a light blue sweater that his parents had given to him for Christmas last year.

"So you had kind of mentioned before about your book release and a tour? When does that start up?" Chris inquired.

"The book is out the first Tuesday in December, and the tour begins that following week—first in Boston, then here, and then Philadelphia."

"Aren't you also in your friend's wedding in December? That seems like a lot going on for you." Chris stopped to buy a pretzel from a cart.

"Nah—I actually called him yesterday to beg off from being in the wedding. Too much other stuff going on, I decided, what with the tour and Mom's treatment and all." Sam tore off a piece of his brother's pretzel, preferring the extra salty bits.

Meanwhile, Chris choked on a bite of his pretzel. "Dude—isn't that a little harsh?"

Sam peered at his brother bewilderedly. "What do you mean?"

Chris looked aghast, "Canceling on a promise to be in someone's wedding just months before the wedding? I mean, didn't they have a tux ordered for you? You can't be this clueless—you had your own wedding!"

"Technically, I suppose, but Amanda planned all of our wedding. I wasn't keyed in to the finite details." Sam hesitated a moment, "Josh seemed okay with it when I called him. Besides, I wasn't even originally supposed to BE in the wedding: I was a fill in for one of his cousins."

Chris calmed down at that. "Oh, I see; well, that makes a difference. Didn't you also have some kind of beef with his fiancée?"

Sam was tired of being the bad guy in the Josh and Tessa romance, and vehemently shook his head. "Wrong—she had a 'beef' with me, if that's what you want to call it. But get this, I finally found out what it was! Josh used me as an excuse for them to break up when he was done with college. He told her I thought they needed space or they needed to grow up or something."

"What the hell? That's low, Josh—doesn't he know the man code is to get pre-approval for that kind of shit? Oh, I get it, now. So she's been pissed at you for interfering in their relationship, when all the time she should have been pissed at homeboy. So she still has no idea or what?"

"That's the thing—I told him he had to tell her, but when I called him yesterday, he still hadn't said anything. So fine, none of my business if he wants to start married life on a lie, but I am not wanting to stand up there knowing she thinks I'm a piece of shit and it really isn't even my fault. I'm sure that now I've backed out of their nuptials, he will continue to remain silent on the whole matter." Sam had a hard time wrapping his head around this version of Josh.

"Wow, I only met him a couple of times, but Josh never came across as such a devious mastermind. I have to say I don't consider what he did to… what was her name again?"

"Tessa," Sam responded.

"Tessa—I don't think what he did was really a lie, but it was misdirection," Chris sounded skeptical.

"You better be careful, bro. Pretty sure Niamh, or any woman, cares about the distinction," Sam warned.

Chris chuckled at that, "Yeah, you're probably right—I definitely do not want to mess things up with Niamh." Chris paused, and then snapped his fingers. "Hey, I just thought of something right now, about the woman you met on the train."

"Theresa? What about her?"

"Did you ever consider that maybe you got her name wrong when you addressed the envelope to her?" Chris offered Sam the last bite of pretzel, which he accepted with gusto.

"I think I know how to spell her name: T-H-E-R-E-S-A."

"Haha, no not like that, but maybe she went by a nickname. Like my long name is Christopher, yours is Samuel…"

"Sure…and?"

Chris stared at his older brother, wondering if he was trying to be dense. "And when you said the name Tessa, it got me thinking about a book series I read by Laura Lippmann, where the character's name is Theresa—you know, you read the series too, when it first came out?" Sam nodded in response, so Chris continued, "Anyway, no one calls her Theresa: they call her Tess. Tessa could be a form of that."

"What? So you think my Theresa is Josh's Tessa?" Sometimes his brother, though very pragmatic, could come up with some eyebrow-raising theories. Which is what Sam was doing right now—raising his eyebrows at his brother.

"No, no, I mean what would be the odds in that?" Chris waved away Sam's theory. "Imagine—you just happened to be traveling on a train the same time your college best friend's fiancée is on the same train?" By this time, Chris was doubling over in laughter. When he had calmed down enough to speak again, he said, "Theresa could be called Teri, Resa, who knows? Which brings us back to the envelope: if you put Theresa on it, but the crew knew her by another name, maybe that's why she never contacted you—she never got the envelope!"

"Okay, but I also put the room number on it," Sam replied.

"Yeah, and I know you: you are a letters man, not a numbers man. I've seen you mess up more than one thing involving numbers."

Sam started tuning out Chris at this point, but not because what he was saying was moronic; in fact, it was the complete opposite, and it tied in to his talk with Josh yesterday, when he said Tessa's sister 'Ruth' was there. It couldn't possibly be true, could it? Could Tessa and Theresa be the same woman? Wait—no way, this was insane. That would have meant that Theresa was engaged, and he knew for a fact she was NOT wearing a ring on her finger. His hands had been all over that delectable body, and hers had been on his body, and at no point had he seen or felt a ring.

Sam shook his head and brought himself back to reality. "You're nuts, and here is our theatre."

Because they had gotten their tickets separately, they weren't sitting together, but had agreed to meet up at the bar on the first floor during intermission. Sam headed to his seat down in the orchestra, and Chris had a seat in the balcony. Sam found his seat and looked at his watch: he had fifteen minutes until the start, so figured a trip to the toilet made sense, and ambled back up the aisle, and downstairs to the toilets. As he was walking past the basement bar, he heard a whispered "Sam?" Turning fully around, Sam stopped dead in his tracks. Finally.

CHAPTER
Thirty-Eight

Tess

Tess could barely catch her breath, let alone believe her eyes. She and Ruth had arrived at the theatre, and immediately headed to the toilets. Tess had been quick, but Ruth was moving much more slowly these days, so Tess had gone out to the lobby outside the bathrooms to wait for her sister by the bar. After ordering a white wine, she was content to people watch while waiting for her sister. It was then she had noticed a tall man enter the lower level of the theatre, and her heart had constricted, because she immediately thought it was Sam, but she also knew that was impossible—what would he be doing in New York City, at the exact same theatre she happened to be in? What did not help matters was the fact that every tall, dark-haired, sexy-as-hell man with glasses she saw, she always did a double take. Everybody eventually finds themselves in New York City, right? She thought to herself.

Ruth was never going to believe this, and Tess hoped she came out soon so she could show her this Sam lookalike. The resemblance was remarkable, Tess thought. And then, as she was taking a sip of her wine, he raised his hand and dragged it through his curls, which were much shorter than she remembered; that movement, though, that was Sam. She should know, because she spent an entire night watching him do this same motion, and every time it had filled her with desire; then she had done the same to him, slowly running her hands through those dark, delicious curls, while also whispering to him how badly she wanted him, how desperately she needed him. In his room that night, Sam had ever so gently brought both of their bodies down to the bed, where he had begun to kiss her neck, and the tops of her breasts that were pushing up over her neckline. When he had stared so intensely into her eyes, she had known that this man she would never be able to resist. And she had admitted to herself, without a doubt, that she had fallen in love with him.

As this man was passing by her, she whispered to herself, in disbelief, yet filled with yearning, "Sam?"

Sam felt as if was floating in a dream, standing still in this lobby, but staring at Theresa. Finally—after searching the face of every curvy red-haired woman he saw, here she was standing before him, and she was breathtaking. Her hair was straighter than when he last saw her, but it was streaming down her back and over her shoulders. Those glorious green eyes seemed even brighter, perhaps due to the color of her dress? That dress, though, was making his hands itch to reach out and touch her. This was madness; she couldn't be here, and yet he uttered, with absolute long-ing, "Theresa?"

Tess's eyes could do no more than stare into his, his reflection mirror-ing her disbelief and relief at finally finding each other again. "What are you doing here?" As much as she longed to throw herself in his arms, she also felt an undercurrent of awkwardness: why wasn't he rushing to her to embrace her? He was the one who had left without a word after the night she had thought could be the beginning of their story.

Sam was using every power of restraint he had to not sweep her into his arms and out of this theatre immediately. In her eyes, though, he saw a slightly guarded look that kept him from moving physically forward. Why wasn't she asking him about his letter, and telling him why she hadn't reached out? These past three months had been filled with despair and loss whenever he thought of her. At first, he thought maybe she had needed time to finish her traveling, so he acknowledged it may take a couple of weeks for her to contact him, but then after one month passed, he began to sense that perhaps he would not be hearing from her after all, and a piece of his heart had broken every month since.

"My brother is in the show," he mumbled. Was he mumbling? He wasn't sure. He knew he meant to speak, but his mouth had dried, leaving only marbles and dust behind.

Tess heard him, though, as she had always heard every word spoken from his beautiful mouth. "What? Really? So are you here for the weekend only?" God, this was the worst small talk ever, Tess chastised herself. What is wrong with her? She had no shortage of witty comebacks on the train, and she hadn't even known him then. So why was this so hard? She supposed because the truth was, she had never truly known him

Sam coughed and then offered plaintively, "I've missed you. So much. I kept expecting to hear from you; why didn't you call me or send a text?" he was well aware he was at the point of desperation, but he had known no bounds with her since their first meeting. He also felt their time right here, right now, was fleeting.

"What do you mean call or text you? I never had your number. You left the train, without a word to me. I went to your room to get my glasses, and you were gone," Tess was close to her breaking point: too many conflicting emotions coursing through her—elation, devastation, relief, disbelief. Which way was she supposed to feel? She lifted her other hand to tuck her hair behind her left ear.

"Is that…are you…" fuck me, Sam thought, he had missed his chance with her. Sometime between the train and now, she had met someone, fallen in love, and gotten engaged. Sam's throat tightened, as if he were being strangled.

Tess froze: oh my god, oh my god, oh my god. It was all over. Her ring, this huge diamond she had never really cared for. She had told Josh "keep it simple" when hinting about ring styles. How had she ever mistaken that key ring for this monstrosity? She wanted nothing more than to rip it off her finger and throw it across the room. Suddenly the lights flickered and an announcement came overhead, informing the audience that it was five minutes to showtime.

Finally Sam managed to ask, disbelievingly, "Are you engaged?" He needed to verify, for his own sanity. To his devastation, she nodded.

Sam began to turn away from her, and Tess, desperate to keep from losing him once again, called out, "It's not what you think." She couldn't let him go without trying to explain, without getting him to understand. All she had ever wanted was to see him once again, and when she finally had now, it was all going so terribly, incredibly wrong.

He slowly turned back to her, "What do you mean—it's not what I think?" Please, he begged to a higher power, let that ring be a complete misunderstanding. Maybe even a terrible hallucination, anything but this sickening reality.

Tess, with tears rolling down her cheeks, "Everything. I was wrong. You just left." Why was she speaking in these haphazard sentences? She made no sense, even to her own ears, but those fucking bells were playing again, and time was slipping away from them. She was choking on her mistakes, her regrets, her fleeting love for this man.

Sam could no longer hold himself back and strode up to her. Craving to touch her, he smoothed his hands on her damp cheeks, and stated, "I didn't just leave—I wrote you a letter, professing every feeling I had about you, toward you; I gave you my cell number, my address, my email, any information you should need so I could possibly hear from you again, and I gave it to a porter to deliver to your room. I have been out of my mind every day since I left waiting to hear from you, hoping every time my phone made any noise at all, that it would be you. I answered every single unknown number, talked to every person from Mumbai to Beijing, just in case you were finally calling me. I have wanted you since I first saw you, hell, I have loved you since I first saw you…"

Sam started bringing his mouth down to hers, when from behind them, a voice insistently called "Tess?"

CHAPTER
Thirty-Nine

Ruth

Two months later

Ruth had the most perfect daughter, it had been decided by the entire family. Eloisa Violet had been born two weeks ago, having arrived five days ahead of her due date, and exactly one day after Thanksgiving. At first, Ruth had thought she had eaten too much pie during Thanksgiving (who doesn't, she told herself), as she started having some cramping late afternoon. Near bedtime, Sean had enough of her groans and made her admit to both of them that she was in labor. About ten minutes later, there had been no denying the labor anymore, and Sean had rushed her to the hospital. Luckily, her parents, Sean's mom, Tess, and all of Sean's sisters were all in town for the holiday, so Eloisa was able to meet almost her entire family. Ruth and Sean had named her after a grandmother each, although the most difficult process was deciding which grandmothers. Sean had smiled and said, "We'll name the next one after the other grandmas," and Ruth had been too enraptured with her brand new baby girl to raise an eyebrow.

A few days after Eloisa's great entrance into the world, Auntie Tess had headed back to Brooklyn, as she had much baking to do, especially with Christmas approaching, and her wedding in three weeks. Why her sister had chosen to have a Christmas wedding was, in Ruth's humble opinion, completely insane; Tess kept correcting her, saying it WASN'T a wedding on Christmas, because technically it was the Friday between Christmas and New Year's. Who the hell distinguished that finite detail? Ruth then had to remember to "check her language at the door", one of Sean's new phrases to try and ensure their daughter didn't grow up to sound like a longshoreman.

Feeding Eloisa always gave Ruth lots of contemplation time: the girl could eat, no doubt, just like her mommy. If Ruth had thought Tess had been frantic with wedding plans after the whole "Sam Train Affair", she had doubled down after what Ruth had dubbed, in her own mind, the "Sam Musical Affair"; Ruth attempted to make light of it to herself, if only to take away the pain she had witnessed in her sister's face that night.

Closing her eyes, she took her mind back to that night. When Ruth had stepped out of the restroom, she had started toward her sister, amused to see her holding a glass of wine. Tess had never been one to drink that much, but would enjoy a cocktail or two when they would go out together, but only if Josh wasn't present: "he doesn't like me to drink" she had told Ruth, after being questioned. Ruth was considering whether to order a soda to drink when she realized Tess was talking to a man, and then OH MY GOD it hit Ruth—that's Sam! What were the odds, in all the places in all the world, that Sam would happen to be in this theatre. Wow, okay, fate, whatever you have planned for my sister, I heartily approve, she thought, if that is what brought Sam back to Tess. Ruth had ducked around to the other side of the bar, where she could surreptitiously keep an eye on her sister. Never before had Ruth ever seen anyone cycle through so many emotions right before her eyes: happy, sad, scared, and all of them seemed to want a piece of Tess's facial landscape. The moment her sister lifted her left hand, Ruth could see the light glinting off her ring, and she had groaned to herself—there was no way Sam would miss that honker. Ruth had always thought the ring was beautiful, but it was WAY too ostentatious for Tess, especially with her being a baker. She constantly complained about getting flour between the prongs and butter under the diamonds. A look of utter defeat crossed Sam's face, and Ruth could feel his sense of loss from across the bar. Her sister looked like she was trying to grab Sam, to not let him leave, when he turned back toward Tess, and placed his hands on her face. Ruth wasn't sure what was going to happen (okay, she actually was POSITIVE she knew what was going to happen) so she quickly made her way back around the bar over to them and called her sister's name. Once it sank into Sam that Tess was engaged, Ruth was terrified he would be either furious or extremely hurt, so she had to stop them from kissing. Not the right time, not the right place. Tess had then asked Sam to meet her after the show—she would wait for him on the corner of 49th Street and Eighth Avenue, and would explain everything then, she implored Sam. Ruth had suggested to Tess for the two of them to leave the show, maybe go somewhere and talk about what had just happened, but Tess insisted they stay. Ruth had studied the playbill, and spotted the name she assumed was Sam's brother—Eric Charles. Tess had stayed in her seat during intermission, but Ruth had to use the toilet, and waddled her pregnant self down to the lower level again, where she bought a bag of nuts and Raisinettes for herself and her sister. Unfortunately, Ruth had hoped to run into Sam in the lobby, but didn't see him during the intermission, and had reported so to Tess.

Putting her shirt back into place, Ruth lifted Eloisa up to burp her, gently rubbing her back. "Oh, baby girl, poor Auntie Tess: she got herself in such a tangle," she murmured to her daughter. Sam did not meet her on the corner, needless to say. Ruth had waited across the street in a coffee shop, eating a piece of pie and keeping a careful eye out the window. Tess had waited there, so forlorn, for half an hour, until Ruth couldn't take it anymore and went out to rescue her sister, who had stood in that one spot all that time, with a mix of hopefulness and dread on the face that Ruth had loved since she was two years old. Her sister—the one person Ruth has always counted on to stand by her side, and until her daughter was born, the one person Ruth would walk through fire for.

Ruth looked up as her mother came through the door to the nursery, holding up Ruth's bridesmaid dress. "I have all of the alterations done, my dear Ruth. Do you want to try it on now?"

Ruth groaned, "ugh—not really. Have you talked to Tess today?" As far as Ruth knew, neither of their parents knew anything about what had happened two months ago. Of course, they knew the bare minimum about what had happened with Sam on the train. Tess had not wanted anyone to know, especially after the incident at the theatre. Ruth knew genuine heartbreak when she saw it, and her sister had it. Ruth prayed every day to whomever would listen—god, idol, fate, whatever—that Tess would call off this wedding. Couldn't anyone else see how miserable Tess was? Was Josh completely blind? But, it seemed like Josh was spending more and more time at the hospital, and now he was working on getting published. Was it Ruth's imagination, or was Josh creating reasons why he should never be at home with his fiancée? If Tess was hoping to have a baby anytime in the near future, she had better become a keyboard, because he spent more time pounding that than he did her sister.

"Yes," her mom responded, "I talked to her this morning. It sounds like she found a veil she likes. Isn't that something? All these months, she said no veil, and then all of a sudden, she wants a veil. I guess Josh made a comment about how regal she would look in one. Oh well, they seem to know what is best, don't they? Here, let me take Eloisa and put her in her crib for her nap." With Eloisa slumbering in her crib, Ellen left to go start another load of laundry—how does one tiny human create so many dirty clothes?

Ruth decided to scroll through her social media, and came across a post by the Moon and Stars Bookshop in downtown Philadelphia, one she had discovered after Sam had given her the list of books on the train that he thought would be beneficial to her students. "Oh my god!" She squealed, disturbing Eloisa in the process. Could it be this simple? She asked herself, as she rocketed out of the chair, down the hall, and into her bedroom where she kept her purse. Ruth pulled out what she had been holding on to for the past two months, not knowing why at the time, but clearly, once again, the universe did. This, thought Ruth, could be the key to everything.

CHAPTER
Forty

Sam

He was always energized by the crowd, but the crowds for his first few signings in Boston had been stellar—a mix of fans who had been readers of his first two books, and then the new readers who had discovered this series after the release of book three. Although it had only been released last week, this new book was getting a lot of attention. Already a bestseller, his agent had called him yesterday morning with the news that Hollywood was interested in making it a television series. "Sam," Brock had said on the phone, "you should be flying! CBS wants to book you for their morning show next week."

"Absolutely not, Brock," Sam said adamantly, "I am not comfortable getting in front of a camera to pander to people who don't have the good sense to walk into a bookstore to find my book."

"Huge mistake—you're a good-looking guy who is here to SELL your book. The audience would eat you up." Brock was nothing if not coercive.

"Listen, can I just get through these first few book signings? I still have tomorrow in New York City, then the day after in Philadelphia, and the day after that in D.C.; then I fly out to the west coast—remember? You are the one who booked me for these, after all." Sam had tried to keep the annoyance level down in his voice.

Today, however, since he was in New York City, Brock had surprised him and shown up for his first signing of the day, and his agent was currently smiling at the bookstore manager; Sam was convinced he was hitting on her. Not surprising, really, as Brock had also flirted with several women who had come for the signing. Sam had never spent this much time with him before: for his past book tours, Brock had stayed low-key and done his wheeling and dealing from the sidelines.

While tapping on his phone, Brock again brought up the television interview; he then looked up and waved his hand in front of him, "Well, you would just fly back to New York, do the interview in between book signing dates."

"At the risk of repeating myself—absolutely not. The fact that I am flying AT ALL is a huge concession on my part; I am not going to fly from California, or wherever, back here, and then fly BACK to California. You know I hate flying!"

"I just thought that was a bit you did—playing the part of the famous author who has to have a shtick or something, and yours is 'I hate flying'."

Sam stared incredulously at his agent, wishing for the good old days when Brock was better entertained by his other clients and absorbed in his phone. Well, somebody out there loved him, because Brock's phone started ringing, and he answered immediately, "Brock here—go."

Sam started packing up his messenger bag, preparing to head uptown for the other signing this afternoon. He had been in New York since last night, and it was bringing mixed emotions for him, especially when he allowed himself to think of seeing Theresa. Hell, who was he kidding? He did almost nothing BUT think of her and that night. Seeing her in the theatre, she had taken his breath away again; he had wanted nothing more than to take her in his arms and show her how much he had missed her. Any confusion he had felt at the theatre over Theresa not contacting him had quickly faded away—all that had mattered was the here and now (or rather the then and there, he supposed).

Sam lifted up his glasses, and rubbed his eyes. He hadn't done much sleeping since then. That fucking ring. He had felt, really, like an idiot; sure, at first he had naively considered that she had met someone in the time between the train and whenever she had gotten engaged, and had allowed himself to continue thinking that for the first half of the show. However, when he and Chris had met up during intermission and he had told Chris all that had occurred earlier, he could come to no other conclusion than admit his brother was right: Theresa was Tessa, which meant that Theresa was also Josh's fiancée. Unfortunately for him, that meant that Theresa loathed Sam. He had almost gone to meet her on the street after the show, but all he could envision was her look when she looked at him, knowing he was Josh's best friend from college. It was no surprise she didn't remember what he looked like—she only had eyes for Josh, and there had been so many of the fraternity brothers there that night. And now that he knew she thought he had encouraged Josh to break up with her? How would he ever get her to move beyond that? Short of throwing Josh, her fiancée, under the bus (which he actually wouldn't mind doing, but not metaphorically) he saw no way out.

Of course, once he had left New York, his train ride had been ex-cruciating, as all of the truths he hadn't wanted to admit to himself were no longer able to be avoided. Theresa, Tessa, whatever she wanted to be called—the woman he had fallen in love with on the train had already been engaged to another man, and the man was someone that Sam also loved, as infuriating as Josh could be. Sam was cognizant enough to recog-nize that he should be furious with Theresa for misleading him, no matter what the truth was of her situation. And he had been, for about an hour, until he had too many questions circling in his mind. Had her dalliance with him been nothing more than exactly that—a mere dalliance? Think-ing back on things, it was clear she had been upset more than once, by something or someone NOT on the train. Had she been lashing out at Josh—using Sam to get back at him? That didn't seem her style; she had been so hesitant at first to open up to him. No, she hadn't gone looking to have a meaningless hook up. But why hadn't she been wearing a ring? A woman like Theresa doesn't betray a man she has fully committed to, of that he knows deep into his bones. None of it made sense, at least to Sam, but his Theresa had broken his heart.

Sam got up and headed out the door, signaling to Brock, who was still on his phone, that he was going to walk uptown. The truth was, even if he wanted to get in touch with Theresa, he still had no contact info for her, short of asking Josh, and that was a non-starter. "Hey, Josh, I just happened to be riding a train and fell in love with your fiancée. We actually spent one mind-blowing night together, but then I had to leave suddenly—can I get her number?" He guessed it was just as well that he had pulled out of the wedding, and it seemed he had been disinvited to it all together, since no invitation had ever arrived. He wasn't even sure when the wedding date was, since he hadn't put it in his calendar. He had only been a fill-in groomsman, after all, almost paralleling his time with Theresa on the train.

Having reached the destination and location of his next book signing, Sam looked around for someplace to get a bite to eat, and stopped dead in his tracks, unable to believe who was rounding the corner. "Josh?"

"Fitz!" Josh called excitedly. "I was hoping I would catch you here! I know your signing doesn't start for another hour, but I hoped that you would be here early."

"What the hell? How did you even know about it?" By the way, I am in love with your soon-to-be-wife.

Josh pointed to the window, indicating the poster in the display with Sam's face staring back at them, a hint of a smile on it. "My hospital is right across the street. I've been looking at this face of yours for the past two weeks! I can't stay for the signing, unfortunately, but I did want to see if I could catch you."

Sam was shocked. "I had no idea you worked up here. I mean, I knew it was in this area, I guess, but wow—even in New York City it's a small world." Sam could no more stop a speeding train than keep himself from glancing around hopefully and asking, "Is Tessa around by any chance?"

"Tessa?" Josh looked confused. "No, she hates going above 14th Street. Plus, she's busy getting all the last-minute stuff done for the wedding."

At the mention of the wedding, Sam felt his chest constrict. "And how is she? Is she good?"

Josh took a breath, "Listen, man, I still haven't told her the truth about our breakup, if that's what you're inferring, but I will, I swear. But I was thinking that now since it's so close to the wedding, perhaps may not be the best time. I don't think she hates you, though. I mentioned you last week, telling her that I was hoping to hear from you, and that maybe you could still be in the wedding: she barely made a comment. She has been so calm about everything, and it has been nice, especially with me working such late nights. We barely see each other right now."

Josh was completely clueless—did he even realize how lucky he was to be marrying Theresa? It didn't seem to even bother him that they spent so much time apart. What was their life going to be like after they got married? And what about his description of "calm Tessa"? It made her seem pretty lifeless, which was the exact opposite of how Sam had ever seen her.

"Hello? Fitz? Fitz? Sam?" Josh said insistently.

Sam looked up, "Sorry, I was just thinking about the signing, I guess. What did I miss?"

Josh laughed, "I was asking if I would see you at the wedding?"

"I never got an invitation, actually. I thought maybe I wasn't invited, since I canceled on you."

"What? No way, Fitz. Not sure what happened, but I apologize for the confusion. I'll make sure to ask Tessa about it later." Josh seemed to fume.

"No worries—you can just text me the details, if that's easier. I still don't know if I can make it."

"Oh, that sucks. Is it your mom? How is she doing?"

"Oh, yeah, she's grand. No, it's my book tour. So many dates, sorry." Not the actual truth, as Sam had no dates scheduled between Christmas and New Year's, and it suddenly dawned on him that's when the wedding was. For certain, the last thing Sam wanted was to be a witness to Theresa vowing her love and commitment to a man who most assuredly would never treasure it.

CHAPTER
Forty-One

Tess

Tess thought she would get through at least one day without crying, but no. Today is not that day. Unfortunately for her, yesterday was not that day, either. Every day she seemed to annoy Josh about something, or he annoyed her. Shouldn't they be in a blissful state right now? Yesterday had begun as blissfully as she expected her days to go, until Josh had called.

"What are you talking about? Of course I did," Tess said vehemently into her phone. She knew it was a mistake to answer it; one look, seeing Josh was calling, had sent waves of apprehension through her, not to mention an underlying current of annoyance. She was baking every morning, then making her deliveries until the afternoon, and then going home to work on anything that needed to be done for the wedding, which was coming up faster that Tess could believe.

"Do you know how humiliating it was? To stand there, after having sought *him* out, telling me that you never sent him an invitation to the wedding. Do you really despise him that much?" Tess could practically feel Josh seething on the other end of the phone, and it was not sitting well with her.

"What the hell are you talking about Josh? You ring me up during the day, after having explicitly told me to not bother *you* at work with questions about the wedding—but it's fine for you to call *me* up and chew *my* ass out?"

"I am not chewing your ass out," Josh hissed angrily into the phone. "I asked you if all of the invitations for *my* guests had been sent. Simple question that should have a simple answer. You seem to have enough time to go cake tasting and decide what we're serving at the dinner reception, so I'm confused as to why you didn't have enough time to properly sort our invitations."

Mortified at both his tone and his words, Tess said, with exaggerated calmness, "Unless you begin to make yourself more clear instantly, I am hanging up. Ruth was here to help with the invitations two months ago— she addressed the invitations for your guests and I took care of the ones for my side, in case I missed anyone."

'Well, you did, Tessa—you missed Fitz. I just saw him at his book signing, hoping to surprise him. Well, I was the one left surprised. Because you fobbed off your job, Fitz never got an invitation." Josh huffed, "Never mind—I'll call Ruth myself. Anyway, Lana is calling me, and I need to go. We had better talk tonight, in case anything else got messed up." Once again, though, Josh had gotten home after she had gone to bed, so their disagreement still hung in the air, like a cloud of doom destined to follow her until it was somehow resolved.

It was only a few weeks until their wedding, and she imagined most couples were somewhat stressed preparing for their big day, but this was extreme. Josh was spending more and more time at his office, when she knew he had no surgeries to prepare for, and she wasn't entirely sure what he was doing with his days or nights, but if this was his behavior before the wedding, how would he be after? Not only that, the modified honeymoon weekend they were going to take to Montreal had been postponed, and as usual, done without first discussing it with her.

She took off her glasses to wipe her eyes. Nothing had been the same since Ruth had been here that weekend. Tess thought of Sam constantly; nothing had been as lonely as standing on that corner waiting for him to meet her. If he had just given her a chance to explain—but that was as far as she ever got when she tried to replay the events of the night to give them a different ending. What would she have done? Called off her engagement? Asked him to wait for her while she sorted things out? Run away with him, right then and there? She doesn't know for sure what door she would have walked through, and each choice felt like a betrayal to both Sam and to Josh. Without a single doubt in her head or heart, she knew she had fallen in love with Sam on that train, and knew she loved him still—but where did that leave Josh, and the life she had created with him for the past two decades? So much effort, time, and emotion—would she have really tossed it all away? Josh was stability, and maybe she didn't always love what he did or said, but he could be counted on to always be there for her. At least that's what she always told herself.

After drying her eyes and blowing her nose, Tess called her sister, who answered after only one ring. "Hi, Tessie, I was just going to call you. I just got off the phone with your fiancé, and boy, was he lovely."

"God, I'm sorry. I should have called you immediately after getting off the phone with him yesterday; I was just so upset over it all, and even thinking about it now had me emotional again," Tess said with a note of apology in her voice.

"No worries—I took care of business and told him that all invitations that needed to be mailed had been sent. This is what he chooses to get bent out of shape about? Has he helped with anything else for the wedding? Frankly, the way he acted on the phone just now with me, I can't even begin to imagine how he was yesterday, which is exactly why I didn't answer the five other times he tried calling me. I knew he'd have something ridiculous to say, and I was right. Why is he being such an ass?"

"He is under a lot of stress with his possible fellowship, and he and Lana have a lot of paperwork to do; that's what he tells me, anyway. I don't know—I barely see him. He comes home super late, and then I get up before dawn to go to work, and he's always gone when I get home. I don't think I have even *seen* him in over a week. I feel like I'm marrying a ghost. Is this how it was when you and Sean were getting married?"

"No, but you know Sean—he likes to be involved in everything, whether I want him to be or not," Ruth chuckled.

Tess sighed, "Let's talk about something nice—like Eloisa! How's my gorgeous niece? I can't wait to see her again."

"She's eating right now, and she was so excited when I told her Auntie Tess was coming down for the weekend."

"What if I'm making a mistake?" She whispered into the phone.

"What was that? Tess, did you say something? Sorry—Mom has decided that now is the perfect time to vacuum."

Tess cleared her throat, "No, nothing. I just asked how Mom and Dad were doing." The last thing Tess wanted to do was have Ruth voice aloud any of the apprehensions Tess had been pushing further and further down; she knew her sister was worried about her, and had been since THAT NIGHT. If Tess could just learn to accept her future with Josh—the future she had been dreaming of up until five months ago—she would be happy again. She sometimes wondered if Josh ever really looked at her. He never asked how she was. Sometimes she felt so miserable she was sure it must be stamped on every feature. How could Josh not see it? What would it take for him to see she had been crying? To acknowledge that the last time he had heard her truly laugh must have been weeks ago. She supposed it was easier to not see those truths if he was never around.

"Oh, Tessie, Mom wants to say hi," said Ruth, and then her mom was on the phone.

"Hi, honey, how is everything going?" Asked her mom.

Ellen Lefferts was one of the gentlest, kindest souls, and hearing her mother's soothing voice brought fresh tears to Tess's eyes; her mother always had this effect on her. If Tess was not feeling well, either physically or mentally, as soon as she heard her mom's voice, she broke down, and today was no exception. She couldn't stop herself from sobbing into the phone, "Mom, I'm so confused—I don't know what to do. How do I know if I'm making a mistake?"

"Tess, sweetie, what is it? Did something happen? It can be a very emotional time leading up to your wedding, I know. I was just commenting to your father this morning that I have been feeling so nervous lately. I just want both of my girls to be happy—are you happy, Tess?"

No, she thought, I am not happy. "I just want everything to be perfect. I want to be perfect. And I'm failing," she admitted, haltingly.

"Tess, you have been so hard on yourself ever since you were young. They say the second child should be more easy-going than the first born, but you broke that mold—always so serious, and so much in your own head. These are golden qualities, though. Sometime, in life, though, there is no right or wrong. Look at what happened to your dad and me. I left him, Tess. Cut through all the other nonsense I ever said about what happened, and the truth laid bare is that I left him. Out of nowhere, if you asked him—blindsided him, which I suppose to some extent is true, but if he had looked at me, he would have seen that I was lost. We were both lost; if he hadn't been as lost as me, he'd have recognized my sadness and discontent. I'm not blaming him, just pointing out that there are two people in the game of love, and if one of them isn't working, that means neither one is working. Whatever you're feeling now, it's not 'wrong', it simply 'is'. I know you and your sister have your secret society, but I am not blind or deaf. I know something happened on the train, Theresa, and I know you were affected deeply by it; otherwise, you would not be in so much pain right now. I also know that your relationship with Josh would never have been affected if it was working. You have three weeks to figure out how you want your life to be, and whatever choice you make, we will support you. And need I remind you: you are perfect in your imperfections."

"But what about Dad? I don't want to disappoint him. He loves Josh like a son."

"And you're his daughter. Your father takes time to come around to something new, there is no denying that. There's also no denying that he is so proud of you, but he worries just as much as you about the future and the past. Sometimes you need to stay in the present. Oh, goodness, Ruth is waving at me—she has to pop out to the bookstore for a bit, so I get to have Eloisa all to myself. I love you, my angel." Then her mom was off the phone, enrapt with her grandchild.

CHAPTER
Forty-Two

Sam

Sam had noticed her as soon as she had walked into the bookstore. He remembered telling her about Moon and Stars Bookshop when they were on the train—their children's department had an amazing poetry section. He couldn't stop himself from looking for her sister, disappointed when there was no Theresa at Ruth's side. Will he always think of her as Theresa: his Theresa, even after she married Josh? He had his biggest audience yet, here in Philadelphia, so many couples showing up arm in arm, excited to be reading the same series of books together. In New York, he had a couple tell him they had gotten engaged while reading the book aloud at night to each other: "completely spontaneous" they had reported, "the most romantic book ever", he had heard. Sam had doubts as to the truth of that phrase, but he had no doubt that, for him, it was indeed the most romantic book ever—a book born out of the love he had felt for the one woman he could never have. Sam guessed that for him, it was also the most tragic book ever. He had dreamt of Theresa being by his side for this tour, being able to look up and see her in the audience, and having her at his side as they traveled from city to city together. Obviously he hadn't expected her to quit her life, or put it on hold for too long, because he loved the baker in her, but surely she would have joined him on these East Coast signings. How do you get over a loss of someone when you never had them fully to begin with?

With one Sharpie dead on the table, Sam looked up to signal to Brock to bring him a fresh one; usually Brock was on top of whatever his author may need, but then Brock had never had Ruth in the audience. Sam smiled, and felt for Brock, as he had clearly come under the spell of a Lefferts sister, and that was a spell that was hard to break. He saw Brock blanch, and then leave Ruth's side, bearing a full box of markers. "Did you see that hot blonde over there? Turns out she just had a baby two weeks ago, and I now know more than I need to about what stains could be on her sweater," he said, shuddering, which made Sam chuckle and appreciate Ruth all the more.

Sam finished signing the last of the books for people in the audience, and then turned to the bookstore back stock, trying to sort out in his head what Ruth could be doing here, especially since she was alone. When he had signed the final copy, he leaned back in his chair and took a minute to compose himself. When he opened his eyes, he saw Ruth pulling out the chair beside him, and watched her take a seat.

"Do you have any idea how much easier it is to sit when you're not pregnant? Course you don't, but I won't hold that against you." She smiled at Sam warmly, "Hey, Sam, long time no see, huh?"

Sam nodded, "Been a minute or two. You're looking well; you should know that you may have damaged my agent for a lifetime."

"Haha—that guy? Good-looking guy, but WAY too smooth for my taste. I like a little more bumbling flirtation, and my husband happens to excel at it." Ruth proudly declared. Then, holding up a copy of Sam's newest book, she continued," This book is beautiful, by the way. Never been much of a sci fi person, but once I knew who you were, I bought your first two books. Definitely helps having the romantic subplot, I think. I read this in two days, right after my daughter was born and we were home. A couple of long nights for the both of us—she was a little colicky for the first week, but if I nursed her, she was content. So, I would prop this book open on my pillow and read for hours. I was so exhausted, but never wanted to stop reading." Ruth stopped and Sam felt her studying his face.

"High praise coming from a new mom—aren't you supposed to have no time for yourself anymore?"

Ruth laughed, "Oh, trust me, I don't anymore. I probably shouldn't have had the time then, but then I would have missed out." Sam stared into the eyes that were twins to Theresa's.

"Oh yeah? Missed out on what?" He asked casually.

"Missed out on reading about the author falling in love with my sister." Sam watched Ruth's eyes dampen with unshed tears. "The things you wrote, your beautiful language—I see my sister through your eyes, and I have never seen anything more spectacular," and now Ruth was crying freely. "Why didn't you come and meet up with Tess after the show in New York? I know you love her—it's written all over this book. Hell, I saw it six months ago on that train."

"How could I? Tell me how I could come and meet your sister after seeing that rock flashing on her finger!" Sam turned in his chair so he was fully facing Ruth. "Do you have any idea how that made me feel? Seeing her again, after all those months. Months that I spent alone, wondering why she never reached out—no call, no email, no text. Hell, I even included my home address for her."

Ruth looked perplexed, with her eyebrows drawn together, "What do you mean you included your address? Included it in what?"

Sam fell back in his chair, "We never got to talk about it that night, I guess. Ruth, I wrote her a letter before I left the train, explaining why I had to go, but also telling her exactly how I felt about her—how she had inspired me, how I had fallen in love. I gave her all of my info—cell, address, email. I wrote "Theresa" and put your room number—Room 123–on the outside and gave it to the porter."

Upon hearing this, Ruth put her head in her hands, "Oh, Sam, we were in Room 132, not 123, and of course, you knew her as 'Theresa' which is, her actual name, but one she rarely uses. All this time: wasted."

"Why did she introduce herself to me as Theresa if that's not the name she uses?" More than anything this was what puzzled Sam.

"It was on a whim, and before you go there, not some plot she thought up ahead of time to confuse you or lie to you. She said she felt 'free' on the train, like a different person, and in a way, she was, but she was also the Tess I knew but hadn't seen in a long time."

"So she never got my letter? I mean, I had suspected as much, because the Theresa—Tess, I guess—would have reached out to me. Or so I thought."

Ruth reached out and grabbed his hands in hers, "I can guarantee one hundred percent she would have called you. Sam, she was more herself with you on that train than I've seen her in years—and I have missed that woman."

"How did you know who I was? I never got to tell her my last name, and if she didn't get my letter-" Sam questioned, before Ruth cut him off.

"It was Josh, actually, and either I'm telling you something new, or you already guessed it, but your college buddy, Josh, is her fiancé. He called her phone the morning after she was with you. She had left it behind in the room, and he called, so I answered it. He said he had to tell her something about his roommate from college-Sam Charles- and then he said your nickname-Fitz-the one Tess knows you by, and I just put two and two together."

Sam rubbed his cheeks. "Unbelievable—what are the odds? Does Theresa know? Tess, I mean? I guess I don't know what to call her."

"You can call her whatever you want, but no, she doesn't know. I didn't know how she would take the news of you being Fitz: first after she came back from your room, or then later, when she thought you had left without a word." Ruth took a deep breath, and then continued, "So what was the deal with all that? Why did you treat her so horribly all those years ago? She was crushed by it; she was beyond nervous about going to see Josh for the first time in college, and then to get brushed aside? Treated like an embarrassment. And then you convince Josh to break up with her? Sam, that doesn't seem like you, so what the hell happened?"

Sam shook his head, as if to forget all about what occurred back in college. "That weekend she came, it was homecoming, and a mess at the frat house. Josh was drunk, I mean we all were. It was no place for her. I barely even met her that night, so I can't speak to the impression she got. Their breakup, however, I had nothing to do with, despite what Josh has told Theresa; in fact, he promised me he would 'fess up and tell her the truth."

"Let me guess, Josh broke up with her on his own volition but blamed you?" At Sam's nod, she continued, "Goddamn, Josh, why do you do stupid shit? He's always been like that—he hates getting in trouble, so when he makes a stupid ass decision, he never wants to take credit for it. Idiot."

Sam ran his hands through his hair, then leaned over, resting his elbows on his knees, and then put his head in his hands. He looked up at Ruth, "What I don't get is where was her ring? It's hard to miss a ring that size, so why didn't I see it on the train?"

"That first day, Tess took a shower after we settled in our room; she always takes the ring off when she showers, but then she and I were in a rush to leave the room and she forgot to put it back on, and at some point it somehow got bumped or fell to the floor—we're not entirely sure when or what happened. When we were back in our room she remembered and we looked for it but couldn't find it then," Ruth explained.

"Okay, but she obviously did find it again, and what? She wanted to amp up the single lady aspect?"

"No, no, nothing like that. She didn't find it, Sam: I did. And I kept it from her. Until she was ready."

Sam sighed, feeling extremely frustrated. Ruth was slowly parsing this story out, when all he wanted to do was understand why Theresa had kept the truth of her engagement from him. "Ready for what? You said you were keeping it until she was ready…"

Ruth shook her head, "I don't know and it's hard to explain how I was feeling. Sam, my sister is vibrant and full of life. She is so brilliant and talented, but I have seen her draw into herself over the past many years since she and Josh got back together. He can be so critical of her, and makes her doubt herself: everything is Josh's way. And then we were on the train, and she was coming back around to being Tess with every hour we were on that train. And then you were so clearly interested in her, and she was sparkling and bright again. I wanted to see more of that Tess. And honestly? She wasn't even as bothered as she should have been by not finding her ring. So, when I found it, I tucked it away." Ruth paused to take a deep breath. "After you left, I stuffed it into the pocket of her jeans in her suitcase; she doesn't even know that part."

Sam looked at Ruth in astonishment, "You sure seemed to have covered all the bases. I have to say, it's pretty impressive, even if it was your machinations that were somewhat responsible for me getting my heart broken."

"My name is Ruth, and I have a problem thinking I know what is best for my sister, and then trying to make sure that happens." Ruth reached over and took one of the bottles of water sitting on the table for Sam's event, opened it, and drank half of it. "Confession always makes me thirsty. Look, in the name of full disclosure, I also have this," and she pulled an ivory-colored envelope out of her purse and handed it to Sam. "Word on the street is you never got one of these."

Sam stared at his name on the envelope, unable to make himself reach for it. "I'm guessing you are behind that also?"

Ruth nodded, "Again, Tess knows nothing about it. Sam, I'm afraid my sister is going to make the biggest mistake of her life, but nothing I say, or my mom says, is dissuading her. Even Josh, who's been saying some pretty stupid shit lately—that alone should be making her come to her senses. It seems like it will take something huge to wake her up out of this stupor." Ruth rose to her feet, continuing, "Look, use it, don't use it, I don't know. You seem like a pretty incredible guy who has his act together. I just wanted to make sure you were fully informed."

Ruth then placed the invitation on the table in front on Sam, and turned to walk away. "How do you know I'm an incredible guy?" he called out to her.

She turned and looked him straight in the eye, "You'd have to be, for my sister to fall in love with you."

CHAPTER

Tess

It was finally going to be the day Tess had been waiting for: her wedding day. She had dreamed of pledging her life and love to Josh since she met him almost twenty years ago; how could she ever have wanted anything else? He had loved her when she was afraid to wish for someone who would love her like that: completely and wholly. He'd never taken anything from her—only given: his love, his trust, his faith; so how was it now that she stood at the doors that held all the dreams she had ever had (as long as she stepped through them once they were opened), and she was too immobilized to make her feet take one more step? She thought of her wedding dress: the stuff of fairytales, and after several fittings and alterations, it was now her dream realized—champagne colored, with plenty of beading and lace, form-fitting and also flowing. Tess had never felt more beautiful, and when her mom had first seen her in her dress yesterday, she had begun sobbing. So now here she was, with people waiting for her to walk down the aisle, and with the ushers standing by for her motion to open those same doors. Why was she hiding (maybe not actively or physically, but certainly mentally and emotionally), Tess asked herself?

Over and over in her head, her regrets over the last six months raced and doubts for her future circled, as they had since the moment she had stepped off that train in California. Sometimes it felt as if she were being strangled by her silent screams, begging for some signal, for someone to tell her what to do. Her biggest issue had always been that she had never thought herself completely worthy of him, and with her lapse in judgment with her questionable behavior, she had finally proven herself right. Why had she taken so long to do it? Honestly, she had expected to fuck things up years before now, driven by her insecurities. Maybe this had all been a self-fulfilling prophecy? Her thoughts were, lately, often mercurial, first laying the blame solely at her feet, and then putting some of the blame on Josh: why hadn't they gotten married years ago, before any of this had a chance to happen? Maybe he had been the one with cold feet all along! He was, after all, the one who had broken up with her over a decade ago, and now she knows it was his decision, and his alone, a fact he had only shared with her last week, after he had revealed that Fitz would be able to be in their wedding after all. When he had confessed to her that it had been only his idea all along to break up with her, and not instigated by Fitz at all, she had been stunned, feeling a sense of loss and betrayal. Why tell me now? She had implored him, and he had stated frankly that it was time for her to know—that her anger toward Fitz all these years was hindering Josh's friendship with him, and that Fitz had agreed to be in the wedding as long as he was honest with her. She still didn't know if she was ready to fully accept Fitz into their joined life together, though, and so far she had been spared seeing him yet. He had only arrived this morning due to some previously scheduled business he had to see to first. She was, however, prepared to see Fitz in a new light, and as someone she could (perhaps) someday welcome as a friend.

Breaking out of her introspection, Tess pulled herself back to the present, and all that was waiting for her behind those closed doors. Luckily, Sean was one of their ushers, and he smiled at her as if he knew she needed the support. Her sister, Ruth, had totally won the jackpot the day she had met Sean. Sean and Ruth had met on an utter fluke on the internet, back when Ruth had still lived in South Dakota, and Sean in Pennsylvania.

They had taken a chance on love, and trusted in their mutual respect and attraction. Funny how now they were going to be moving to South Dakota, and Sean could live in the world in which Ruth had grown up.

All she had to do was put one foot in front of the other, and the day would be closer to being over. She could move past all of this loathing she had felt for herself for the past six months. Did she owe Josh the truth, especially after he had told her his truth? What would he think of her if he knew? Deep down, Tess feared there was a chance he wouldn't care, or even believe any of it had happened. Without a doubt, she knew he could give her the life she had wished for all these many years: love, reliability, children. Of course, he had also promised her a honeymoon, and look where that had gone: tossed aside in favor of his career. What was that saying? "It's not you, it's me"—it wasn't completely her, but since she was the only one standing here, for now it was true. Was it her, though? If Josh had been marrying, say, Lana—would he have so callously cancelled the honeymoon? Would he have told Lana that she needed to just be a doctor, not a surgeon? Implied that Lana wasn't built to handle the stress? If Tess had so many doubts about her wedding, her impending marriage, why was she even standing here? Stubbornness? Desperation? Was there any love left to salvage?

"Deep breath, deep breath, deep breath—you can do this" she whispered to herself as she rounded the corner to the doors. Tess and Josh had been very traditional, so due to Ruth's suggestion, they hadn't seen each other or each other's attendants before this moment, the night of the rehearsal. She knew who his attendants were—two of his cousins, his teenage best friend (who had also been hers at different moments during her life), his friend from med school, and his college fraternity brother, who she had detested on first sight; the feeling she had always assumed had been mutual. Or so she had thought, for years now. What if she had been mistaken about Fitz? Could she have unjustifiably held such a grudge for years? Normally, she prided herself on having impeccable intuition about other people: if that were true, though, why was she currently fostering doubts about Josh?

"You good, Sis?" Asked Ruth, not just her maid of honor (despite being married and a new mother, she refused to be referred to as "matron of honor'), but her best friend and devoted older sister. "Need a drink before we go in?" Ruth and her other attendants had already walked up the aisle; tomorrow the men would escort the ladies during the procession. Josh had expressed some concerns about the rehearsal being done slightly differently that the actual wedding, but he had acquiesced for tradition. "I wasn't sure what the hold up was, so I just sauntered my happy ass back down the aisle. I may have implied I need to feed my baby, so nobody blinked an eye," Ruth said as she cupped her breasts. Her sister had never had much of a filter, and it didn't seem that being a mother was going to change things. Tess finally smiled at that thought.

"No—just gathering myself. Everybody all set?" She wasn't ready. She wasn't ready. This is wrong. Tess started to take a step back—maybe no one would notice if she just slipped out this side door?

"Yep, just waiting on us, and Dad. Have you seen him?" Ruth looked around for John Lefferts' silver head.

"He was here and then vanished," much like she longed to do now, Tess mused; and then here came her dad, his tall frame climbing the stairs from the church basement, his silver hair glinting from the light. Then he was rounding the corner, and Tess could see he was holding out shots of Squirt, her favorite childhood drink. Trust her dad to think of everything, and to be able to bring a glimmer of hope to her right now. Tess had always believed that as long as her dad was with her, she would be safe, and he would catch her every time she fell.

"Got the good stuff, in honor of your sister", he told Ruth, "if I'd known you were joining us, Ruthie, I would have brought you some." Then they clinked cups and downed the Squirt. "Now, ready, Kid?" John's green eyes, identical to those of his daughters, gave her the strength and reserve she so desperately needed.

"Let's roll," Tess used a favorite expression of her dad's, and her sister turned the corner, kissed her husband and motioned to him to open the doors; Ruth started down the aisle, once again, and the notes of the cello wafted to greet them. "Dad, I may have messed up," Tess said faintly, but her dad was staring straight ahead at their mom, who he had loved and then lost and then loved again. All she had ever wanted was a love like her parents had—minus the divorce about thirteen years ago, of course. Now that they were back together, they were more helplessly in love than ever—is that how it will turn out for her and Josh? Tess gripped her father's arm, and before she knew it, they were halfway down the aisle. How had she gotten here? She wasn't ready to be with Josh yet—too many things left unsaid, and too many secrets in her heart. She stopped abruptly to catch her breath and looked at her childhood sweetheart, wondering if it was hot in the church. Was everyone else beginning to blush? Did anyone else feel a bead of sweat run from their hairline down the back of their neck? It was at that moment she looked beyond her groom, and over to his groomsmen, and she stumbled. Clutching her dad for support, she drew herself upright, sure that her eyes were playing tricks on her. Maybe there was a gas leak, and she was hallucinating?

What the hell? She asked herself. It couldn't be—maybe her contacts were drying out. The odds were stacked so high against this happening right now. She didn't recall any of Josh's family having such dark hair and eyes. And then his eyes, those endless, intense brown eyes, locked with hers, recognition flaring, cheeks flushing, and realization dawning. How could she not have known?

CHAPTER

Forty-Four

In all of his thirty-six years, Sam had never been more nervous than he was at this wedding—the wedding of one of his best friends and the woman both of them, it seemed, loved. What the hell was he doing here? He had asked himself this question at least once every five minutes since his arrival earlier today. Since Ruth had handed him that explosive invitation, in a moment that seemed frozen in time, Sam had been torn apart. How had he gotten it all wrong—every decision he had made since leaving the train was the wrong one—hell, leaving the train had been the wrong decision. If only he had stayed, he and Theresa (it said so on the invitation!) could have had one more day, and then one more magical night, together, just the two of them, wrapped up in only each other. Certainly they would have sorted everything out and then—and then what? All of this would still need to have been dealt with. Josh was still clueless about it all, and when he had called Sam last week and told him he had told Tessa the truth about their breakup, Sam had felt relieved that he was off the hook for the blame; he had also been conflicted. Now if Theresa found out who he was, his true identity, how would she take it? Probably she would feel betrayed, confused, and conflicted because that's what he was still feeling.

Sam also recognized he needed to be at the wedding, to see her, to ensure she possessed all the information before saying "I do". He had told Josh he would be able to be in the wedding after all: his schedule had opened up. So now here he was, awaiting Theresa's arrival down this aisle. He had made sure to stay well out of sight of the bride, but her maid of honor had seen him this afternoon, as soon as he had stepped out of his Lyft. Ruth's expression, he hoped, would be the same one he would see on her sister's face. Ruth had made a beeline for him, hugging him and whispering "I knew you'd come", before kissing him on the cheek. She had then pulled a stocky red head over to her, introduced him as "Sean, my husband", and instructed Sean to usher him to where Josh's attendants were hanging out. As he and Sean had walked around the building and into an annex, Josh had also been heading to the doors, but to leave as they were entering.

Josh had greeted him warmly "Hey, Fitz! I'm glad you could make it to the rehearsal." Then Josh had turned to introduce him to the rest of his groomsmen, all of whom Sam noted he had already met at least once. Was it ironic for a surgeon to not pay attention to minor details? As long as Sam had known Josh, he had always done that—he never made a note of his friends and if they had met before.

Sam had given Josh what felt like a Judas hug, knowing he wanted more than anything to find Theresa immediately and beg her not to marry Josh, but grand overtures would not take this wedding down; only subtlety laced with surprise could do that, and that is exactly how he would handle it. Theresa had to be the one to make the decision for herself.

Before he had left Boston, Sam had Chris come over to help him plan his attack, and that meant letting Chris choose his wardrobe for him—he killed when it came to fashion. Chris had perused with disdain the options already laid out on his bed. "Is this a funeral you're packing for or a siege?"

Sam had laughed, "Are you telling me my choices are shit?"

"Bro, you are going down there to, hopefully, steal away the bride from her own wedding. You need something that pops, not all of this dour-looking crap. Do you have anything NOT in black? Maybe something you didn't buy in the super goth section of Torrid?"

"Torrid? Don't they only sell women's clothes?" Sam asked doubtfully.

"How in the hell would I know—do these pieces LOOK like I shop at the mall?" Sam loved to irk his brother, knowing full well Chris got most of his clothes custom-made. "Besides, aren't malls passé now?"

Sam attempted to regain control of the conversation, "Anyway, I'm not necessarily going down there to steal the bride-"

"Bullshit," Chris interrupted, "and if you don't steal that glorious woman I saw you with at the theatre, I am taking you to the nearest facility to get your head examined." Chris paused, then asked, "Would you get an MRI for that, do you think?"

At that moment, Niamh had popped into Sam's apartment, "Chris, are these the shirts you wanted?"

"Oh, now I need your girlfriend's help, also? Why not parade me around Boston and get the public's opinion?" Sam was affronted by the lovebirds tagging up on him.

"Don't worry," Chris assured him, "Mom is coming over also." Chris then doubled over in laughter, "You should see your face right now."

"Could we please get back to me?" And Niamh came over and held up one of his brother's custom-made shirts, a brilliant blue with a chevron pattern in yellow and gray.

"Oh, this will be gorgeous on you, Sammy," Niamh pronounced. Since when had he agreed to be known as "Sammy" to his brother's girlfriend?

"I was thinking this," Chris suggested, producing a purple shirt with a paisley pattern in assorted pinks.

"Absolutely not—do you actually wear that in court?" Sam asked skeptically.

Chris looked affronted, "Do you realize how many cases I've won wearing this shirt? Just try it on. It might be a little snug on you—I've witnessed first-hand your love of carbs." And Chris started to help Sam take off the shirt he was wearing. Sam batted him away.

"I certainly don't need you to be my lady's maid—valet, yes, but I think they have more boundaries." And boundaries are what Sam desperately needed here with his brother and his girlfriends. Suddenly this huge apartment with the three of them in it seemed stifling. Sam took his shirt off and donned the shirt from Niamh, who also whistled at him as he undressed. He didn't recall asking to be humiliated today.

"You've got to be joking—you do know that a valet would bathe his master, right? And you're the writer," Chris scoffed, "do some research, man."

"Both of you idiots need to shut up! Sam, that shirt is so fucking fit on you! Chris, look at how it hugs his shoulders. Sam, I never noticed before how broad your shoulders are. Nice," she nodded appreciatively. "Now we just need some pants that will accentuate his-"

"Okay, you two clowns have done enough. I get it, I get it." Sam stepped into his bedroom to see his reflection in his mirror. He had to admit, the shirt did look halfway presentable, but he refused to give his brother any credit. He went back into the living room and asked, "Seriously, is this me?"

"No," Chris responded, shaking his head, "better than you—it's me. And Niamh is one hundred percent right here. This is your destiny shirt."

Now here Sam was, wearing his destiny shirt, and standing at the altar waiting for the doors at the back of the church to open, and then suddenly they parted, and beams of sunlight streamed through all of the windows; his heart rose in his throat, seized with the most overwhelming sense of anticipation he's ever felt. He watched as Ruth strode down the aisle, with that same sense of purpose Sam had begun to recognize in her. Where was Theresa?

Suddenly, the lights parted as if they were curtains, and the most intensely magical woman Sam has ever experienced was gliding down the aisle, on her father's arm. Only, on second thought, she wasn't gliding— she was haltingly walking, stopping after every few steps, the greatest look of apprehension on her gorgeous face. Dressed in a long-sleeved scarlet dress that flowed around her whenever she did move, and those sensual curls of hers seemingly all wrapped up behind her head. As he watched her, one long curl popped over her shoulder, having sought and earned a hard-won freedom.

Theresa's eyes tracked up to the altar, landing on her groom, and Sam desperately tried to read her expression, but she was giving nothing away with those emerald eyes, until slowly they moved over each groomsman, when at last they found his. She looked away, and then her gaze flashed back to him. Theresa's mouth opened in surprise, her eyes widened in shock. He watched as all color drained from her face, and her body seemed incapable of movement. Her dad attempted to pull her forward, to no avail, and the hand holding on to his arm visibly shook—with excitement? Surprise? Dread? Every cell in Sam's body screamed at him to take some action: go to her! They seemed to yell. She needs you! They implored. He couldn't though, he had to restrain himself from moving. His good sense so far overtaking his base instincts. As much as he yearned to sweep her off her feet and run away with her, he could not make any decisions for her; this most imperative choice must be hers alone, for he had already made his.

Theresa turned to her father and whispered something, that only he seemed to have heard, and she unlinked her arm from his, slowly walked two steps backwards and then turned around and fled the church.

CHAPTER
Forty-Five

Tess

"Tessa, what the hell was that? What kind of stunt are you pulling?" Josh demanded.

After fleeing her own wedding rehearsal, Tess had gone back to their apartment, and Josh had found her there shortly after, which was unfortunate, because what she wanted, and needed, was more time to gather herself. How would she begin to explain her actions to Josh, when she had only come to admit the truth to herself, one she had been trying to deny for six months.

"It's not a stunt, Josh, and I have been trying to get you to understand something for months now. How you could even suggest that I would play some kind of game with you is indicative of our entire relationship." Tess looked at Josh, and truly saw him, for the first time in years.

"When is the last time you think we were happy, Josh? I tried to imagine that time this morning, and nothing came to me. All I felt was a void." Tess whispered.

"Those are just nerves, Tessa," Josh sputtered, "you have always been this way when a big decision needs to be made, and you know that. Remember when you couldn't decide whether to move to New York after we got back together? It took me to point out to you that you weren't exactly setting the world on fire anywhere else."

"Right there, Josh—that's part of our problem," Tess replied, becoming bolder.

"What problem? I didn't even know we had a problem until you had your little fit at the church." Josh was indignant.

"A little fit? I hardly think me running out of my own wedding rehearsal is a 'little fit'. I actually think it was a BIG FUCKING FIT!" She screamed at him, and instantly knew that losing her cool would not get her, or them, anywhere.

"Okay, let's take a deep breath and try to mitigate the hysterics. I am wanting to have a calm and rational discussion about your actions today, before we have a hundred people in that church tomorrow, who will be there, at our invitation, to witness our nuptials."

"Josh, sometimes I don't even think I can breathe. When I imagine our future, I feel like I am being suffocated," Tess confessed, trying and failing to keep her emotions at bay. Anger was one thing, but she did NOT want to feel sorrow. "You make me feel so small sometimes." She breathed in deeply, "Wait—I feel small sometimes, but that's on me, I have come to realize, and I need to stop blaming you for that. You are only treating me the way I have given you permission to treat me, and I'm not sure when I started caring so little about myself that I allowed it."

"Now hold on," Josh interjected, "You never wanted to make the big decisions, so I made them, and if that made you feel small, I apologize for that; but as you said, you seemed more than happy to let me do it. Tessa, we have our whole life together planned out—you and me in Brooklyn, for now, but we had been talking about a move to Manhattan, to be closer to my hospital. You can bake anywhere, but I've been telling you that you might not have time for it in the future with being a surgeon's wife. That's part of the reason I have advised you against starting your own bakery. And then we want to start a family in a couple of years, right? Remember when we talked about having two kids? Isn't that still our plan?" Josh reached out to take Tess's hands, to draw her closer to him, but she pulled back.

"You're not listening to what I'm really saying, Josh. I don't think I am ever actually being heard. Everything I hear you saying is all about YOU—your career, and moving into the city for it, and me quitting what I love, again for your career. You career is not MY life, and it's not OUR life. What about our honeymoon—we talked about that, too. I wanted a honeymoon, and you agreed to it, but then went behind my back and erased it all," Tess sobbed, "I feel like I'm being erased and you're trying to mold me into who you expect your wife to be."

"The honeymoon again?" Josh said exasperatedly. "God, I thought that was behind us—you had moved on from it."

She nodded again, "I did, I moved on—what choice did I have? All of this, it's a thousand small cuts and I am bleeding out. Your constant comments on my weight, disguised as worry about my health; your refusal to even discuss me opening up my bakery. Hell, me even living in New York City; every aspect of my life has been decided because I am, or was, wanting to only please you. Where does that leave me?"

Josh stared at Tess as if he did not recognize the woman before him. "I'd say that leaves you sitting in a pretty nice apartment, leading a pretty amazing life thanks to me. All my hours of work, of being at the hospital, they were for you!"

Tess shook her head in denial, "Be honest with yourself, Josh: they weren't for me; they never were. It was only for you. We have barely even SEEN each other in months, and we are not even married yet. You shouldn't be okay with NOT making love to me since I got back from my bachelorette trip—had you even noticed that? Wondered why I never waited up for you anymore?"

"I am not completely blind, Tessa; you have been different ever since you got back, like a wall had been put up. I was sure Ruth had spent the whole time talking you out of marrying me, and sure enough, here we are!" Josh came to Tess, and put his hands on her shoulders. "This is total Ruth, you know—filling your head with ideas, making you believe things are possible that aren't."

"NO, Josh, this isn't Ruth, this is me. And you're right: I have been different, I just never expected you to notice." Tess thought to herself that now was the time to confess, tell him everything about meeting Sam, and all that had happened between them. Yet this wasn't about Sam—it was about Tess, and Tess becoming Theresa, and letting go of Tessa. She had discovered her true self on that train.

"Where does this leave us, Tessa? How are we going to move on from this?" Josh demanded.

Tess sighed, "We can't; we won't. I am not the girl you broke up with and then lied about it when you wanted me back—when it was convenient for you. I'm not the woman who waited years for you to propose, who had to hint year after year about wanting to be married." Tess twisted her engagement ring for one final time, and looked at the man she had always thought would hold her future. "Josh, I'm going to do something I should have done a long time ago. You were the boyfriend I needed when I was fifteen, but you aren't the husband I need at thirty-two."

"Oh, that's perfect, Tessa—so what? You're breaking up with me? What about what I need? Please, don't do this—we can work it out; let's take tonight and I'm sure by tomorrow you will be ready to put on your wedding dress and walk down that aisle."

Tess shook her head mournfully, "Josh, we were already broken; I am giving you what you need, which is space to find what makes you happy. Oh, and this," and Tessa tearfully pulled off her engagement ring and handed it to him.

"Now what do we do?" Josh looked stunned. "You have always said that all you ever wanted was to marry me; then I finally give in and propose, and this is how you act? How do we tell everyone invited to the wedding that there will be no wedding?"

"I don't know, Josh, but you've been pretty good with canceling everything else with me lately; I'm sure you won't have a problem canceling your wedding."

With that, Josh stormed out of the apartment, a bag of hastily packed clothes slung over his shoulder, telling her that if she came to her senses he'd be at his office at the hospital. After he left, Tess sat at their kitchen table, staring at her empty hand; taking off that ring had felt like a weight being lifted from her entire body. She walked into the bedroom and changed into a pair of yoga pants and a long-sleeved t-shirt, and shook her hair out from the complicated twist it had been wrenched into for the rehearsal. She supposed at some point that she should call her sister or her parents, and then her phone suddenly rang, showing that Ruth was calling her. She answered her phone as she stretched out on her bed, with the comfort of Rapunzel curling up next to her.

"Ruthie, I did it," she sobbed into the phone, knowing that she would never need to explain to her sister what she meant, and it turned out she was right.

"I know, Sis. Josh just called and gave me an earful. Dude never did know when to draw the line," Ruth commented darkly. "If he thought I was going to sit there and be blamed for his wedding falling apart, he was sadly mistaken." Ruth paused, and Tess felt her sister's concern coming through her phone. "How are you, Tessie?"

"After admitting so many things to Josh that I have kept pushing further and further back, and accepting my new reality? I'm doing better now. Honestly, it's a relief to just be done with it. How are Mom and Dad?"

"Oh, you know Dad—he will take a beat to adjust to not getting a surgeon as a son-in-law. Mom is thrilled that you found your voice. They are taking care of notifying the priest and the caterer. Just so you know, all of the food has been arranged to be donated to several shelters in the area."

"Ruthie, what a mess I've made—how do I tell everyone? Where do I start?"

"Don't even worry about that; word has been spreading like wildfire. I'm surprised your phone isn't blowing up." Ruth was beginning to sound as if she was out of breath. "Do you want any company?" Ruth asked hesitantly.

"That would be great," Tess replied emotionally, and then as if by magic, her doorbell rang. Tess smiled at that, and shook her head, because she shouldn't be surprised: Ruth always was one step ahead of everybody else.

Ruth had handed Tess a package as soon as she entered her apartment, "I don't know what you're going to do with all of the other gifts over there," she said, nodding to the stack of wedding presents in the corner of the living room, "but this is just for you. I will be here as long as you need, Sis. You and me, the Lefferts sisters, back together again. Sean has Eloisa, and they are hanging with Mom and Dad."

The sisters ordered in Chinese food, and Ruth ranted when Tess needed it (Ruth was so much better at ranting) and been silent when Tess had to cry (Tess really was an excellent cryer). Tess took Ruth's gift into her bedroom and eventually fell asleep many hours later with it on her pillow.

254

CHAPTER
Forty-Six

Tess and Sam

The next morning, after gleaning a location from her sister (why did Ruth always seem to hold the information she needed) Tess grabbed her book and walked the two blocks to the subway, where she rode it to Brooklyn Heights. While on the train, she made a playlist that she felt would fit her mood for the next several months. Exiting the train, she climbed the stairs to the street level, and followed the directions on her phone.

Walking into the lobby of the hotel, Tess stood nervously in front of the elevator before pressing the "UP" button. After she entered it, she then took it to the fourth floor and found the correct room. Tess pressed two fingers against her throat, and felt the fluttering of her pulse, trying to recall a time she had been as nervous and excited as she was now. Reaching up, Tess pushed her glasses up from the end of her nose and finally knocked on the door, which was answered immediately by Sam, whose tousled dark hair told her he hadn't slept much the night before. She felt her chest tighten at the sight of him, and longed for him to take her in his arms. What was taking him so long? What was he waiting for?

Sam was both shocked and relieved to see her standing at the door to his hotel room, and she looked as vulnerable as he felt. He had been pacing the floor of his hotel room for most of the night. After Tess had left the church, Ruth had approached him, asking him where he was staying. He gave her his details, and she had told him "Sit tight—I may need some reinforcements later." She had then reached over to him and squeezed his hands, "You're a good man, Fitz," she said with a wink, and off she went. After getting to his hotel, he had made his first stop the hotel bar, and two Irish whiskeys later, had headed to his room. Sam had never been a patient man, and it had taken everything in him to not prowl the streets of Brooklyn. Not having any idea where Tess lived was a good deterrent, though. He had vowed then to himself that when he next saw her, the first thing he absolutely had to do was finally get her phone number!

Seeing the stunned look on Josh's face at the rehearsal had not been pleasant, and Sam knew at some point in the future, regardless of what happened, he would need to reach out to him and explain. What Sam had no intention of doing, however, was apologizing. If that had been Sam at the altar, watching Tess walk down the aisle to marry him before doing a one-eighty and running out? Sam would have been hot on her heels, but Josh had just stood there, looking like he had expected her to come back at any minute. You don't let someone who steals your breath with every glance just walk away from you, yet that was what Josh had done.

Looking down at the woman who was, currently, stealing his breath away, he suddenly felt ineffectual. What an ass he was! Chastising Josh for not chasing after Tess, when wasn't that exactly what he had done (or not done, as the case may be)? Sam struggled to speak, but at last managed, "I wasn't sure if you would need time, or how much time, or even if you would actually want to see-" and then he was unable to continue, as Tess launched herself into his arms, and framed his bristly face with her soft hands.

With tears streaming down her cheeks, unable to wait any longer for him to make the move, she pulled his head down to her level, and kissed him, with all of the pent-up love she had been denying herself for six months. As much as she had yearned for him to kiss her, she ultimately knew it was her move to make. When she came up for air, she began trying to explain, "I'm so sorry I didn't tell you, but I didn't know it was you. I never meant to hurt any-" and then Sam silenced her with his mouth on hers, and ran his hands down her body, pulling her flush with him. He had been aching to do this for so long, and felt as if his whole life were, right now, wrapped up in his arms.

"Shh," Sam said, "I don't care about any of that; the only thing that matters is you being here with me right now. I haven't left this room in case you came to me. I'm an ass for not coming to you. Just so you know, if you hadn't shown up by this afternoon, I was coming to you. Somehow, some way I would have found you, once again. Just like I found you on the train." He wiped the tears from her flushed cheeks, and cradled her face in his palms, and, making up for lost time, kissed her again. He ran his tongue over her lips, tasting her sweetness, over and over.

Tess took his hands from her face, kissed his palms, as he had done to hers all those times on the train, and then she reached for her bag, "Last night I received one of the most amazing gifts ever, in my entire life, and it's the reason it took me until this morning to come to you. I read it all last night; it's beautiful, overwhelming, and completely left me stunned—you really wrote this on the train?" She questioned in disbelief, while holding up the gift Ruth had given her last night, a copy of Sam's book, <u>Excess Baggage</u>.

Sam smiled, shaken that his book was the reason for her delay. His words were so intimate in the book, and he felt he had bared his soul for the entire world to see; yet the only one who truly mattered was standing in front of him. The knowledge that it was those words and the emotion behind them was the reason she was looking at him with a mix of awe and desire was about to bring him to his knees. "Not all of it, but the first six chapters, at least. I lost count, truthfully, because it didn't matter to me anymore where I wrote it—all that mattered was who I was writing it for, and that person was always you, my undeniable and unavoidable muse. Tess—okay that might take some time to get used—from that first glance out of the train car window, I was drawn to you: your passion, your laughter, your sense of humor, your heart, your soul" with every declaration, Sam drew her deeper into his arms, until at last space ceased to exist between their bodies. His kiss this time conveyed devotion and commitment.

"I am a selfish man, and I want it all, and I will only find it with you." Sam took the book from the arm he had pinned to her side in his embrace and opened it to the dedication page, reading aloud "For T, and our memorable train ride." Sam closed the book and put it on the nightstand. "I just said 'T'—I didn't know if I should call you Theresa or Tess, and then I didn't want the wrong eyes seeing it: it would just be my secret ode to you," he confessed as he turned back to her and folded his hands around her much smaller ones, relishing the feel of her naked fingers.

"No one has ever said the things that I see you saying to me in this book, Sam; for so many years, I was afraid to take a chance on myself, until you. With you I gained courage, wisdom, and the strength I needed to be who I've known I always could be." Tess took a shaky breath, and let the tears fall. "Knowing my Sam, I'm sure you had to restrain yourself from following me down that aisle. I'm glad you didn't, though. It was my turn to come to you; you have shown me, over and over, in so many ways how you feel. I couldn't do that for you until I ended things with Josh—and you deserved more than to be waiting in the wings. I was so lost in all the dreams I thought I should have, but seeing you yesterday, waiting for me at the end of the aisle? I didn't see a dream Sam, I saw love."

Sam breathed in deeply, desperately needing to have all his cards on the table right now. "All these years, what I regretted, more than anything else in my life, was how I reacted to you at the frat house, back in college. I was drunk, stressed about my writing, but more than that I was jealous."

Tess shook her head in confusion, "Jealous about what?"

"All the stories I heard about 'Tessa': I knew I had never had that kind of love before—that kind of woman. I was beyond nervous to meet you that night, and then when I finally did meet you, I pulled my whole 'Fitz' act and acted like such an ass. I've always hated that nickname because it represents that night in my life." Sam pressed his forehead to Tess's forehead, leaving them skin to skin and sharing their breaths. "I am forever sorry about all of it."

Tess felt Sam's tears of regret on her own cheeks, mixing with her own tears, knowing she was also guilty of her own bad behavior on that night. She stroked his face, and pulled her head back to look into his soulful eyes. "That night represents all of my insecurities coming to the surface. I had also heard so many stories of the amazing Fitz, and here I was, still in high school, coming to see my college boyfriend in his frat house. I was terrified someone was going to make me a target, and everything was completely unknown to me. So, I put on my best armor and attacked first. I was so nasty to you, and have felt ashamed about it ever since, so I made 'Fitz' an enemy in my mind."

Sam and Tess each took a moment, thinking about their past mistakes, about what could have been, but what had now brought them each to this moment years later.

"I think we both realize that without what happened that night at the frat house, we wouldn't be where we are right now. I wasn't ready for you then, too much growing to do. But I have never been more ready for any-thing—EVER—than I am for my future with you, Theresa Lefferts."

Tess looked deep into Sam's eyes, while stroking his face. "Well, Samuel Charles, I do have one more confession for you, though—with all that I've gained since we *truly* met on that train platform, I did lose something, too."

"Oh," Sam asked curiously, "what was that?" She could confess any-thing to him, for as long as he lived, as long as she was in his arms.

"I lost my excess baggage," Tess replied, smiling, and then they both started laughing, which passed quickly when it dawned on Sam and Tess that this moment was the beginning of their forever.

Sam kissed Tess passionately, sinking his hands into her mass of curls. Breaking slowly apart, Tess took out her phone and played the first song on her playlist, "Tupelo Honey". As she began to sway to the music, she reached to Sam, and took his hand in hers; staring into his fathomless brown eyes, she whispered, "Dance with me, Sam."

EPILOGUE

It was finally going to be the day she had been waiting for—for the past year, anyway. Looking back on their relationship these past twelve months, she often forgot that they hadn't known each other forever. So deep and abiding was their love, they only knew the present and the future now, and everything that had brought them here, on this day.

No rehearsal was needed for this wedding, because Sam and Tess planned to speak from the heart, in front of their families. Everyone had been able to be here for this day; had in fact gathered yesterday, and they would be in each other's company for the next three days. Sam's family: his parents, Scott and Jane, who had successfully completed her cancer treatments and stayed seizure-free; his brother Jamie, wife Tamzin and year-old daughter Emily; his brother Bobby and his wife Lorelei, who was pregnant with Sam's first nephew; his brother Chris and fiancée Niamh; and his brother Eric and boyfriend of six months Hudson. Tess's family: her parents, the newly remarried Ellen and John; her sister Ruth, pregnant with their second child, husband Sean, and nine-month-old Eloisa.

Tess stood at the doorway to the viewing car on the AMTRAK train, drawing in a breath, but not out of anxiousness or nervousness, only excitement. It was taking everything in her to not race down the aisle of the car to where Sam stood, surrounded by the world passing them by outside and their beloved family members inside. Tess didn't need her father to walk her down this aisle today; she was giving herself to Sam, as she had since she met him. Wholly and fully.

Sam looked down the car to his Tess, as he had grown to love calling her. She would always be Theresa to him, but the name was saved mostly for their most intimate moments, an homage to their initial time together. He had no idea how in the hell such an ethereal creature decided she would lower herself to meld her life with his, but he thanked his lucky stars every day that he had the good sense to fall head over heels for her. He nodded to his brother, Eric, who started the music that Tess would walk up the aisle to: "Someone Like You" by who else? Van Morrison, and he looked around as tears were forming in the eyes of all the people he and Tess loved. Sam had already been dominated by his own waterworks since he entered the viewing car. All the sadness he had felt here the first time was replaced with love and hope.

Tess began gliding down the center aisle of the train, wearing the dress she had actually bought last year for her non-wedding. She had taken it to a seamstress and had it altered and changed, so it did not resemble the dress originally chosen, but now reflected Tess on the inside. Her red curls flowed over her shoulders and down her back, and she had eyes only for Sam, so tall and breathtaking in his purple paisley shirt. In truth he was drop dead gorgeous, and she looked forward to telling him that over and over tonight, in Room 132.

Sam smiled appreciatively at his fiancée's appearance directly in front of him, and resisted the urge, once again, to sweep her off her feet and back to their room. He cleared his throat, and took her arm in his, and together they turned and faced their officiant, Todd, who turned out not only to be their favorite waiter on the train, but also an ordained minister, which they had found out when he had shown up at a book signing of Sam's last spring. He had divulged that he had known since meeting them that they would end up together.

Now here they were, starting their lives in the same place they had fallen in love, only this time with no excess baggage.

SERIES NOTE

Excess Baggage is Book One in the series "Love, South Dakota Style". If you loved this book, be sure to read the other titles: *Cutting Losses* (Book Two), *Mixed Messages* (Book Three), and *Second Chances* (Book Four). You will get to read Josh's redemption story and how he finds his way back to Effie, a woman from his past, how Liam and Lana fall in love after their one-night stand, and revel in Henry finally getting his happy ever after with Charlotte.

The love never ends, so scan the QR code below to go to my website JodiCulliney.com to enter my world of books. Stay tuned for announcements concerning my book currently in progress.

ABOUT THE AUTHOR

JODI CULLINEY, FORMER BOOKSTORE CLERK AND LIFELONG LOVER OF books, grew up in South Dakota, where she lived a peaceful existence until she met the love of her life and made the move to Brooklyn, NY. She has a Bachelor's degree in English from Black Hills State University and is working on her next novel.

Scan this QR code for a link to my Substack, https://jodiculliney.substack.com/ - It's called Reader Becomes Writer and it is where I write about how I started my journey and talk about my books!

Thanks for reading.